THE SILENCED

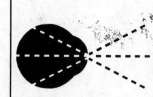

This Large Print Book carries the
Seal of Approval of N.A.V.H.

THE SILENCED

HEATHER GRAHAM

THORNDIKE PRESS
A part of Gale, Cengage Learning

GALE
CENGAGE Learning·

Farmington Hills, Mich • San Francisco • New York • Waterville, Maine
Meriden, Conn • Mason, Ohio • Chicago

GALE
CENGAGE Learning®

Copyright © 2015 by Heather Graham Pozzessere.
Krewe of Hunters.
Thorndike Press, a part of Gale, Cengage Learning.

Thorndike Press® Large Print Core.
The text of this Large Print edition is unabridged.
Other aspects of the book may vary from the original edition.
Set in 16 pt. Plantin.

LIBRARY OF CONGRESS CATALOGING-IN-PUBLICATION DATA

Graham, Heather, author.
  The silenced / by Heather Graham.
    pages cm. — (Krewe of Hunters) (Thorndike Press Large Print Core)
    ISBN 978-1-4104-8032-3 (hardback) — ISBN 1-4104-8032-1 (hardcover)
    1. Missing persons—Fiction. 2. Psychic ability—Fiction. 3. Suspense fiction.
4. Large type books. I. Title.
PS3557.R198S54 2015
813'.54—dc23   2015017820

Published in 2015 by arrangement with Harlequin Books S.A.

Printed in the United States of America
1 2 3 4 5 6 7 19 18 17 16 15

Dedicated with love and appreciation to
Cindy Kremple, Sharon Murphy,
Patty Harrison,
Janice and Thomas Jones, Pat Walker,
Ginger and Larry McSween,
Molly Bolden and Kay Levine,
Susan and Kevin Cella,
and Rebecca Barrett
for all the behind-the-scenes
help you give
so often at Writers for New Orleans.

And with very special thanks to
Sheila Vincent
and the Hotel Monteleone.

PROLOGUE

Lara Mayhew held her cell phone to her ear, trying to reach her friend Meg as she hurried along the length of the National Mall. She moved as quickly as she could; she'd never intended to be out so late — or so early, whichever it might be. The buildings she loved by day seemed like massive living creatures at night, staring at her with a strange malevolence. She loved the White House, the Capitol building, the Mall and, maybe more than any of them, the Castle building of the Smithsonian with its red facade and turrets.

They suddenly seemed to be looming hulks of evil. It was the hour, of course.

She told herself she was being ridiculous.

The ringing finally stopped and Lara got her friend's voice mail. Of course. Why would Meg be up at 2:30 a.m.?

But Lara could at least leave a message that might save her friend from worry when she disappeared.

"Meg, it's me, Lara. I wanted to let you know I'm going home. Home, as in getting out of DC and heading for Richmond. I'm going as soon as it's daylight. I'll talk to you when I can. Love you. Don't say anything to anyone else, okay? I have to get out of here. Talk soon."

She clicked the end button and slipped the phone into her bag. Meg was her best friend. They'd both been only children — and they'd both wanted siblings. They'd decided once that they'd be just like sisters. And they were.

She wished she'd managed to get ahold of Meg, that she could've heard her voice.

She walked briskly along the dark and empty sidewalk and yet she was certain she could hear all kinds of noises. Furtive noises.

Get a grip, she warned herself. She wasn't prone to being afraid — not without good reason.

Yet the night . . . scared her. And for *no* real reason.

Maybe because what she suspected was bone-chilling?

She considered calling 9-1-1. *And saying what?* She didn't have an emergency. She was stupidly walking around on dark city streets, suddenly afraid of trying to make her way home in the early-morning hour.

She reminded herself that she was near the White House, for God's sake, the Capitol, the Smithsonian buildings — and the Washington Monument. Despite the darkness and the shadows, she was fine.

She'd just never been in the area so late. Then again, there'd never been a night quite like this one. She was so upset about what she suspected that she hadn't thought about the time when she'd made her indignant retreat. She hadn't had the sense to be afraid as she dashed out.

She hadn't thought to call a cab, either, and there weren't many of them on the streets right now.

She mulled over her fears about what was going on, the situation that had caused her to stay so late, spend so many hours talking. Of course, she and Congressman Walker had often stayed at the office late. Not this late, though. Well, maybe, but he always saw that she got home safely. And most of the time, she'd left feeling exhilarated.

She had adored him. She worked on media and communications, but she was also an adviser, a problem-solver.

It was about a month ago that she'd first begun to feel uneasy. She'd wanted to call Meg then, but hadn't. Meg had been in the middle of her FBI training. So she'd gone home to Aunt Nancy's for a day and then done a quick circuit of the things she and Meg had done as children and during their breaks at college. She'd followed what they called their trail. All places that were cheap and historic and wonderful. And she'd left a message in the hollow of the broken marker in the Harpers Ferry graveyard, as they'd done when they were kids. One day — who knew? — she might go back to pick up the message. If her suspicions proved groundless.

She was angry with herself. She wasn't naive. She'd just wholeheartedly believed in what she was doing. Then she'd begun to realize that there were little erosions in those beliefs — which had become big erosions.

She thought about her friend again, wishing Meg had answered her phone.

They'd been such dreamers. Meg had always focused on law enforcement, she on law and governance. Her love of history and the story of America had made her understand and value the importance of good government, and she still believed in the passion for justice and freedom that had forged her country. There had been painful lessons along the way; among them, a bloody Civil War, which had taught

Americans some of those lessons.

Longing to work in DC — to fight for justice and equality herself — she'd found Congressman Ian Walker, who was a dreamer, too.

And an idealist. One who did, however, recognize that in a country where different people had different ideals, compromise was often necessary.

What to do, oh, Lord, what to do . . .

Today, she'd been shocked, absolutely shocked. Before that, she'd thought she had simply been imagining things. And then today, she was faced with all the talk about Walker's Gettysburg speech, what he should say — now that Congressman Hubbard was dead.

She should've been more careful. She shouldn't have suggested that she was worried about the fact that such a decent man had so conveniently died.

Leave. Go home. That made the most sense. Get the hell out as soon as possible. Go home to Richmond, figure out the proper thing to do about the situation here, decide what she really wanted to do with her future.

It was crazy, she told herself angrily, to give up her passion because of *this.*

But she hadn't given up. She just needed

a change for a while; there was still good-ness in the world, and lots more op-portunity, and she needed to sample some of it. Then, one day, perhaps she'd come back, using her skill with words to champion the right man or woman again.

Once she found safety, should she tell the world her suspicions? She had no proof. She'd be laughed out of court; no lawyer would take her on.

She could always approach her media contacts. Throwing the hint of suspicion out there could change everything.

There was also the possibility of being sued for slander, since she had no proof.

There was Meg, but she had to reach Meg first.

And the faster she walked, the more afraid she felt.

Get out of Washington! It's a nest of vipers!

She still believed in the dream. In men and women who couldn't be bought.

But there were other things she could do.

Take a job with a media company or PR firm in Richmond. What about Harpers Ferry? Tourism there grew every year. Then again, Harpers Ferry was small. Maybe Richmond would be best. And she loved Pennsylvania — especially Gettysburg! They'd gone there so often, she and Meg, and made interesting friends.

No! Not Gettysburg. Not after tonight!

She needed somewhere far, far away from DC.

She did love the Blue Ridge Mountains. There were smaller towns out that way, towns that flourished because of tourism. She could find work with a tour company or something. Anything except this.

Baltimore?

Maybe she needed to go much farther afield than the states of Virginia, Maryland or West Virginia.

She looked around the shadowed streets, walking as swiftly as she could. She'd worked very late before now — well, till one in the morning, anyway. She hadn't been nervous those other nights, not at all. Congressman Walker was a good man; it just seemed now that he was a man who could be swayed, who could be fooled and manipulated into changing his views and his policies — into working with others to undermine what he had once believed in.

But she still felt that he was, at heart, a good man.

No matter what she'd learned today. No matter what she'd expected. No matter how disappointed she was. She *had* to believe he was a good man.

Was he really innocent of any knowledge of a man's death?

She could be wrong; she probably was. But she couldn't help suspecting that someone in his political camp had wanted Congressman Hubbard out of the picture. It was just a suspicion, she told herself again, and it could be unfounded!

Her fear tonight was simply a result of the shadows and the darkness. By day, tourists and lawmakers crowded these streets. Children laughed and ran around on the grass. The Smithsonian's Castle stood as a bastion to the past and the country's rich history — as the USA became a full-fledged country, one that had withstood the rigors of war and knew how to create the arts and sciences crucial to a nation of dreamers.

She could see the Washington Monument ahead of her in the night, shining in the moonlight that beamed down. Yes, she loved Washington, DC, but it was time to leave.

Her heels clicked on the sidewalk, echoing loudly in her ears. She prayed for a taxi to go by.

A beat-up van drew near and seemed to slow down as it passed her. She walked onto the grass verge, suddenly even more afraid. With her luck, she'd be worrying about the fate of the nation — and get mugged by a

14

common thief.

Not long ago, a young woman had been found on the shore of the Potomac River. Naked, her throat and body ripped open. Police and forensic scientists were having a problem because river creatures had played havoc with her body. No "persons of interest" were being questioned in the death; the police feared they were dealing with someone suffering from a "mental disorder."

Lord, she was stupid, taking off in the middle of the night like this! It was just that . . .

She'd been so upset, so indignant, so . . . perplexed that personal danger hadn't even occurred to her!

She hardly dared to breathe. Why had she stood up and said she no longer wanted any part of it? Why had she taken off the way she had? *Get a grip,* she told herself again. The hard-core politicians she knew wouldn't be stalking her; they weren't suffering from any mental disorders. Wait — not true. *Anyone* in politics was suffering from a mental disorder!

She tried to laugh at her own joke. No sound came.

She quickened her pace; her feet, legs and lungs hurt. She kept her phone in one hand, trying to look fierce, as if she was ready to press 9-1-1 at a second's notice.

Her heart was pounding.

It was a van.

Everyone who watched TV knew that evil men in vans caught victims on the street and *dragged* them in by a side door and then . . .

The van drove on.

She felt giddy with relief and smiled at her unjustified panic.

A moment later, she saw a sedan in the street. It slowed and she squinted, looking toward it.

"Lara!" The car slid to a halt, and a deep male voice called her name from the driver's seat. "Come on. I'll give you a lift!"

She *had* to know him; she should've recognized the voice. It must be muffled by the night air. She was being offered a ride by someone who was obviously official. Someone she knew, someone who knew her.

Maybe Ian had sent a driver out after her. Maybe he'd realized what time it was and that the streets might not be safe.

Her relief made her feel weak.

She dropped her phone into her purse and ran across the street, grateful and shaky.

But the man didn't get out of the car. And for some reason — perhaps the warning voice inside her that reminded her she now knew too much — she grew suspicious.

Ian's people would have gotten out of the car, opened the door for her!

She turned to run.

Where? Where should she run? The streets were empty, the Mall was empty . . .

Lara prayed the beat-up van would come back.

She nearly stumbled.

She paused briefly. She would *not* trip and fall and look back screaming the way idiots did in horror movies when giant reptiles were coming for them. She took the seconds required to kick off her heels while digging in her bag for her cell phone.

She did nothing stupid.

But that didn't save her.

He was fast. Surprisingly fast.

He slammed into her and down on her like a tackle in a football game. She opened her mouth to scream.

Who the hell was it? She still couldn't see him! Did it matter? Escape!

She couldn't turn her head; he was behind her, forcing her down. And then . . . she felt his hand coming around her head. He was holding a rag. She smelled something sickly sweet and she began to see black dots. The smell gagged her. She had to keep fighting; she was going to die if she didn't.

So she fought . . .

But as the scent overwhelmed her, she thought, *Oh, God, no, I really am going to disappear.*

The blackness took her.

He'd studied the information available on serial killers with the same concentrated attention he'd always given textbooks; what had to be done had to be done, and he had to do it the right way. He knew FBI men, behavioral scientists. He was careful never to talk too much, but he was an excellent listener. He never undertook any task lightly.

He'd invented an alter ego for himself, a man he called Slash McNeil. Slash McNeil was now fully part of his personality. Slash? Well, it made sense. McNeil? Why not? It seemed to go well with Slash. Not that he needed a name to sign to confessions or letters to the editors or police. He just liked it.

McNeil had been born *off,* as anyone who knew this manufactured alter ego would say. Even when he was a toddler, he'd enjoyed smashing bugs. As he'd aged, the bugs became small reptiles; McNeil liked to set snakes on fire. Once he grew older, the animals he tortured became kittens and puppies and then cats and dogs.

When he was sixteen, he committed his

first murder. It hadn't been particularly good, well planned or satisfying. He'd teased ugly Sarah Rockway, letting her think he wanted a make-out session with her, and lured her to a bridge. He'd kissed Sarah — and then tossed her over the bridge. In McNeil's mind, at least, the girl had died happy.

But he hadn't wanted Sarah Rockway — nor had he wanted the murder to be so swift. He'd wanted to slash her, cut her, as he had the kittens and puppies.

And he'd really wanted Celia Hampton. Celia, the cheerleader, the leggy beauty who would barely give him the time of day. He wanted her naked, doing anything he asked, begging him for her life.

But murder was an art to be properly learned, and practice improved any art.

It took him another two years to lure Celia Hampton away with him. He'd waited for a frat party. Waited until she was drunk and vomiting and offered her a wet towel — doused with a drug, of course. Then he'd slipped her into his old van and out to the woods in Virginia, far from the city. He hadn't had to strip her; he'd shown her his knife and she'd done everything he wanted. After that, he'd cut her. First her throat. Slowly. He'd let her bleed out . . . while he sliced open her gut.

He'd thrown her in a river — weighing her down by stuffing her with stones. By the time she was found . . . the river had washed away all evidence.

In the beginning he'd been able to live on the memory for years. Then, more recently, he'd felt the need to kill again. But now things were different. The need came faster. He got work that allowed him to travel, and it had afforded him opportunities for murder. He was controlled, always controlled and always careful. He studied his victims. They were never ugly again. They were the pretty ones. But he made sure that when they were found, he couldn't be. They might know about him — since communications among law enforcement officers were pretty good these days — but they didn't know who he was.

He always took a souvenir.

The tongue.

Serial killers often took souvenirs. He'd determined that would be his souvenir of choice.

They would recognize his work.

Then again, maybe not; he left his victims in water, weighed down with whatever he could find. And the water concealed any evidence there might be.

Yes, he had an alter ego. And he'd paved the way. Two dead already, just in the past month. Now . . . this one. And there'd have to be more.

He'd watched the first girl, Sarah, not with malice, but with purpose. He hadn't done anything out of hatred or viciousness. He'd been inexperienced then, still learning. With Celia, the second girl, it had been easy. It wasn't that he *liked* what he'd done. He'd seen the need early on and he did his job as he understood it.

It was just necessary. Like dressing every morning, driving, breathing, eating — making a living.

He wished he could be sorry. He wasn't.

He did what he needed to do, and that was all.

He'd become Slash McNeil.

For a moment, he paused. It was messing with him this time. He had it figured out — and damned well, too. The girls, the type, the psychology.

But this one . . .

This one was different. The way he handled her had to be different. And he sure as hell didn't like it, not one bit.

Still . . .

He was prepared. He'd prepared for this possibility months ago, and in actuality,

21

there were things about it that were even more appealing than usual. This involved wits and careful machinations and a certain danger that made it all the more exhilarating; it gave him a high that was greater than the rest.

He smiled and thought about the woman — her flair, her grace, her confidence.

And he thought about what she'd be . . .

When it was all over.

1

Meg Murray's alarm went off with a strident ring that made her nearly jump out of her skin as well as the bed.

She groaned and rubbed her temples. Keeping up with the guys wasn't easy — not as easy as she'd hoped, anyway.

But she, and Sandra Martinez and Carrie Huang — the two other young women in her academy class — were holding up nicely. And they'd made it. Meg was proud — and relieved. She knew that only one out of every hundred applicants got into the academy.

And not all made it through.

She'd been determined. Just as some kids knew they wanted to grow up to be actors, artists, veterinarians or zookeepers, she'd known she wanted the FBI.

She and her class had learned legal and investigative processes and passed every physical test of strength and coordination.

The men and the women in her class had all done well. Meg hadn't beaten Ricky Grant — considered by most of them, including Ricky, to be the toughest cadet in their class — but she'd kept up with him. In fact, her class had excelled.

They'd graduated; they'd had their ceremony. They were officially agents now, and they'd celebrated.

She wasn't sure why she'd felt compelled to keep up with Ricky in all things.

She hadn't gotten wasted last night; she'd been extremely temperate while pretending to imbibe far more than she had. And she wasn't hungover; she was tired!

The trials, the strain, the classes, the yearning — they were over. It was exhilarating, and it gave them all a flutter of fear. Time to go into the world as rookies. Time to prove themselves.

And, of course, it was time to move out of cadet housing and into places of their own.

That wasn't a worry for Meg. She'd always believed she'd graduate, so she'd already made arrangements to rent a small town house just down the road from headquarters at Quantico. She was going to be assigned to the criminal division there. They had a few days to clear out and she simply had to switch from housing to her new home.

Awake, she lay in bed, a little dazed. This was really it. She had two weeks before heading in to her first assignment.

Her television, on a timer, sprang to life with the news. Meg paused, watching it, before she went in to shower. Police were still seeking clues in the brutal murder of a Jane Doe discovered by the Potomac a couple of weeks ago. More troops had been killed overseas. A truck had stalled on the beltway, causing a ten-car pileup. Investigations were still under way regarding the death of Garth Hubbard, the indie presidential hopeful beloved by so many that he might've been the first man to take the White House on such a ticket. The cause of his death had been deemed natural. He'd been at home with his wife, alone in their bedroom. Paramedics had been called; his family doctor had come, too, and signed the death certificate. But this was Washington, DC, so, of course, there was talk of conspiracy.

"Ah, yes, good morning!" she muttered to herself.

The news anchor — after waiting an appropriate beat or two — offered her viewing public a wide, toothy smile and went on to recount some of the good news of the day.

Maybe it wasn't such a bad morning. An attractive reporter related a story about the heroics of a young man as he dived after a woman, a stranger, who had nearly drowned while tubing in West Virginia. She then had another story about a young girl saved from an abusive teen by the intervention of a stray dog — the dog now, happily, had a home.

Meg realized she was just staring, somewhat hypnotized, at the television.

She had to get going. There was an orientation class she was required to attend and she wanted to get through it quickly so she could concentrate on moving into her little town house before her life began anew.

As she relished the hot water pouring over her in the shower, Meg considered the life she was about to start.

As a child, she'd dreamed of changing the world. That had meant to her that she had to be a policewoman or run for president. Maybe a policewoman — and *then* the president.

And when she was ten years old, her family had fallen victim to a horrible crime.

She would never forget it. She could still remember that time as clearly as if she'd just lived it. Her cousin, responsible and steadfast, had gone missing. Then the ransom note had come.

But Mary Elizabeth's body had been found. Meg had known they'd find her before they did. Everything about those days, that experience, had been shattering and devastating, and for a long time, she'd thought she was crazy. But she hadn't been.

And now . . .

Now, all she could only hope to do was put away some of the bad guys. Just as they'd put away the man who'd taken Mary Elizabeth.

In her classes, they'd recently had guest speakers, agents and scientists from the behavioral science units. Listening to what man was capable of doing to man had been horrifying, despite what she already knew. The academy classes lost students along the way because sometimes it was too much to bear.

In her case . . .

She was even more determined. She had every reason to be.

Because it hadn't ended with Mary Elizabeth.

Sometimes she met people who'd been tortured.

And killed.

And she'd wanted to help.

She liked to feel that she'd grown strong.

27

Her superiors and teachers knew about her past — about Mary Elizabeth being kidnapped and murdered. She was honest about her desire to be with the Bureau. She was careful not to dwell on the past in case someone believed that her previous experience might hinder her work.

It would never interfere with her work; she was sure of that.

Dressed and ready for the day, she checked her reflection in the mirror. She wore a blue pantsuit, very regulation. Her shirt was white, but she was allowed pinstripes, thin lines in a pale blue. Somehow, they made her feel a little brighter.

She was young, but at a height of five-ten she was often assumed to be older than her actual age of twenty-six. She had a wealth of thick, nearly black hair, which she'd pulled back into a bun. She almost turned away from the mirror, but then studied her reflection more closely. She thought her mouth was too big, as were her eyes. At least they were a clear, dark sky blue. She studied herself critically and decided she looked presentable. And especially dressed like this, she seemed to exude confidence, maybe even authority.

With a shake of her head, she finally

turned away. She really wanted to believe that she had the right stuff. She'd gone through college, studying criminology, become a cop in Richmond for a couple of years and then been accepted to the academy. It was the career she wanted; she'd gone after it step-by-step.

She reached for her phone in the charger at her bedside and realized the message light was blinking.

Lara had called her. She frowned; the call had come in the middle of the night. Lara never called her that late. She listened to the message.

"Meg, it's me, Lara. I wanted to let you know I'm going home. Home, as in getting out of DC. I'm going as soon as it's daylight. I'll talk to you when I can. Love you. Don't say anything to anyone else, okay? I have to get out of here. Talk soon."

There was a second call, a second message. But Meg heard nothing — except what sounded like a rush of wind and a muffled thump.

A purse dial?

Perplexed, Meg played the message again and tried to phone Lara back. The call went immediately to voice mail. Her friend had seemed breathless, so she'd probably been walking when she'd made the call.

29

But she'd sounded distracted — and a little frantic.

Meg left a message herself. "Call me back. You've got me really worried. Please, call me as soon as you possibly can."

Disturbed, she added a last "Please!"

She told herself that Lara had just become disgusted with politics; many people did.

Not Lara! she thought.

Lara had been a media and research assistant in the offices of Congressman Ian Walker. Lara had admired the congressman from his first speeches, when they were still in high school in Richmond. Walker was passionate about equality, whether racial, religious or sexual. He was also critical of irresponsible spending, the unusual politician who managed to be both fiscally responsible and socially liberal. He fought hard for his causes on the house floor.

Why would Lara suddenly decide to go home? It didn't make sense!

She lay on the silver gurney as if she were sleeping, and Agent Matt Bosworth believed that she'd once been a lovely young woman.

Death had not been kind. She was now a bloated, pallid corpse, ravaged by the river and creatures of the water. It was difficult to tell where the autopsy Y incision had actually been made; he knew she'd been ripped from throat to groin, disemboweled and stuffed with rocks. But time had caused the rocks to dislodge from their human cave and she had floated to the surface and then the riverbank, where she'd been found by the boat motor of a pleasure sailor on the Potomac.

Matt knew that another woman had been found at the beginning of June — but she'd washed up on the Maryland side of the river.

The woman now lying on the gurney before him had shown up on the DC side. She'd come to the office of the chief medical examiner, or OCME, for the District of Columbia. It was a relatively new, state-of-the-art facility that handled about seventeen hundred cases a year — of death by violence, death unattended by a physician, unexpected death or death with the possibility of spreading disease.

The offices were large and also housed forensic labs, reception areas to provide information to family and friends, and staff who offered counseling. The workers here were often distraught when the public thought — due to numerous television shows — that answers were revealed within the space of an hour.

Death was seldom so easy.

But Matt had faith that whatever could be learned about the deceased would be learned here. All in all, he was glad the FBI was involved — and that everything on these murders would be handled as one case. While Matt wasn't surprised that it had so quickly become a federal case, he *was* surprised that the Krewe — a specialized unit — had been called in.

DC wasn't geographically large, not compared to other major metropolises. But with Capitol police, District police, Maryland and Virginia police and the FBI, jurisdiction might have become a bit confused. However, since these two murders were in Maryland and the District, it seemed logical that the FBI would take the lead. There were dozens of elite units at headquarters that might've been called in.

But it had been the Krewe.

Matt hadn't questioned the details yet. He'd come into work and Jackson Crow had informed him that they were heading out. In time he'd find out what had happened — and what was going on now.

He'd been with the Krewe for about eight months, invited in after he'd explained to his superiors that he'd been "lucky" when he'd wandered into the bar where a serial killer had stalked his victims. It had actually been the ghost of a young victim who'd shown him the way. Matt figured that Jackson — Special Agent in Charge Jackson Crow — and Adam Harrison, Krewe director, had watched his work.

And known that he'd be right for the unit.

Matt had never understood why he saw the dead — or why the dead seemed to talk to him. He hadn't had a traumatic life; he'd had a good one, with great parents and a solid education. A family friend had assisted in getting him into Virginia Military Institute. He'd served in the military, and after that, he'd decided he wanted the FBI. He'd heard about the Krewe of Hunters and known he wanted in. He also knew that the Krewe invited its agents to join; it wasn't something you applied for. So he'd waited patiently.

He'd seen and communicated with the dead since he was a kid, but he'd realized that others didn't. And he'd also realized that if you wanted to be taken seriously, you didn't tell anyone that you spoke to the dead.

After several years in the FBI and that one particular case, he'd been invited in. He'd been happy to be with the Krewe. No more pretense.

So, that morning, he hadn't questioned

Jackson. They'd find out soon enough exactly what they were looking at.

It hadn't taken them long to reach the OCME; their offices in Alexandria weren't that far from it. He liked their new location, a pair of beautiful old row houses that were also host to FBI internet personnel, other agents and some civilian employees. They could easily commute to the Capitol and the facilities at Quantico.

So far, Matt had learned that they'd been specifically called in when the second body was found. While three killings officially called for a serial killer investigation, the brutality done to both women had caused the captain of the Maryland force to alert the FBI. The assistant director at headquarters had called Adam Harrison, and Adam had directed Jackson to take the case.

But while the situation was grim and the perpetrator obviously a heinous killer, there didn't seem to be much reason for the Krewe to be called in. Nothing seemed to hint at the paranormal; this was murder at its most brutal, but sadly, such killers had existed before and would again. He'd eventually learn the whys of this case. Right now, they needed to learn what they could from the body — and from the DC cop,

Carl Hunter, who'd been the detective called to the scene.

"The cause of death was the slashed throat?" Matt asked, after the ME, Dr. Wong, finished listing the injuries to the body. He spoke through a paper mask, as had the doctor. The smell of decay was strong.

Wong was a bright man in his early forties, clear and concise in his manner. He looked at Matt and nodded. "The throat was slashed. It would've taken the victim time to exsanguinate, and some of the slicing on the body was performed before death, but she was so heavily drugged that I don't think she felt anything, including the slash to her throat."

"I understand it was a right-handed killer," Detective Hunter said. "That's correct, Dr. Wong?"

Carl's voice sounded scratchy. Matt understood. Carl was a good guy; they'd met during a few earlier cases. The man was a dogged investigator, putting in long hours. He was nearing retirement, but hadn't slacked off in the time or determination he gave a case.

He'd seen a lot.

This was still hard to tolerate.

"Yes," Wong said. "He was right-handed

35

and very certain in his movements. No hesitation marks at all. The guy's done this before."

"Were any organs taken?" Jackson Crow asked.

"The tongue is missing," Wong said. He cleared his throat. "Bits of organs are missing — but that's because the ripping of the stomach caused pieces to . . . fall out."

Matt leaned forward to see the atrocity Wong showed them, setting a hand on the dead woman's shoulder as he viewed her ruined mouth.

Her shoulder was cold, cold as ice. It was shocking what the body felt like when life was gone, so still and cold, as if the soul, the very essence of what had been human, had flown and left emptiness behind. "Same as the victim found on the Maryland shore," Carl Hunter said, turning to Wong. "I talked to Jared Welch from the Maryland force before I came in. People might say that cops are territorial, but we're both glad as hell that the feds are in. God knows, we might have got into this thing first, but we haven't come up with anything. Both bodies brought in with no purses, no IDs, hell, no clothes. Just unidentified bodies, naked and ripped to shreds. We don't have any leads at all and this killer . . . *has* to be stopped."

Wong told them, "I haven't seen the first body yet, but I have the report. The other victim will be transported here. As you requested, Special Agent Crow, we're treating them as murders committed by the same perpetrator or perpetrators."

"Right," Jackson murmured. "The taking of the tongue — it's a definite signature. I'm afraid it suggests this killer isn't finished yet. We'll need every law enforcement officer in the area on high alert."

Two dead in less than a month, Matt thought.

"But we haven't matched her up with anyone?" he asked.

"We're working on fingerprints and X-rays and hope to have something soon," Wong replied. "As I said, I didn't perform the autopsy on the first Jane Doe, but I've studied the sheets. To summarize, I can tell you that the murders were performed the same way. I believe both women were taken by surprise — since there appear to be no defensive wounds. They were drugged with an inhalant, and then —" he paused to show them the inner right elbow "— injected with propofol, a drug commonly used in surgery. Actually, our tox reports aren't back yet, but that's what was used on the Maryland victim and I'm betting this is going to be the same."

"Interesting. So you think they were unconscious when they were mutilated?"

Wong nodded.

"That means he didn't get off on the cutting," Jackson mused. "And no sexual assault?"

Matt knew that the first victim hadn't been raped or molested. Not as far as they could tell. While the bodies were badly decomposed, medical science could still provide them with evidence.

Wong shook his head. "No. Probably not. Doesn't fit what we're seeing here. I'd say the killer takes them, sedates them, rips them from stem to stern, stuffs the bodies with stones and tosses them. They're found naked and heavily compromised by immersion in the water. As you can see," Wong said, lifting the sheet, "she's been nibbled on by many creatures."

Matt *could* see — far too plainly.

"She was about five-six or -seven in life."

"Long blond hair, five-six and a half," Wong said.

"Almost identical to the first girl, according to the Maryland reports," Carl offered.

"So, that's his type," Jackson said. "We'll get the warning out. Press conference. I'll ask you to handle it, Matt. Dr. Wong, please

38

keep us apprised of anything new."

They left the autopsy room, discarding their masks in the proper bin. Matt felt as if the smell of decomposition clung to him.

Carl paused in the hallway. "I'm not shirking," he muttered. "I know this might be my last case, and I'll be out there, working it as hard as ever. But . . . God, I hate cases like this. Like I said, we've got nothing, and until we get identifications, we don't even have anyone to question. The killer knew what he was doing, disposing of the bodies. No trace on them — or not any that forensics has found as yet. Dump 'em in the river and you pretty well destroy any clue there might've been." He paused. "We all know that some killers get away with it. I sure as hell hope it isn't this guy."

"We won't let it be," Matt said quietly.

Hunter nodded, but his expression was uncomfortable. "Gotta tell you, I don't get the shakes easy. But . . ."

Matt was curious. Carl was as practical as a man could be. He seemed jittery, though, and Matt sensed that it was due to something other — something more — than the sheer horror of the case.

"What is it?"

"I got this awful feeling that she . . . that she looked at me when I first got to the scene. Impossible, of course. Her eyes . . . well, soft tissue. You saw . . ."

Matt glanced over at Jackson.

He'd touched the body. Whatever soul, whatever essence of life there'd been, was gone.

Carl shrugged. "I'm on it — task force, anything you need. I seem to keep saying this, but I'm glad you guys are in on this one. And no, we can't let him be the one who got away." He lifted a hand in farewell and hurried down the hall.

Jackson turned to Matt. "Right now, we have to be careful. Really careful. We need to get on the air, though. Say as little as possible," he said. "But we need a warning out there. And we don't know whether he might choose another type, so all women in the District and the surrounding area should be especially careful."

"You don't want the media folk at headquarters to handle this?"

"I think we need to take it from the start. I'll arrange for clearance."

Matt nodded. Headquarters had a division to deal with the media. But sometimes the Krewe worked on their own. He knew that he was often chosen to give press conferences because, according to Jackson, he had the all-American football player look. He could seem both stern and stoic — and, most important, trustworthy, reassuring to a worried public.

He wasn't sure how anything about this situation could be reassuring; whether it was their usual kind of case or not, it was exceptionally disturbing.

And now he knew why the Krewe had been called in. Carl Hunter would've been careful about what he said and to whom. His own coworkers would have ribbed him mercilessly if he'd said that a corpse had looked at him. But somehow, he'd gotten that information through to the right people.

"When is the press conference?" Matt asked Jackson.

"As soon as we can organize it," Jackson told him. "We'll call an emergency task force meeting, bringing reps from the area. Meeting won't take long. We don't have anything to say yet. Then we'll get on the air. You'll speak, along with representatives from the DC police, Virginia and Maryland. You won't be on the hot seat alone."

Matt didn't care about being on the hot seat; he was used to it. There was the truth — and there was the matter of telling the truth so that it afforded the greatest protection to the public while suppressing enough details to make sure law enforcement knew more than any kooks or would-be psychics out there.

They'd keep a lot quiet, he was assuming. Grotesque details did nothing but stir up sensationalism — and sometimes provide a killer with the notoriety he sought.

Jackson and Matt reached the big black sedan set for their use. Jackson let Matt do the driving. He was one of the best things about the unit, in Matt's opinion. He was half–Native American and well aware of the diversity of people and beliefs around the country. He also had an aura of calm about him and an ability to listen to those who worked with him. He wasn't a micromanager, and yet he expected the best from those around him. If he trusted you, it was with complete confidence.

Matt liked to believe he'd earned the man's trust.

He also liked to believe that he was worthy of it. He thought he was; while their backgrounds were dissimilar, they were also much alike.

He wondered if Jackson's thoughts were similar to his. Jackson grinned over at him and said, "You still don't look much like a Native American." Matt grinned in return. He was, like many, many people in the

United States, someone who could actually trace his ancestry back to Pocahontas.

"A heritage sadly diluted by time."

"Let's just hope we both have some of that mystic wisdom we're supposed to have," Jackson said wryly. "We're going to need it."

The day felt long to Meg as she attended her sessions. At every opportunity, she tried calling Lara's number.

Her calls continued to go straight to voice mail.

She tried calling Nancy Cooper, Lara's aunt in Richmond, but Nancy hadn't heard from Lara, either. Meg ended the call quickly, not wanting to worry her.

She tried a few of the mutual friends they had in the area. She even tried Lara's ex-boyfriend, Clark Walden, despite the fact that the two had split up at least six months earlier. Clark was in the military; she discovered he'd been deployed overseas a month ago.

She called Congressman Walker's office and was informed that Lara no longer worked there. No, she'd left no other information.

Despite failing with her calls, it wasn't until she'd finished for the day and was sitting in the cadets' lounge that she really began to feel a sense of panic.

And that was when the TV news came on.

A second body had been discovered. She remembered hearing about the first woman, who'd been found a few weeks back. The case had seemed particularly sad to her. Police had discovered a young blonde woman between the ages of twenty-five and thirty. She'd stood about five-seven and, while alive, had weighed approximately a hundred and twenty pounds. She had yet to be identified. There were no suspects in the case, and police had begged the public for any help they could give.

The newscast that came on made her sit straight up and spill her coffee.

The second murder victim had also been about five-six or five-seven. And she'd also been blonde. Because of the condition of the body, forensic scientists were seeking her identity through dental records. Fingerprint identification was being attempted but, once again, the police were seeking help.

Meg's heart began to flutter with fear.

The body had been discovered that morning.

She stood, stumbled around the lounge until she could grab the remote control and turned up the volume.

She listened to a lieutenant from the DC police issue warnings and inform the public that extra police officers would be on the streets. An officer from Maryland spoke next.

And an officer from Virginia.

And then, a rep from the FBI took the microphone.

He was tall, a striking man with sandy, close-cropped hair, the shoulders of a linebacker and a ruggedly chiseled face. His voice was rich and deep; she assumed he was a regular spokesman for the agency.

But as he finished his speech, hotline numbers were flashed on the screen. She heard the assurance in his voice when he added, "We at the FBI will not stop our intense hunt until this killer is apprehended. Until he is, however, responsibility lies with every man and woman out there. If possible, don't go anywhere alone. As of now, he has selected two blondes. He has seen to it that identification is a difficult process. Keep in mind that his choice of victim could easily change. When Ted Bundy was stalking women, most that we know about had long, straight brown hair. Because of that, many thought they were safe by dying their hair. We have very little information on this killer

45

as yet, and that means *everyone* could be in danger, blonde or not. Although the killer, whom we're assuming to be male, has targeted only young women so far, it's quite possible that women of all ages and descriptions — and conceivably men — could also be at risk. While you shouldn't panic, you must be vigilant. You've been given the call number — any and all suspicious behavior needs to be reported. We are relying on the public for assistance. We need to combine public awareness and the dedication of every law enforcement officer out there. We vow not to hold back any pertinent information — and we'd appreciate it if the media refrained from affording this man a nickname, as a label or a title. He's a vicious killer and deserves no recognition."

He went on to thank his audience, which included reporters from various news organizations, and stepped away from the podium. The DC mayor came forward again and began to speak.

But Meg didn't hear him. Her heart seemed to slam against her chest. She saw that the agent who'd just finished was standing in the background, talking to an elderly white-haired man in a pristine suit.

Adam Harrison.

Meg got up. She *had* to speak with Adam;

she didn't want to simply call a hotline.

She'd intended to go to him eventually for another reason altogether. She'd always wanted to be part of the Krewe of Hunters — and she felt she belonged there. She'd wanted to graduate and enter the criminal division first, a matter of pride, perhaps. As in, *I've taken all the right steps. I've worked my hardest. I believe I've excelled and I believe I have the skills you need . . .*

There was no waiting now.

She had to go to him; she knew he'd help her.

And she desperately needed help. She had to find out about the victim.

Because Lara was a blonde, five-seven, lovely and fit and about a hundred and twenty pounds.

"Margaret!"

Meg wasn't sure why Adam Harrison even remembered her. He must have met hundreds of people through the years and she hadn't seen him in more than a decade.

He was a very dear man. Ramrod-straight, dignified in manner and appearance, he had to be in his late seventies or early eighties. She'd been surprised that the phone number he'd given her all those years ago still worked. Her call to him via that number

47

had gone right through, almost as if he'd been expecting to hear from her. How that could be, she didn't know.

Years ago, Adam had arrived at her home, although the police and even Meg's own parents had been skeptical. He'd come with the FBI agents who'd been called in because her cousin's case had begun as a kidnapping.

While the family worked to put together a ransom, Meg knew that Mary Elizabeth was already dead. She'd known because she'd awakened to find Mary Elizabeth sitting at the foot of her bed. At first, she'd been joyous, certain that her older cousin had been released and come home while she was sleeping. But Mary Elizabeth had drawn a finger to her lips, shaking her head. She'd tried to speak, and Meg had heard a rustling sound. And then she *thought* she heard her cousin speaking, telling her that she had to let them know the truth — that the family couldn't go on believing when there was no hope. Her body was in the cemetery, hidden behind a mausoleum. Meg crawled out of bed. The grown-ups were all awake; officers crowded the house, and everyone waited by the phone.

Crying, Meg went to her mother and whispered what she knew. Her mother was horrified, not wanting her dad's sister and husband to hear. She'd pulled Meg away and chastised her in the kitchen. But the older man who'd come with the FBI people had followed. He'd listened to her story and, back in the parlor, told someone to check the cemetery.

Where they'd found Mary Elizabeth's body.

At first, Meg's own mother had treated her as if she'd been possessed by Satan. She'd quickly gotten over that, but Meg would never forget the way her own family had looked at her. Thanks to her, they'd caught the killer almost immediately. Forensic evidence left at the scene made short work of identifying him, since he was a repeat offender and therefore already in law enforcement databases, and of proving his guilt.

She saw her cousin one more time. At the funeral, by the graveside. She'd been beautiful, dressed in the white confirmation gown in which she was buried, shrouded in brilliant gold light. Somehow it had been comforting. And she'd actually comforted her aunt and uncle; her conviction was so strong that Mary Elizabeth was in heaven.

Adam Harrison had been at the funeral. He'd been so kind to her, and Meg had never forgotten.

Standing outside alone, she'd watched while he paid his condolences to her family. When he saw her, she thought she'd start crying all over again. But he came to her and said, "You're a very brave and special girl, you know."

"I'm a freak," she told him.

He shook his head. "No, Margaret, you're not a freak at all. You're special," he repeated.

That made her roll her eyes. Her older cousins liked to tease her and call her "special" when they were making fun of her.

He'd smiled. "No, you really are. You can't bring Mary Elizabeth back, but you've allowed her to be at peace. And the man who killed her, he'll never kill again. We found her body quickly because of you, and found the evidence we needed to arrest her killer. There are monsters in this world, Margaret. And it takes very special people to stop their power. If you ever need me, call."

He'd handed her his card. Later, without ever using it, she'd put the number in her cell phone.

Over the years, she'd read everything she could about Adam. He was rich, but he didn't spend his money on cars or vacations. Without being a member of any police force, he assisted various agencies with what were referred to as "unusual" crimes. He'd been appointed a "directing consultant" with a specialized unit at the FBI.

That was when she'd known she'd wanted to be part of the FBI.

She'd never contacted him; she'd just worked toward her goal.

But now . . .

When she called him at the cell phone number that was still, miraculously, the right number, he told her to come over.

His home was in northern Virginia, so it hadn't taken her long to reach him — no more than forty-five minutes — even though she stopped by Lara's on the way.

"You've graduated, Margaret. Congratulations!" he said as he welcomed her into his home.

"You . . . knew I was in the academy?"

"Of course. I thought maybe you'd find me. If you hadn't, I would have sought you out. Do you want to be with the Krewe?" he asked her. "Oh, would you like some iced tea or coffee — or a drink?"

She shook her head. "I need help," she said.

"Oh?" He seemed surprised. She realized he'd assumed she was coming to inquire about becoming part of the Krewe.

"My friend Lara Mayhew is missing. I saw the press conference about the woman discovered in the river. Adam, Lara fits the description to a T."

He frowned, obviously not expecting this. "It's a long shot to think your friend might be this girl. When did she go missing?" he asked.

"She left me a message at around two-thirty this morning, about leaving DC. She said she *had* to get out of there. And she seemed really distressed."

Adam was silent for a minute. Meg knew he'd lived through a great deal of stress and heartache through the years. "But . . . if she said she was leaving, it's quite possible that she . . . left."

"There was something wrong with the message, Adam. She didn't sound all right. She almost sounded as if . . . as if she planned to go into hiding."

"Maybe she did," he said gently.

"I know, but her message scared me."

"So you'd say she's been missing, what, about fifteen hours?"

Meg nodded unhappily. She knew that the length of time Lara had been missing wouldn't fit the official interpretation of "missing." It hadn't even been twenty-four hours.

"And you haven't been able to reach her?"

"No, and I made several other calls, too." She hesitated, then added, "She was involved in politics. Not that I'm suggesting politicians are evil or anything."

Adam laughed. "We could take a poll on that one," he said.

"The whole situation really worries me, Adam. She worked in media relations for Congressman Walker, and I tried calling his office. They seemed to be saying she quit, but I couldn't get any more out of them. They gave me . . . the brush-off."

"I won't get a brush-off," he assured her, his voice grim. "Those offices are usually busy, and unless you represent a powerful lobby of some kind . . . Well, let's just say that the days when a man could walk into the White House to chat with the president are long gone." He paused, then offered her an encouraging smile. "Remember, though, your friend may be fine. Try not to stress too much. If she said she was leaving, she might have done just that."

"Adam, I *know* that something's wrong."

"Ah," he said quietly. "I'm so sorry."

"I — I need to see her."

"Of course. You mean you need to see the victim. If she can be identified, it'll certainly help the investigation. You realize it's not easy?"

"I went through the academy. I've seen all kinds of horrors."

"Yes," he said, "but this is the real world you're entering — not a video of what others have been through or a lecture about what they've discovered. This will be up close. And it might well be personal."

"I've been to an autopsy before."

"However, it may not be your friend at all," he pointed out.

"But then again, it may be. I can't reach her, Adam," she said, even more urgently than before. "I tried repeatedly. I called her aunt. I called other friends. And, as I told you, her office wouldn't give me any information."

"So they say she quit?"

"Yes, sometime yesterday or last night, I assume. Actually, they didn't use the word *quit.* They used the words *no longer here.* And they suggested I speak with her if I wanted more information about her future plans."

Adam was thoughtful for a moment.

"Have you . . . *seen* this friend?" he asked her softly.

Seen. As in seeing her ghost or whatever

54

remained of the person who had once been Lara.

"No, but like I said, I'm absolutely certain that something is very wrong. She loved her job. Plus, her message seemed so strange. And there was another call from her phone but no message. I figured at first that she'd redialed by accident." Meg shrugged hopelessly. "Adam, believe me, I tried all the people and venues I could. I had her landlady check, but Lara didn't answer the door at her apartment. I checked her place myself on the way here. She didn't respond. I have her spare key so I went in. She's not there. Her purse and keys are gone, but she hasn't packed to go anywhere. I'm aware that she hasn't been gone very long and yet . . . her resemblance to the victim is so close."

"I understand."

"I just — I need to see the woman they found, Adam."

"The body is badly decomposed," he warned her.

"Still . . . I believe I'd know if it was Lara."

"I agree that you need to see her," Adam said.

"I noticed that the Bureau is handling the case."

"Yes, the Krewe specifically, and yes, I can

make the arrangements. Are you ready now?"

She nodded.

"You drove here?" he asked her.

"I did. So we can go to the morgue right away?" Meg asked.

"We'll stop there first, although we probably don't have to. I'm sure that if this *is* your friend, her fingerprints are in the system, since she works on the Hill. I believe the corp— the young woman was not . . . Well, it may take them time to get prints, but I can find out where the ME is with that."

He made the calls as she drove. They reached the OCME and a receptionist was waiting to let them in. Adam was familiar with the morgue and led her down a hallway.

They were met by the man she'd seen on television. She was tall, but he seemed to tower over her. She tried to remember the name she'd heard on TV. Agent . . . Boswell or something like that.

It didn't matter. Adam introduced them. He was Special Agent Matthew Bosworth. He was polite but restrained during the introduction, and assured Adam that Dr. Wong was already there, prepared to show the body.

Meg was brought into the room where the

woman lay. The air was pungent with the combined scent of disinfectant and decomposing flesh. She swallowed fiercely to fight her gag reflexes. She'd seen death before, but never like this.

It was difficult to view the body . . .

She had to. She began to shake. Tears welled in her eyes.

"Is it your friend?" Agent Bosworth asked her.

2

Matt had long been accustomed to the horrors in this world and yet every time he saw the handiwork of a killer he felt as though his heart and soul had been torn apart. All that made it bearable was the fact that he confronted those monsters. Someone had to, and perhaps because of his own past, he was more determined to confront them than others.

Yet watching Meg Murray as she stared at the dead woman seemed more wrenching than dealing with death himself.

He wondered if she really *could* make an identification — the corpse was so mottled and distorted with swelling and decomposition.

Even Dr. Wong, who spent far too many hours gazing upon the horrors inflicted on one person by another, seemed moved as he studied the young woman. But Wong didn't usually get to observe, up close, what seeing the ravaged body of a victim did to those who had cherished that victim in life. Making the whole situation even harder was the fact that Meg was one of them now. And she had a past with Adam Harrison, although Matt knew very little about it.

Wong cleared his throat.

As he did, Matt remembered when it had been his turn to stare down at the dead, dreading the possibility that the remains would belong to someone he loved.

He glanced over at Adam, who was looking back at him.

Matt set a hand on Meg Murray's shoulder. "Is it your friend Lara?" Meg was straight and tall — and shaking. She had enormous and striking blue eyes. She blinked hard, trying not to betray emotion. Watching her was painful; she was beautiful but seemed fragile, yet she also had the rigid stance and stoic control of a hardened law enforcement officer.

He forced himself to be just as impassive. The seconds ticked by.

He wondered if she'd heard his question.

"No."

She was shaking even more badly now.

She turned suddenly, almost colliding with him. He was afraid she'd fall and awkwardly tried to comfort her, holding her upright, patting her back.

"No, no," she said. "It's . . . it's not Lara."

Her hair smelled sweetly clean. For a moment, when she clung to him, her body racked with emotional spasms, he felt as if they'd been transported from the decay of the morgue to the realm of daylight and life.

"You're sure?" he asked huskily.

She nodded.

"You realize that the face and body have been badly . . . compromised," he began.

"It's not her. I'd know Lara."

She took a huge breath and steadied herself, shoulders straightening as she moved back, and shrugged with embarrassment. "I'm sorry. I just . . ."

"It's fine," he said.

"I was so afraid . . ." Her voice shook. "I should have better control."

"We should never have complete control. We wouldn't be human," he said.

Matt had never met her before tonight, but he'd heard about her. Unless circumstances brought them a perfect candidate for the Krewe, Adam and Jackson introduced prospective agents they'd heard about to the rest of the group — and then the possibility of an interview was broached. They were a tight clan.

They spoke freely among one another.

But *just* one another.

They were closemouthed, careful to smile casually when other agents teased them about being the *supernatural* crowd. If they responded, it was merely to say that they considered *all* possibilities on a case. He'd first heard about Meg — or Margaret Colleen Murray — in a meeting. Adam had mentioned that a "prospect" was coming through the academy.

If she was on Adam's radar, there had to be a reason.

"Well, then, there's hope," Adam said. "Meg? Don't you agree?"

She'd been looking at Matt with an expression of relief mixed with horror. She turned to Adam and shook her head. He stepped forward with her, urging her closer to the corpse.

"You're sure?" he asked, just as Matt had.

Meg seemed frozen for a minute or two, then reached out and gently touched the dead woman's arm. "Yes . . ."

"My heart bleeds for this poor girl," Adam told her quietly, "but as Matt said, at least there's hope for your friend Lara."

Matt sent Adam a silent question, gesturing toward the door.

"Shall we go?" Adam suggested. "Dr. Wong, thank you."

Matt followed Adam and Meg out to the hallway, thanking Wong for coming back in at a moment's notice that night.

"It's difficult, huh?" Wong shook his head. "I'm very glad for Agent Murray — but it means other people out there will mourn this woman. I wonder sometimes what I was doing when I decided to become a medical examiner. There's an old joke about doctors who go that route. As an ME, you can't make fatal mistakes — because your patients are already dead. But . . . I like to think that at least we speak for the dead, that we're a voice. The voice that may lead to justice."

"Yours *is* the voice that leads to justice," Matt declared.

Wong nodded slowly. "There's something off about this. I can't quite figure out what it is." He lifted one shoulder in a shrug. "When I have both bodies here, maybe I'll see it."

"Keep me posted."

"You heading this one up?"

Matt glanced at Adam and Meg as they moved down the hall toward the exit. "So it seems. Jackson Crow officially, but definitely our unit." Jackson Crow spent long hours in the office. He was in charge of supervising the Krewe and overseeing the unit in New York. He coordinated data searches that came to them, organized specialized work as needed and kept his expert eye on every case in motion.

Since Matt had been summoned to the morgue that morning, he assumed he was now responsible for this one.

"I'll call you immediately with anything I have," Wong promised him.

Matt thanked him and hurried after the other two.

While Jackson Crow did the real supervisory work, Harrison was the creator of their unit and the overall head; Harrison dealt with the Bureau chief, mayors and other law enforcement — paving the way for Krewe members when that was needed. Adam and Jackson made a good team; Adam Harrison left Jackson Crow free to concentrate on the work at hand.

Matt had thought Adam and Meg would leave, but they were waiting for him, speaking quietly.

When he reached them, they left the building.

"What made you think your friend might have been one of the victims?" Matt asked.

"I received a strange message from her, saying that she was going home," Meg replied.

Matt couldn't help it; he raised his

eyebrows at Adam. He said, in what he hoped was an even tone, "Then, perhaps, she *has* gone home."

Meg Murray stiffened. He almost smiled. His reaction might be a whimsical one, but he felt she had the look of a dark-haired pagan queen — not a fledgling agent — at that moment. She might become a force to be reckoned with, if she wasn't one already.

"She *didn't* go home. I called her cell phone, her landline and her home in Virginia. She always has her cell — and she's not answering it. Her parents have both passed away, but I've spoken with her aunt, who hasn't heard from her, either. And now, of course, she's worried, too."

"But she might have taken a longer route . . ."

"Home could mean two other places," she broke in, "aside from her apartment, and she's definitely not there. Harpers Ferry is where she spent half her time, or it could mean Richmond, where her aunt lives. There is no route to Richmond or Harpers Ferry long enough to take all day," Meg said tightly.

At least her anger with him had stopped her shaking. There wasn't a thing about her that seemed fragile now.

"Thank you for making these arrangements, Agent Bosworth. I won't trouble you again."

She turned and headed for her car. Adam Harrison watched her stalk off, a concerned frown on his face. "She has good reason to be worried," he said.

"And that reason would be?"

"I don't know the whole story yet. For starters, we need to have that phone message analyzed. Her friend Lara Mayhew worked for Congressman Walker. Lara called Meg very late — as in 2:30 a.m. Lara was upset. The kind of upset that worried Meg," Adam explained. "And Lara used these words — *I have to get out of here.*"

"But this call only came in last night, or rather, early this morning," Matt pointed out. "I'm not trying to be skeptical. I'm merely playing devil's advocate."

"I've heard the message. Well, messages," he said.

"Messages?"

"Two of them," Adam told him. "I'll have her play them for you in the morning. The second one sounds like an accidental call — just background noise. Might have been wind. We'll need to have it analyzed, as well."

Matt mulled that over. "So, there *could* be trouble. It could mean someone took the

65

phone away from her, for instance. But it could also mean that her friend's gone into hiding, which is what the first message implied."

Adam nodded. "She could have, but I know Meg. And Meg . . . Well, you should understand. Sometimes people just . . . know," he said.

"Yes, I remember you had your eye on her when she was in the academy."

"And now she's out. Her graduation ceremony was yesterday. She's been assigned to the criminal division. Anyway, I'll make the appropriate arrangements and bring her in."

"You think this is a real case? This business about Lara Mayhew? Adam, we do have two savaged bodies. And Meg's friend wasn't one of them."

"But her friend *has* disappeared. There's a killer out there. And I don't like the idea that Lara was working for a congressman. I hate to say it, but . . ."

"Yes, scandal has erupted in those circumstances before." Matt frowned. "But if there's ever been any scandal around Congressman Walker, I've never heard it. His wife is gracious, a well-known hostess and fundraiser for assorted charities. And Walker's been in office so long his kids go to school in DC. Does Meg Murray — do you — believe that Ian Walker has done her friend in over a sex scandal?" Matt was skeptical. Not that congressional scandals didn't exist and not that appearances couldn't deceive, but as he'd said, Walker's reputation was that of an honest, upstanding family man.

"Meg hasn't suggested that her friend was saying anything negative about Ian Walker. Then again, you never know." Adam sighed. "She's worried. And her friend and the two dead girls fit the same description. She might be this killer's type." Adam looked away for a minute. "I'm bringing her into the Krewe. She has . . . instincts. We're going to help her find Lara."

"But should we be chasing someone who might want to stay hidden? Whose disappearance might be entirely unconnected? Sir, we have the makings of a serial killing spree here. One more will make it three."

"Yes, and her friend just might be the one to raise the body count to three," Adam said. "I'm going to let Meg focus on this situation until it's solved. And, Matthew, you'll work with her. My office, first thing in the morning, if you will."

Was she dead?

Lara Mayhew saw nothing but a world that was black. Maybe it was limbo, maybe it was purgatory.

If so, death came with all the pain of life. Her limbs hurt; her head pounded. Opening her eyes seemed to be a Herculean task.

Death. Did death come with thirst and hunger and cold, too?

No.

She wasn't dead, but she was in hell. Hell on earth. She could smell the soil around her; she could feel a damp chill seeping into her.

Buried! she thought. Buried alive.

A sound escaped her lips and she knew that before death came the ability to feel fear. Terror. She tried to move and found that she could. She stretched out her arms and felt the hard dirt beneath her. Yes, buried alive.

She rose to her knees and felt around her.

Scream? Don't scream? Was the killer nearby?

On her hands and knees, she crawled forward — until she struck hard rock. She felt the pain in her knuckles. Yes, that proved she was alive!

She backed up and started moving in a different direction, inch by inch.

And then she hit a wall. Earth, more earth.

Earth all around her. And stone, and metal.

She began to scream and cry out.

She was buried underground, and the dirt walls seemed to swallow her screams.

She screamed and screamed . . . until she could scream no more.

Meg had spent her last four months living dorm-style on campus at Quantico with the rest of her class. She was lucky, however, to have a small room to herself. She'd had a roommate who'd dropped out after their first week. Glenda had thought she was up to it, that the academy was what she wanted. But the physical training, along with some of the graphic videos they'd seen, had changed her mind. Forensic art had been her forte; Glenda was going to leave and work as a consultant for her local police.

Arriving in her room at the complex, Meg switched on her iTunes and fell onto the bed, emotionally worn out and physically exhausted.

She was glad she'd made it through the most grueling part of the training already; she wasn't sure she would've been up for it after seeing the girl on the gurney tonight.

She was still surprised that Adam Harrison could change things with the snap of his fingers — or so it seemed. She'd expected to start working for Supervisor Marshall Dunn on Monday of the following week. Tonight, with Adam, she learned that she'd been assigned to Jackson Crow's unit by special request.

She'd never forgotten Adam, and she'd had her heart set on eventually working for one of his units. She certainly hadn't imagined that he'd remember *her.*

Or that he'd instantly take her into the Krewe.

Or even that he'd believe that this situation with Lara could be important. An emergency!

While she was grateful, she wasn't at all sure why she'd been assigned to work with a man who evidently believed she was an alarmist. Special Agent Matthew Bosworth. He was extremely attractive — and confident. But the man looked at her as if she were more than green. As if she were an outright burden.

And she was humiliated at the way she'd fallen apart, so relieved not to have seen Lara on that gurney, she'd nearly collapsed. Maybe if he hadn't come across as the most seasoned and superior agent in the entire world, she wouldn't have felt so . . . yes, green, when she'd fallen apart.

It doesn't matter, she told herself. She

wanted to find Lara. Regardless of what her friend had said, she wouldn't just have disappeared without getting in touch with Meg again. Without a phone call, at least, to say she'd arrived safely.

Meg was seriously worried. Thank God that Adam believed her — and believed *in* her.

"I would've waited," he said as she drove him home, "given you a chance to meet some of the Krewe. But I'm convinced we're dealing with unusual circumstances. Tomorrow you'll report to my office. You and Special Agent Bosworth will trace Lara's movements, interview the people she was working with and talk to any other friends." He paused. "I've followed you, you know. Your education, your career."

And Meg was glad. It was like learning she'd had a guardian angel watching over her through the years. She grimaced as she recalled the unfortunate incident with Agent Bosworth — and the fact that she'd informed him she wouldn't bother him again.

Adam must have more agents, many more! Why did she have to work with this one?

She'd deal with it. She had to.

The important thing was that now she

didn't have to drive herself insane wondering and worrying about Lara — and end up looking like the worst agent ever after doing so well. She would've spent all her time obsessing over Lara's fate, her whereabouts, when she should've been giving her all to the new job. But now Lara *was* her new job.

Was it better to know the fate of a loved one? People always said it was. And yet it could also mean the end of hope.

Years ago, knowing that Mary Elizabeth was dead hadn't eased the pain of her loss.

But perhaps seeing justice done did create what they called closure. Her aunt had known that her daughter's suffering was over. That her killer was locked away. Actually, he wasn't locked away anymore. He'd been killed in a prison brawl.

Her aunt had told her that the killer's death shouldn't have made anything better for her. But it had. Christian or not, she'd said, it had brought her some resolution. She hoped he'd suffered.

And now . . .

Now Lara was missing, after leaving a cryptic message.

Maybe she'd gone into deep hiding. But if she had, she'd done it for a reason. And the only way to find Lara was to find out what that reason could be.

Meg sat up, considering the possibilities, trying to sort out where Lara could be. Probably not in Richmond, or at least not at her aunt's house. But Lara had a small house in Harpers Ferry, left to her by her parents when they'd passed away. She and Lara had often visited during their college years, both in love with hiking and tubing on the river. They hadn't been in quite a while; she didn't think Lara had been out there recently, but she'd hired a service to handle maintenance and security, and she even rented it out now and then.

Maybe she was there. It was a direction to pursue, at any rate.

After a minute, Meg rose and walked into the bathroom. Time to get ready for bed.

She liked to shower first thing in the morning. It seemed to start the day right, really wake her up. But since she'd begun training, she'd discovered she needed a night shower, too — in order to be able to sleep.

Tonight, the odor of the morgue seemed to linger on her. She didn't just want a shower to sleep, she *needed* one.

She took a long shower, with very hot water and lots of soap and shampoo.

Wrapped in a towel, she got out her toothbrush and toothpaste. The mirror was heavily fogged, and she wiped it with the edge of her big beach towel.

She looked thin, she noted. Thin and haggard. Well, nothing she could do about that right now.

She studiously brushed her teeth, glanced in the mirror again — and froze.

The mirror was misty once more and yet she could see her own face. And another. Behind her.

Lara's face.

Lara's mouth worked; her eyes seemed filled with pain. No audible words came to her lips, and seconds later she began to fade away. And yet Meg thought she knew what Lara had tried to say.

Not *help me,* but *find me. Find my remains.*

Meg whirled around just in time to see the last vestige of her friend disappear into the soft swirl of fog left by her very hot shower.

"I met Margaret when she was a child," Adam was saying to Matt. "The Krewe didn't exist back then, but local law enforcement in West Virginia called me in. They knew I could find the right people to help us discover the truth. I was also friends with an agent working kidnapping cases for the FBI." He sat behind his desk, a cup of coffee in front of him, his hands folded on the desk. He raised them as he said, "There was hope that it was a ransom case, that the missing girl would come home. But her little cousin knew. She told me, although she wouldn't tell anyone else, that she saw Mary Elizabeth sitting at the foot of her bed. She was gone, Meg told me, and she could be found in the cemetery. It changed the case. We found the body before the ransom drop, and because of the forensic evidence at the scene, her killer was easily caught. So I've kept tabs on Meg. I was going to wait until she'd graduated and taken a position at the academy and then introduce her to Jackson and the Krewe, but . . . well, life intrudes and changes everything. Life — and death."

Matt nodded, well aware of the truth of his words.

He looked out the window onto the beautiful old street. He loved their location in Alexandria, and he was glad the Krewe had left the modern building where they'd once had their offices. There was something about looking out at the old row houses that seemed good for the soul; history had marched through these streets. The houses had been there when the nation struggled for freedom. They'd continued to serve as homes during the bloody conflict of the

Civil War. Alexandria was so close to Washington, DC — yet it had been part of the Confederate state of Virginia.

Of course, he loved the Capitol, too. He was no romantic when it came to war, but the history of his nation's struggle was both powerful and heartbreaking to him. He was fascinated by the life of Abraham Lincoln. He was equally interested in the lives of men like Stonewall Jackson and Robert E. Lee.

When he was young, his parents had purchased an old tavern west of Richmond. In a roundabout way, it had been owned by Thomas Jefferson, who'd purchased the place for a cousin and been repaid over a period of years. Matt had dreamed that he could sneak into the parlor area at night — and find Jefferson sitting by the fireplace.

He never did see Jefferson. He did, however, encounter the spirit of his cousin, Josiah Thompkin. Thompkin had regaled him with tales of famous congressmen, battles, the Underground Railroad and more. Matt's parents had thought he spent too much time with his books and that he — like many children — had an invisible friend.

One of his great-aunts had known, however, and when his mother had spoken to him about her concerns, Genevieve had winked at him and told him that "imaginary" friends could be the best. They mirrored the soul, she'd said, and furnished the mind with information.

Great-Aunt Genevieve was long gone now, but he always remembered her with a smile. She'd made it to ninety-five, full of laughter and vigor to the end.

She'd assured him she *wasn't* coming back. She'd lived a long life — and she knew the light was waiting for her.

"You and Meg have similar pasts," Adam said, returning Matt's mind to the present.

Had Meg grown up with imaginary friends, as well? Unlike Meg and him and the rest of the Krewe, Adam's background was somewhat different. His son, Josh, had been granted the gift — or the curse — of precognition; he'd known what might happen. He'd known what people were thinking. He'd been ill throughout his life, and he'd died young. There seemed to be no rhyme or reason when it came to paranormal ability. Matt felt sad that there were people worldwide who kept their secret, trying not to give themselves away in case the world considered them crazy.

There was a knock at the door. Agent Murray was certainly punctual.

Matt remained by the window, staring out

as Adam invited her inside. He turned, curious about the young woman. She could be no more than midtwenties, but she carried herself with a grace and poise that belied her age. Her dark hair was pulled back and she seemed even more attractive than he had realized. Today she was wearing a medium-length business skirt and matching jacket, and he couldn't help noticing that her legs were wickedly long and well shaped. There was an unselfconsciousness about her, and he sensed that she had no idea of her own appeal.

"Meg, come in. I have a few more of our local Krewe working this. They'll be getting onto research, credit card trails and the like. I think you and Matt should start at the source. Head over to Congressman Walker's office. I've arranged that he'll be ready for you at ten," Adam said.

"She's dead," Meg told him.

"You *know* that?" Adam asked.

Meg nodded, glancing at Matt as if she didn't want to speak in his presence.

"I know she must be dead, yes."

"You saw her?" Adam asked.

Meg glanced at Matt again and lowered her head in a nod.

"It's all right, Meg. You can speak freely. Don't worry, Matt has friends around the

78

city who only appear to him. I'm just so sorry that we won't find your friend alive," he said very softly.

She'd been crying, Matt saw. He felt a tug of sympathy.

It hurt so badly to lose people.

"You're absolutely sure?" he heard himself say. He didn't mean to doubt her; he sincerely hoped she'd been wrong. His voice sounded rougher than he'd intended.

She turned to him. "Agent Bosworth," she said coldly. "I never say that someone is dead unless I believe it to be true." He could tell he'd offended her. But that wasn't necessarily a bad thing; anger helped dissipate pain.

"Until we find her, you can't be certain," he said, then asked, "You've never had a living person in desperate trouble try to reach you?"

"No," she said, the one word like a cube of ice in the room.

"Did she speak to you, Meg?" Adam asked.

Meg hesitated. "She couldn't quite manage to speak, but . . . I think she asked me to find her. And I — I believe she wants us to find her body."

Matt felt that Meg Murray had no intention of giving his opinions any credence, but he didn't feel the need to respond. He'd been around for a long time — as an agent and as one who knew the existence of a sixth sense. She'd learn.

The other agents arrived then.

Adam rose to make introductions. Jackson Crow had come in with Angela Hawkins, Will Chan and Katya Sokolov.

"Agent Murray will be joining this office," Adam said. "This, as you can appreciate, is a difficult time for her. Meg, everyone's been briefed on the situation with Lara Mayhew and the two murders. Agent Crow is your boss and I never interfere. Okay, I *seldom* interfere. Agent Hawkins sorts through our many requests and tries to send out the right people. Since we're near Washington where everything seems a bit unusual, we're quite busy here. That was a joke — or an attempt at a joke, anyway. Agent Sokolov is a medical examiner as well as an agent. She'll visit Wong today and inspect the bodies."

Meg solemnly shook hands with everyone. She asked Will Chan, "What's your specialty?"

Will smiled. "I was an illusionist," he told her.

"I see," Meg said in a pleasant tone that nonetheless relayed her confusion.

Will's smile grew wider. "My specialty is film, sound, cameras — and now and then, a bit of a performance if necessary. Although occasionally we all have to perform. In any case the team you see here will be working with you on this particular case."

"Can you play the message your friend left?" Matt asked, not meaning to be churlish, but they weren't at a getting-to-know-you cocktail party.

"Yes."

She pulled her phone out of the black leather tote she carried and set it on speaker. They heard a woman's voice.

One that sounded breathless — and scared.

"Meg, it's me, Lara. I wanted to let you know I'm going home. Home, as in getting out of DC and heading for Richmond. I'm going as soon as it's daylight. I'll talk to you when I can. Love you. Don't say anything to anyone else, okay? I have to get out of here. Talk soon."

Meg played the message twice.

Jackson cleared his throat. "She did say she was leaving in the morning."

"And I wanted to believe it," Meg said.

There was an awkward silence. Matt wasn't convinced, but Adam had faith in her conviction.

And they all had faith in Adam.

"So, you see," Meg said, "something happened during the day or that night that made her want to . . . run."

"And meet up with our killer?" Will murmured.

"Or another fate," Matt replied.

"In other words, you think there might've been a different motive to get rid of Lara Mayhew — and she was killed by a different perp?" Angela asked.

"Entirely possible," Matt said. "But Ian Walker isn't known for being . . ."

"Slimy?" Kat supplied.

Matt looked at Meg. "Did she ever suggest that there was anything going on between her and the congressman?"

"No. But . . . I haven't spent much time with her since I started at the academy. We talked every other day, but I've only actually seen her twice. As far as I knew, Lara adored him, as a father figure. She lost her parents when she was eleven. I think she saw Walker as a fine man, the way she'd seen her dad."

"Maybe Walker will solve the mystery," Jackson suggested.

"Doubtful," Will Chan said.

"And . . ." Kat began, before hesitating.

"And?" Adam repeated.

"To the rest of the world, the idea that something's wrong is . . . mere supposition. She's a young woman who became disillusioned with politics and left DC."

"There's another message," Adam reminded them.

Meg pressed her phone again. All they heard was a whooshing sound — like the wind — and then a thump.

And the phone went dead.

"I'll check with her cell phone company," Angela said. "Meg, I'll need your phone for the next few hours. We'll have techs try to decipher those sounds."

"Of course."

"You'll be with Matt if we need to reach you for any reason. We'll get the recording and return your cell as soon as possible."

"Whatever it takes," Meg said.

"And you're off to see Congressman Walker!" Angela looked from Meg to Matt. "I don't envy you. Interviewing a politician. I don't think many of them are capable of telling the truth, even when they've got nothing to hide!"

Matt liked Angela. She was down-to-earth, pleasant under the most trying circumstances — and skilled at figuring out past sins that might have emerged in the present. Attractive, in her early thirties, she was light-haired and light-eyed. She was married to Jackson. Matt hadn't been around when they'd done the deed; they'd slipped quietly away for a small private wedding. In this "special" unit, agents being married to each other was acceptable. Will and Kat were a couple, too.

They all had to work so closely together that Matt felt they were more a family than a workforce. He wondered how their new member was going to fit in.

Of course, when he'd joined, the others had wondered if *he'd* fit in.

"Your work sounds intriguing," Meg said.

"It's different," Angela agreed. "It's a million hours a week most of the time. It's travel when you're tired of going places. It's seeing a lot of what can only be described as evil. That would be true whatever position you took after graduation, but then you've been through the academy. You know that."

"Yes," Meg said. She added a little hesitantly, "I'm grateful to be here. I was going to apply when I was able to. This is all . . . faster than I expected."

"Meg is certain that Lara is dead," Adam said flatly.

There was silence for a minute. Matt realized that Meg was doing a worthy job of hiding her grief. And yet he wasn't certain that she was right about Lara's death. He walked over to her. He wasn't sure why he placed his hands on her shoulders except that he wanted her full attention.

She seemed to draw herself up, stand taller, but didn't move or back away.

"Meg, are you positive? Maybe you saw her, but she was in your mind, asking for help."

She still didn't back away. "I don't see people who step out of my mind, Agent Bosworth. Do you?"

"Actually, I have. The dead can reach out, as we all know. But sometimes the living can, too, from a distance."

She slipped away from him and he was almost sorry he'd spoken. She lowered her head. He thought she might have had an expression of hope on her face.

"I haven't had that experience. I honestly believe that she's dead." He asked himself how true that was. He had the impression that she and Lara had often read each other's minds.

"I'm sorry, Meg," Jackson said. "Very sorry. Adam, I have some news. We have a match for our first victim. Her name was Cathy Crighton. She worked at the Big Fish down in Georgetown. Her boss assumed she

85

just took off. Apparently, the pay isn't very high and he has a large employee turnover. Not only that, he considered her a fairly unreliable employee, showing up late and so on. Turns out a friend in Oklahoma, who'd been trying to reach her, reported her as missing. The report took a while to get to us. I'm making inquiries about her last movements."

"Anything about the girl who was found yesterday?" Adam asked.

"No, not yet," Jackson answered. "We'll be cross-referencing all the victims we have on record and missing-persons reports, seeing if we can come up with a common denominator." Jackson looked over at Matt. "I've emailed you all the particulars I have so far."

Adam turned to Meg. "Make sure you have everyone's cell phone number."

"I'll get started on the digital," Will said, leaving the room.

Kat was going off to the OCME, while Jackson and Angela left to research Congressman Walker. It was time for Matt to head out with Meg Murray.

"We'll make a stop at Lara's apartment first," he said.

Meg bit her lip, eyes closed. He could only imagine what she was fearing — that they'd enter her friend's apartment and find her there. Dead.

"It has to be done," he told her calmly.

"Yes, of course," she said. "I've already been to the apartment, though. I have a key. Lara isn't there."

"*Wasn't* there," he pointed out.

"Yes . . ."

"Chances are you're right, but we'll take another look, anyway. I've called the landlady. We'll have her let us in officially — and start fresh. Maybe the landlady will have something useful to say," Matt added.

"Fine, you two get on that, and then go over to the congressman's place. We don't want to lose this first session with him." Adam paused, smiling at Meg. "Scariest part of the job," Adam said lightly as they left the office. "Politics! Scary as hell."

3

Meg wasn't sure why, but it seemed that she and Agent Matt Bosworth were destined to be at odds — over little things that didn't really matter. She didn't mean for that to happen. It just did.

It started as soon as they left Adam's office.

"My car is parked on the street."

"My company car is just below."

"Yes, but I'm going to need mine . . ."

"I'll ask Jackson to see that it's flagged so you won't get a ticket."

"Honestly, it would be simpler if I drove myself . . ."

"We're going in a company car. This is a Krewe case."

Who cares which car we go in? she wanted to shout.

She refrained. He didn't open the door for her; they were both agents. Equals? Not in his mind! She didn't think he was sexist.

She just thought he considered himself superior because of his seniority.

She slid into the passenger's side. Before he drove off, he put a quick call through to Jackson. "Can someone see to Agent Murray's car?" He glanced over at her. "What kind of car?"

"Jaguar."

He didn't say anything; the slight quirk on his face seemed to indicate that a cadet shouldn't be able to afford such a car.

"It's a 2004," she said, trying to sound as if she was just giving a description. She had no intention of explaining that it had been her dad's. "Silver," she added, annoyed with herself, wondering why the hell she was concerned about his opinion. It was all because she'd nearly passed out on the man. A matter of pride, she supposed. Or maybe even denial. She'd gone to the academy with fit, intelligent, attractive people. Agent Bosworth seemed to be all of those things — ten times over. He was hardened by his years with the FBI, she supposed, and guided by the single vision of an assignment. And yet if she so much as brushed against the man . . .

She also wondered if he was so rude and blunt because he recognized his own appeal. Maybe it was his way of telling her,

Hey, back off! Don't touch, don't come too close.

He passed the description on to Jackson, then hung up and drove.

Dread filled her as they made their way to the Capitol Hill area. Lara had rented the most affordable apartment she could find, as close to the Capitol as possible. She lived in a converted mansion, an old family home that had been divided into six units, two on each floor. Lara was on the first.

As Matt parked, Meg realized he'd done his homework. He knew exactly where they were going. He pulled out his phone as they exited the car and headed toward the house.

By the time they reached it, Lara's landlady, a silver-haired woman named Mrs. Shelley, was there to meet them. She extended a hand to them both, smiling at Meg since they'd met a few times, and introducing herself to Matt Bosworth.

"Lara didn't say anything to me about breaking her lease or going away," Mrs. Shelley said. "I do hope that she's all right — she's such a lovely young woman!"

"We're certainly hoping she's all right, too. But Meg can't get in touch with her and we're worried, so thank you for your help," Matt said.

"Of course! Come on in."

Mrs. Shelley led them through the main door to the house. Stairs stretched up to the second floor, with hallways leading to the downstairs apartments.

Taking out a ring of keys, Mrs. Shelley looked through them as they walked to Lara's door.

For a moment, Meg felt as if she couldn't breathe. She was overwhelmed by the same fear she'd felt when she'd come here yesterday evening, when terrible visions had rushed through her head and she'd been terrified that she'd open the door and find the apartment trashed and Lara in a pool of blood. Or that she'd go into her bedroom and find her with her throat slit.

Mrs. Shelley opened the door.

The living room was neat, as Meg had known it would be. Lara had once told Meg that she wasn't home enough to really mess the place up.

"Be careful what you touch," Matt said.

She tried not to glare at him. She *knew* that!

"We'll go through the place later," he said. If he knew how offensive he was being, he gave no sign.

With anxiety dogging her every step, Meg still managed to walk quickly through the living area to the bedroom and the small office beyond.

All the while, she knew that Agent Bosworth was a step behind her. Did he not trust her? Or was he afraid she hadn't looked carefully — that they might stumble across Lara's body?

"I guess she's not here," Mrs. Shelley called out. She hadn't moved from the living room.

"Can you tell if she packed up anything at all?" Agent Bosworth asked Meg.

"I don't think she did. At least, it didn't seem that way to me last night. But I can't be one hundred percent sure without looking through her drawers and her closet. I don't have gloves, so . . ."

"I do," he told her before she could finish, taking out two pairs. "We don't have time for a complete search now, but maybe you can tell if she did pack."

And find out if her friend's body had been stuffed in the closet.

Meg pulled on a pair of the gloves and opened the closet door. Lara's clothing hung there neatly. The black-and-red carry-on Lara took anytime she traveled — her lucky travel bag, as she called it — was on the floor, along with sneakers, sandals and shoes Lara would've taken on a trip.

"I don't believe she packed and left," Meg said.

"Okay," he told her. "We'll pay our visit to Ian Walker and come back for a more thorough search."

They met Mrs. Shelley in the living room. She seemed relieved that they'd found nothing.

"She must've taken a little trip, then," Mrs. Shelley said, smiling. "If she was really leaving, she would've told me."

"Of course," Meg assured her.

"We'll be back this afternoon," Matt Bosworth said. "We're going to see if we can dig up any clues as to where she might be."

Mrs. Shelley nodded and unfastened two keys. "Here you are. The first opens the main door. All the tenants have one. The second is to this door."

Matt thanked her, not mentioning that Meg already had a key.

"Oh! You might want the security video," Mrs. Shelley said.

"You have security tapes?"

"There's a camera just over the entry," Mrs. Shelley replied. "It's a wonderful selling point when I need to rent out the units, although that isn't often. This close to Capitol Hill, I don't have much trouble landing good tenants. You know DC — once people get into a place they like, they tend to stay for the long haul."

"I'm going to have an agent come out for the security footage covering the past few days, if you don't mind."

"Anything," Mrs. Shelley said fervently.

They both thanked her and headed back to the car.

"Shouldn't we be looking at the footage right now?" Meg asked.

"I'm going to have Will retrieve it and then check it out," he said.

"But . . ."

"He's an expert. He'll know if anyone's tampered with it."

She fell silent. She knew she'd been letting her emotions take hold.

"Onward to Congressman Walker's house," Matt announced.

Meg realized she had no idea where the man lived; that was something Lara had never mentioned.

She quickly found out.

Ian Walker lived in the Sixteenth Street Heights in DC in a grand colonial-style mansion — when he was in the city.

The congressman had been blessed with family money. He'd also known how to play the stock market to improve on his inheritance. She knew that because Lara had talked about him so much. While she and Lara had been friends forever, Meg's home was really Harpers Ferry, West Virginia. Lara's parents and family were from Richmond, although they also had a home in Harpers Ferry, where they'd spent summers. Meg had worked and lived in Richmond for a few years after she'd graduated from college there; she was still a West Virginia voter.

"Nice neighborhood," she murmured as they approached the house. "It was his idea for us to come here rather than his office?" she asked.

She didn't use Agent Bosworth's name as she spoke to him. In the car, it was only the two of them. She'd noticed that while most law enforcement agents and the instructors she worked with called one another by their surnames, Krewe agents were on a first-name basis. They knew one another well. Or, at least, they seemed to. *Matt.* She couldn't bring herself to call this man Matt. He obviously thought he'd been saddled with a neurotic beginner.

She wasn't a beginner. She'd qualified as a Richmond police officer and now she was officially an FBI agent.

"Yes. Someone on his staff gave you a hard

time, but Walker himself seemed concerned about the fact that we were worried. Adam told me that to the best of the congressman's knowledge, Lara just wanted to move in another direction. That they'd parted on good terms," Matt said, watching the road. "Be very careful. We're going in there for help. No accusations, okay?"

"I did make it through the academy!" she told him.

He laughed. "Yes, as you've pointed out. And admittedly that's an accomplishment. But I know plenty of agents with plenty of what you'd call the right stuff — and no social skills. Doesn't mean they're not good agents. It just means there are certain places, certain times, they shouldn't be in the field."

"My social skills are just fine," she insisted. She decided not to suggest that he might want to work on his own.

There was a gate, artfully designed, a break in a high wall around the house. Ivy and vines grew along the wall, making it appear that the home was well established and a pleasant addition to the area.

"Capitol police," Matt murmured.

"Pardon?"

He pointed down the street, and she saw a car with the markings of the Capitol police department. She knew that the department was responsible for a two-hundred-block area around the Capitol, but in reality their reach extended all the way around the globe, if need be. They were responsible for Congress when it was in session, but their responsibility to senators and congressmen, their families and staff, went far beyond that. If a congressman from Utah, for example, was speaking back in his home state, Capitol police might be there to look after his safety. In 1801, when Congress moved from Philadelphia to DC, only one man was assigned by Congress to protect the Capitol building. But in 1828, when a son of John Quincy Adams was attacked in the rotunda, the United States Capitol Police Department was established.

"Maybe the congressman thinks he's in danger," Meg suggested.

"Or maybe the patrol car is just doing a drive-by," Matt said thoughtfully.

"It might have something to do with the death of Garth Hubbard," Meg said.

"That's an interesting possibility," Matt said.

They paused at the gate. When he stated who they were and it rolled open, they drove through to the circular drive.

Three men in suits were standing on the porch.

None of them was Ian Walker.

As they both got out of the car, Matt Bosworth took his ID wallet from his suit pocket; she did the same.

The men seemed to recognize Matt.

And they'd been expecting them.

The three on the porch were a varied trio. One was tall, maybe an inch taller than Matt. He was bald and looked like he might have been a biker in an earlier life. Another one was lean, about a foot shorter, with thick wavy hair and a ready smile. The third was somewhere in between, well built, about six-even and with close-cropped brown hair.

"Welcome," the shorter man said. "Congressman Walker is waiting for you. I'm Ellery Manheim, his personal assistant. Nathan Oliver here, to my right —" he indicated the large man "— is also with my office, and Joe Brighton —" he gestured at the man to his left "— is Congressman Walker's campaign and media manager."

Meg had heard about the three of them from Lara. As they shook hands all around, Meg thought of the things she'd heard Lara say about these men — many of which had made her laugh. Ellery Manheim was the one in charge of day-to-day matters, since

Walker was usually absorbed with bigger concerns. "Ellery's fine," Lara had told her, "as long as it's not raining. The man has more hair products than I've owned in my whole life!"

Lara had liked Joe Brighton and called him an interesting man. Brighton had been a marine before going into media. "He could spin it so that a polar explorer would buy an icebox, no word of a lie!" Lara had said.

And about the huge guy, Nathan Oliver, Lara's comment had been, "He's okay, too. Except if you were to crash into the guy, you'd probably have to be hospitalized. I think he's made of steel — or maybe rock. He'd crumble if he cracked a smile. He's called an assistant, but I suspect he's really a bodyguard."

Meg thought she recognized the men, at least vaguely. They hovered around the congressman whenever he spoke in public.

"Come in, come in, please," Ellery Manheim told them. "Congressman Walker is waiting in the den. I understand you've come to see us about Lara Mayhew?"

"Yes," Matt said. Meg realized he didn't intend to say anything more until they were actually with the congressman.

If Manheim had hoped Matt was going to

discuss why they were there, he didn't reveal any sign of it. He just said, "Lara is a phenomenal young woman. Her work for Congressman Walker was exceptional."

They were led through a mudroom to a grand foyer and, from there, to a large office off to the side; it seemed to stretch the length of the house, which must have been seven or eight thousand square feet in size.

Matt glanced at her as they moved along. To her surprise, he offered her a wry smile and whispered, "And this is just his Capitol home. Can you imagine his spread in Virginia?"

Her lips twitched slightly. He was already stepping forward to shake Congressman Walker's hand.

"I understand there's some concern about Lara Mayhew," Walker said after introductions had gone around. Meg noticed that Matt referred to her as Agent Murray — and made no reference to her friendship with Lara.

"Yes, she left friends and family a few very cryptic messages, and no one's been able to reach her," Matt said.

Congressman Walker directed them to comfortable leather seating in the center of the long office. Meg saw that his men had followed them in, but didn't sit. "Lara was with us at Capitol Hill until very late the night before last," Walker said. "And normally, she'd be here now. She was wonderful! But I'm afraid she resigned her position that night. Maybe the hours of the job got to her," he said, shaking his head. "I don't blame her. She was young and probably wanted more of a life than she had working with me."

"You're planning a run for the presidency?" Matt asked.

"Considering it," Walker responded.

"Congressman," Ellery Manheim said, clearing his throat.

Walker grinned. Meg observed that he was a handsome and dignified man, wearing his years very well for a man of sixty-plus. He had retained a full head of steel-gray hair; his eyes were a deep brown and set in a nicely sculpted face. He was extremely fit; Lara had told her he could run on his treadmill and dictate notes or discuss a promotional or communications issue at the same time. Today, he was casually dressed in a light blue pullover and jeans.

He had an easy smile that made him a man to trust.

"Why were you working so late?" Matt asked.

"The evening got away from us." Walker

let out a soft sigh. "You can't imagine the volume of letters I receive, the needs of my constituents. Couple that with studying the quantity of bills that are always on the agenda — and sorting out what's tacked onto what and whether the value of passing a particular bill outweighs the problems. Then, of course, there's reelection — and deciding if I should throw my hat in the ring. Work never stops," he said.

"No, it never does!" That pronouncement came from a woman who swept into the room. She was slim and tiny and kept her hair tinted blonde, and, like the congressman, she carried her age well. She didn't appear to be the recipient of hours of cosmetic work, and the smile lines that crinkled around her mouth and eyes only enhanced her natural beauty.

"Work, work, work!" she said, grinning as she approached the newcomers.

Matt instantly rose; Meg did, too. "My wife, Kendra," Congressman Walker said. "Kendra, special agents Bosworth and Murray, FBI."

"FBI?" Kendra repeated, shaking their hands.

"They're here about Lara," Walker said.

"Lara? She's an *amazing* girl," Kendra said. "If she's in any kind of trouble . . ."

"No trouble, my dear," Walker said quickly. "She's missing."

"*Missing?* She was working with you all the other night!" Kendra said. She frowned, playing with a little silver pendant of the Washington Memorial she wore around her neck. "But didn't you tell me she was moving on — that she felt she wasn't really cut out for politics?"

"Yes, dear," Walker murmured.

"We'll get to the bottom of this," Kendra declared. "Ellery, could you ask Ginger to bring a coffee and tea service in here? You people are so consumed with work that you forget good manners!"

Ellery disappeared out the door as bidden.

Kendra sat, motioning for Matt and Meg and the congressman to do so again. "Born and raised in Virginia by old-school parents," Kendra told them. "And while many aspects of Southern history might be regrettable, Southern hospitality is not one of them. Why didn't you offer these hardworking agents some form of sustenance, Ian?"

"My dear, we hadn't gotten that far!" Walker protested. He looked at her as if he still adored her and the gaze she gave him in return said the same thing. Meg knew they'd been married for nearly thirty years. Their devotion was admirable.

If it was real.

"We're fine," Matt assured her. "And I'm from Virginia myself."

"I hope you voted for me," Walker said.

"Yes, actually, I did," Matt said.

"And you, Ms. Murray? I'm sorry, I mean Agent Murray?" Walker asked.

Meg saw that he was studying her closely.

She'd never met him. Between their schedules, she and Lara had only managed to get together for a few brief breakfasts and dinners. While Lara had talked about her job and the people she worked with, she'd never had a chance to bring Meg to a fund-raiser or any other event where she might've gotten to know Walker. Yet he seemed to know her. Or know about her.

She forced a smile. "West Virginia," she told him. "But if I was registered in Virginia, I'm sure I would've voted for you."

A young woman in a polo shirt and chinos walked in, bearing a silver tray laden with a teapot, an urn, finger sandwiches, cream and sugar and serving utensils.

"Thanks, Ginger," Kendra Walker said.

"My pleasure, Mrs. Walker. The children are being dropped off soon. Shall I watch them in the playroom until you're ready?"

"Yes, please."

When Ginger left, Kendra asked, "Coffee, tea?"

"Coffee, please," Matt said. "Just black."

"Same for me, thanks," Meg said.

"Congressman," Matt began, "Lara Mayhew called a friend after she left you the night before last. In her message she said she *had to* leave."

Meg thought the congressman would appear baffled, that he would claim he had no idea why.

If he'd done something to her, he would know she hadn't been found yet. Or would he? Had he left her body lying somewhere they wouldn't easily find it?

But he shook his head sadly. "I was sorry, sorry because I knew I was losing one of my best employees. But there was an issue that I've determined to deal with in one way, and Lara was opposed to my position."

"What was your position?" Meg asked.

"It had to do with a health issue, but you realize that committees manage to tack all kinds of add-ons to a bill to get other members to vote for it. Once a bill reaches a vote, it might contain a lot of extra provisions, many of which have nothing to do with the original bill," Ian Walker explained. "Lara's opinion was that we should nix the whole bill. After Hubbard died, I was trying to rework it on my own, but others became involved, too. Lara was an idealist. None of us want to admit it, but we aren't capable of creating an ideal world. Or an ideal bill. Not when government requires compromise."

He seemed earnest. And it was plausible.

"Garth Hubbard was a remarkable man. I believe he would have made an exceptional president," Kendra said in a sorrowful voice. Her fingers tightened around her necklace as she added, "Such a tragic loss."

"I thought there was some question about his death," Matt said. "Weren't there accusations flying around that either the far left or the far right had done him in?"

"When a political figure dies suddenly and unexpectedly, there's always a conspiracy theory," Walker said with a wave of his hand. "I loved Garth like a brother. But he had high blood pressure all his life. He told me once that his doctor had said he'd probably die of something heart-related sooner rather than later. He did. Massive heart attack. Better now, I suppose, than if he'd made the presidency." Walker seemed to reflect for a minute, then said, "Lara was disheartened by his death. I suppose she just didn't have enough faith in me."

"Oh, darling, don't say that!" Kendra slipped an arm around his shoulders. "Lara is such a lovely girl. I honestly believe she maintains complete faith in you. She was overwhelmed by all the bureaucracy and red tape that goes with government."

She'd been so polite. Now she looked at Matt and Meg as if they were ogres who had come to threaten a loved one. "Is there anything else? I wish we could help you with Lara. She was a cherished member of our team. But she chose to leave. She said she was going home. But she didn't let us know what her plans were. She wasn't particularly happy when she left, and I have to admit, although I love the girl, she doesn't belong here if she can't be a team player."

So much for Southern hospitality. Kendra was suddenly all but breathing fire.

"What I need to know is where and when you saw her last," Matt said pleasantly, as if he hadn't heard the venom and dismissal in her words.

"I saw her a few days ago," Kendra replied.

"The night before last, we were all at my office," Walker said. "My staff and me, not my family." He smiled at his wife. "Our discussions went on for hours, and she left really late. Like two or three in the morning." He looked sheepish for a moment. "I wasn't aware of the time. She was determined to leave. There's constant security around the Capitol all the time, though. I'm sure she's fine — and that she did just what she said she was going to do. Go home."

He spoke earnestly, and Meg couldn't help believing that Walker genuinely cared about Lara — and that he'd been sorry to see her go.

But what exactly had upset her friend so much?

Matt Bosworth was getting to his feet, and she stood, too. She might have been a solid — even kick-ass — cadet, but he was the appointed agent and she was the new-grad tagalong. If he had risen, they were leaving. Both of them.

"What had been tacked onto the bill that upset Lara?" she asked.

"Oh, it had to do with equal rights in the health bill," he said vaguely. "It's all quite lengthy and complicated to explain, Agent Murray."

She found that an unsatisfactory and, yes, condescending response, but it was time to go.

Matt took her arm. "Well, thank you for your assistance with this matter, and, Mrs.

Walker, thank you for your hospitality. We may need to talk to you again. I'm grateful that you're as concerned about Lara Mayhew as we are."

"Of course!" Walker said, nodding solemnly. "We cared deeply about Lara. Call me anytime."

"Yes, of course," Kendra echoed, but her voice was a little more brittle. "If we can help in any way, call on us anytime."

Ellery Manheim suddenly made a shocked noise.

They all turned to look at him. He quickly hid whatever emotion had accompanied his thought and resumed speaking.

"I heard they discovered a woman the other day . . . A woman who'd been murdered. Like the one they found about a month ago," he said. "My God, you don't think that could be Lara, do you?"

"It wasn't Ms. Mayhew," Matt informed him.

"No?" Kendra Walker asked. She seemed relieved.

"No."

"You're sure?"

"Yes," Matt said, giving no more information.

"Lara's fingerprints would be in the system. She was bonded, of course,"

Congressman Walker said.

"Thank God!" Ellery Manheim said, and he sounded sincere.

There was a rush of laughter and footsteps pounding toward the room. Two little girls dashed in. They were both blonde and thin and full of energy, one about five and the other perhaps eight.

"Grammy, Gramps!" they called.

The kids pushed past Nathan Oliver and Joe Brighton to reach the congressman and his wife.

Kendra scooped up the smaller one and Congressman Walker picked up the older girl, whirling her around. Ginger ran in after the girls.

"I'm sorry!" Ginger said, breathless. "They got past me. They wanted to see you right away."

"It's fine, Ginger," Walker said. "My daughter brings the kids over and takes a shopping day now and then," he told Matt and Meg. "I love to see them!"

"These people were just leaving," Kendra said abruptly.

The child in her arms was staring at Meg. She had curly hair and huge blue eyes and was as cute as a child could be. She gave Meg a huge smile and reached out a hand. Meg reached back and the little girl

110

squeezed her finger.

"Pretty!" she said.

Meg couldn't help flushing. "Thank you. And you're very pretty, too."

"Ellery, will you see the agents out?" Kendra asked, a bit impatiently.

"Can you play with us? *Please!*" the toddler in Kendra's arms begged.

"Oh, now, Brittany, you know grown-ups have to work. And the agents are working now," Kendra said.

"I'd love to stay, play," Meg told the child, "but your grandma's right. I do have to work."

"This way, please," Ellery said.

When they got to the door, Ellery offered them both cards. "I think the world of Lara. If you need anything else, don't hesitate to call."

Matt handed him a business card in return.

Meg didn't have any yet.

"We appreciate that," Matt said. "Now let me ask you this. Lara didn't say anything to you that she didn't say to Congressman Walker, did she?"

Ellery opened his mouth. For a moment, Meg was certain he was going to say something revealing, something unexpected, but he was looking toward the office.

She swung around; the door was just closing.

"She wasn't happy that the congressman wanted to compromise on the health bill and not remain true to his campaign promises. She really was . . . disillusioned. That happens around here. But you can't win. If you stick to your guns, you create a stalemate, nothing gets done and people are angry. If you compromise, then the idealists are angry. It's not easy," Ellery said.

"No, I understand that. Did she say anything to you about home, or going anywhere, at any time?" Matt asked.

Ellery turned to Meg then. "Agent Murray, are you the Meg Murray who's Lara's good friend?"

Lara had evidently talked about her. It seemed pointless to lie.

But she didn't have to answer, because Matt did.

"Yes, Agent Murray and Lara were good friends," he said.

Ellery Manheim smiled awkwardly. "Then you know that she loved Richmond, where she was born, and the place she officially called home. But she talked to me about the past, and said she loved hanging around in Harpers Ferry with you and your grandfather the most. Lara said you and she loved to play at the national park, and that you crawled up to the heights and hung around when the ghost tours were going on. You reenacted John Brown's raid and you actually had a job with the parks department for a while, right?"

Meg knew how to keep a straight face. But she still hadn't managed to control her coloring and felt a flush rise to her face, along with the urge to cry.

Yes. Lara had talked about her to this man.

"That night she told us she'd had it with politics. She was going home," Ellery said. "Ian tried to convince her to stay. I did, too. But she kept insisting that she was going home. When she left, Ian and Joe and Nathan and I kept up the conversation. Then, after she'd been gone ten or fifteen minutes, Ian suddenly stood up and said, 'Lord, it's almost three in the morning!' "

"What about Lara?" Meg asked. "So no one went looking for her, to make sure she got home okay?"

"Honestly, I figured she was fine, that she'd managed to hail a cab or, with the adrenaline she had going, she might even have walked to her place. You know where she lives, right?"

"Of course," Meg said.

"And we've been there already," Matt added.

"You found nothing?" Ellery Manheim asked.

Matt Bosworth smiled. "We didn't find Lara," he said. "Thanks for your help. And I'm sure we'll be talking again soon."

He headed out to the car. Meg followed.

She was tall, and walked with long strides, but she had to hurry to keep up.

Matt was silent as they got into the car.

"Walker does seem to be a real family man," Meg said. "When she went to work for him, she thought she'd finally met a decent politician, a man who meant to do good things."

"What's the impression you got of him?" Matt asked, backing out of their parking spot and then moving forward onto the street.

"His wife is as loyal as they come, the grandkids obviously adore him. I also think he cared about Lara. He was certainly ready and anxious to see us," Meg said.

"Yes. But he could've seen us at his office. Seeing us at his home seemed . . . staged," Matt argued. "I'll admit the kids were a nice touch." He sounded a little — just a little — sardonic.

"You — you think Ian Walker could

have . . . could have killed Meg?"

"I don't know yet. One thing I sure as hell do think is that man's hiding something. What it is, we have yet to discover."

Lara had screamed. She'd shouted until she had no voice.

She'd explored her world of darkness. Dirt, stone, strange metal blades. She was in a space of about ten feet by fifteen, with a giant stone in the middle.

She didn't dare think about the creepy crawly things in this small dark space.

She'd found one plastic gallon jug filled with liquid. Despite her thirst, she hadn't tried the liquid at first. It had to be a trick. She was supposed to drink and find out that it was lighter fluid or drain cleaner or something equally toxic.

Then her thirst had become overwhelming, and she'd known she'd rather die fast, even in agony, than suffer that torture any longer.

She'd still had the sense to drop a little of the liquid on her fingers. She'd smelled it, felt it — and then she'd tasted it. She'd meant to go slow; she couldn't. She had drunk too quickly and then gagged and nearly vomited, except that her stomach was empty and she'd retched with nothing but the water coming out.

It was water, just water. She learned to take one tiny sip at a time.

No one came. The hours dragged on.

She heard nothing; she saw no one. All she could do was huddle in the cold.

She was naked and in the dark. She had to stay alive; she had to hope and pray and not give in to desperation. She'd been dumped here to die.

Why not just kill her?

Because maybe her body wasn't supposed to show up yet.

That thought almost made her laugh. Why were they worried about her *dead* body when no one seemed to know where her *living* body was?

She thought she heard singing. She listened and wondered again if she was dead, if the first stages of death contained all the pain and fear of life. She seemed to be hearing something like a very old hymn, one that might've been sung for centuries, although she couldn't recognize any words.

She tried screaming again. Screaming and screaming . . . begging for help. Until she was hoarse again and no sound came.

She allowed herself a moment's humor. Were the angels singing for her?

Was she in a vault, in some forgotten

graveyard of a godforsaken town?

No, the stone in the middle told her it wasn't a vault. The regular shape of the place was, however, created by man.

She thought she saw figures before her eyes and realized she was shaking.

The cold night had seeped into this place. And yet she felt strangely warm.

She was getting a fever.

Think about Meg. Meg would come for her. She could've sworn that she'd thought so determinedly about her friend that she'd actually seen her face — that she'd actually begged her for help. Was that yesterday? She didn't know. In this world without day or night, without time, she had no idea.

Meg had seen her, too. Hadn't she?

But Meg saw the dead. Soon, she'd be among them.

4

Back at Lara's apartment, Meg went through her friend's drawers and prowled the apartment, looking for anything that might indicate that Lara had been back. Her purse was gone; she hadn't owned a car. Her work had been on Capitol Hill and she'd either walked, which she loved doing, or taken a taxi if she wasn't with friends or business associates. She also used DC public transportation.

Matt Bosworth waited patiently, studying the house.

Meg could see that Lara had apparently made coffee and cleaned the pot the morning before she'd left. Her breakfast was usually fruit and cereal; there was a banana peel in her small compost bin, and a single cereal bowl in the dish drainer. Lara never used her dishwasher unless she had a party. She considered it a waste of energy.

In the bedroom Meg was going through

the closet again when Matt Bosworth called out to her. "She kept a journal? A written journal?"

"Yes," Meg called back.

"Then maybe there's something in her most recent journal," he said.

Yes, Lara's journal! She should've thought of that first thing — before pawing through all her belongings.

Agent Bosworth came into the bedroom, a book in his hand. It was a journal with handsome black binding and an imprinted Green Man tree. He had it open and was reading it.

Meg suddenly realized that they were both delving into Lara's life; she really had no more right to do that than he did.

At least she was Lara's friend.

On the other hand, he'd been around for a while and this was business, this was his job. Delve, pry, do whatever was needed.

He read aloud, " 'Sometimes I want to go back. Way back to the days of innocence when we truly believed. Follow the trail as Meg and I did when we were students. Richmond to Sharpsburg, on to Harpers Ferry where we were *home,* and Gettysburg, where we learned that ideals are everything, and that good men may fight for different causes.' "

He looked over at Meg. "That was her last entry. Dated the day before she went missing."

"What did she write before that?"

He handed her the book. She started to sit down on the foot of the bed — and then didn't. A forensic team might come in and she wanted to compromise as little as possible.

She stood up again and flipped through the entries.

"She noted her meeting the other night, too," she told Matt. "Right before the entry you read. She wrote it earlier that same day. 'Stand by my convictions.' "

"But since the other entry was *after* that," Matt began, "she really might've gone somewhere. Maybe she was preparing to leave, in case things didn't go the way she thought they should. Do you think she might've tried to follow that trail? I'm assuming you did make that journey at some point?"

Meg nodded. "As you know, she was from Richmond, and I was from Harpers Ferry. I still have a home there, a lovely old place." She looked up at him. "Stonewall Jackson never stayed there, but one of his physicians did. My grandfather owned it and his family before him. Lara's aunt loved to come to

Harpers Ferry during the summers. She was a river-tubing enthusiast. That's where Lara and I became friends. Anyway, once we were eighteen, we'd head out every summer from Richmond, where we went to college together. We'd go back to my place — or rather, my grandfather's. He left it to me when he died a few years later. Then we'd go to Sharpsburg and Gettysburg."

Matt looked interested enough that she was encouraged to continue. "Lara studied the Civil War. She could give you whole biographies of both Union and Southern commanders, and she was ardent about Lincoln. She believed that old politics really do influence new politics, that there's a connection. And she was always frustrated with the way politics are now. For example, she used to tell me that when our Founding Fathers finished serving their terms, they went back to their original jobs. They weren't supported forever. They were equal with the people they served. Lara knew that neither the senate nor the house would ever vote to give money back, but she still believed that there were people out there who wanted to serve rather than find a cushy career."

She realized she was telling him far more than necessary; she just needed him to understand what a principled person Lara was.

She lowered her head. She knew she'd seen Lara in the mirror. Once again, she was convinced that Lara was dead. She had to be.

"Sorry, I don't mean to get carried away here. But yes, we both loved the trip. We went to museums, reenactments, churches, graveyards — all over. Oh, in Colonial Williamsburg, she was crazy about the old taverns. Thought they were so much fun. We loved to go up to the Harpers Ferry cemetery up on the high hill. Sometimes we just enjoyed the view of the Shenandoah and the valley below, and sometimes we made up stories about the names we could read on the graves." Meg stopped speaking.

"I'm not sure we'll be able to find her, even if we attempt the journey," he said. "For now, though, I think we've discovered everything we can here. I should go back and check in at the office. I'll get you to your car first," he told her. "We'll call to let you know what's next."

"I'm going to take this and read through it," Meg said, indicating the journal.

"Good plan," he said simply. When he turned and headed out, she followed him, locking up. When they returned to Adam's house, she wasn't sure what she was supposed to do. She started for her car.

"Where are you going?" he asked.

"Quantico," she said. "I have to be out of cadets' quarters by the end of the week."

"We can help you move. You need to come back and report to Adam first. I'll go see what Jackson and the Krewe have uncovered, but you need to see Adam."

When they arrived at the office, she walked in ahead of him, afraid Adam would announce that they hadn't found a thing to suggest that anything had happened to Lara Mayhew.

But she was wrong; Adam had them both come in.

"Do we have anything? Anything that'll justify spending taxpayers' money?" he asked immediately.

"Lara isn't at her apartment," Meg answered. "And I don't believe she's gone anywhere. The suitcase she always uses is there and none of her clothing seems to be gone." She waited, still and stoic, for Matt to speak.

To her surprise, he proved to be an effective advocate. "There's something odd going on. What it is, I don't know. Today Walker attempted to show us what a wonderful family man and good all-around guy he is. I'm not saying he isn't, but he admitted to an argument over the way to pursue a bill he'd been working on with Congressman Hubbard. Apparently, Walker's determination to stand strong died along with his friend."

Adam nodded. "What else do you have?"

"What do we know about the death of Garth Hubbard?" Matt asked.

Adam looked slightly taken aback. "We know there were questions. There always are. But from what I've read, it was all aboveboard. He did have a heart condition. His own physician was there and unsuccessfully tried resuscitation. There was an investigation, and nothing was found other than that he had a heart attack." Adam paused, then said, "Still, something about it bothers me."

Matt went on to describe their visit; he discussed each of the men who worked for the congressman, Ian Walker, Kendra Walker, the children and everything that had happened, everything that had been said. His memory and his ability to relay details were impressive.

"In your view, is there any chance that Walker is somehow involved with Lara's disappearance — and Congressman Hubbard's death?" Adam asked, frowning.

"I don't know what he might be involved in. But I agree with you — something isn't quite right," Matt said. "And it all bears investigating. If we could find Lara — or discover just what happened after she left the congressman's office — I think we'd learn something."

"What about the murdered women?" Adam asked.

"Not sure. At this point they don't appear to be connected. That is, unless we find . . ." He paused, glancing at Meg. "Unless we find Lara Mayhew."

Ripped to pieces and floating in the river, Meg thought.

Adam turned to her. "We'll be in touch, tell you what direction we plan to go in, Meg. Go home now and try to get some sleep. Matt, would you see her out?"

"Adam, thanks, but I don't need to be seen out. Agent Bosworth, have a good evening." She nodded politely. Then she walked out, determined to leave under her own steam.

An official sticker had been placed on her car. She left it where it was.

For a moment, she thought Matt had followed her out, after all. She looked over her shoulder; he hadn't.

She got into her car and started home,

then decided to buy some groceries before arriving at Quantico. Normally, she would've gone to a store on the base, but it would be faster to stop before she got there. All she wanted was to be at home, by herself.

There was a gas station on the way, which carried coffee and cereal and milk. Maybe not the freshest in the city, but it would do.

Meg parked her car, locking it.

Lara's journal was in the car and she didn't want anything stolen while she was inside — especially that.

Meg headed in and made her purchases and came back to the car. She heard footsteps behind her; they sounded furtive.

One hand on the Glock at her waist, she spun around.

There was no one following her. She saw a shaggy-haired man filling his tank. A woman with a child was exiting the gas station store.

She saw no one else.

Still, when she got back into her car, she couldn't shake the feeling that she *was* being followed — and watched.

She stopped at the security point and produced her credentials while the guards on duty swept her car, a measure that was always taken. Driving back, she parked and hurried in, waving to a few friends in the lounge.

"Meg, hey, Meg! Come on down, talk, play. Where ya been?" Ricky Grant said loudly.

"Tomorrow!" she promised. "I'm absolutely exhausted!"

She fled before anyone else could call her.

Once in her room she closed the door. And locked it. She slipped off her jacket and removed her Glock and the small holster she kept it in, setting both on her bedside table. Then she kicked off her shoes and jumped on the bed, instantly digging into her tote bag for Lara's journal.

But she couldn't concentrate. She found herself looking at her door every few seconds. Silly — her classmates were still down in the lounge; it couldn't have been one of them.

Was she paranoid? Had Lara been paranoid?

She had to keep it together. Adam Harrison had almost magically brought her into his special unit, so she needed to be responsible and capable.

She was getting help on the situation with Lara, and she was grateful for that.

She was even grateful to Special Agent Bosworth.

She caught herself wondering about the man. He betrayed so little. In his demeanor, his behavior, he seemed so . . . self-contained. And so contradictory. He could act like a dictator — and then turn around and support her when she least expected it.

She didn't understand why he was so suspicious of Walker, why he suspected Walker might've had something to do with Hubbard's death. Her primary concern was to find out what had happened to Lara!

But what if those two things *were* somehow related?

And yet it didn't make sense. Everything about Hubbard's death had been in the media. The man had been dearly loved by many and practically hailed as the new messiah. He hadn't bent to pressure from any group. His followers had labeled him "the commonsense candidate."

Meg realized that she was as exhausted as she'd claimed to be. It was early — only about 8:00 p.m. She was starving but didn't feel like going back downstairs and winding up in some conversation or other. The energy bars she'd just purchased would be her dinner.

As she ate, she browsed the internet for up-to-the-minute news, but there was nothing she didn't already know.

She got ready for bed, skipping her usual shower, and crawled in. She decided she couldn't take any more bad news — not that night. But she was afraid another body might have been found, so she searched until she found a podcast showing the most recent local news.

No more bodies. Not yet.

She went on a classic movie site and let an old adventure movie with Errol Flynn play. Despite herself, she thought about the charm of Errol Flynn's character — and then about the FBI agent with whom she'd spent the day.

Nothing alike.

But that was just because she'd hardly ever seen him smile. She wondered if he might be as agile as Flynn. He seemed to have the same heroic ethics as Flynn's character in this swashbuckler. She'd considered him an adversary of whom to be wary. Because he was skeptical of her!

But did that matter when he intended to investigate her friend's disappearance and not scoff at her fears?

No, he could be as rude as he liked.

But as she drifted off, she had to acknowledge that there was something about him that attracted her.

Yes, he was lean and muscular and wore a

dark suit very well. He had a chiseled face that was highly masculine and appealed to all her senses.

Meg rolled over and reminded herself that she'd worked with well-built men on a daily basis.

He was . . . different.

Worry about Lara, not him!

On the other hand, maybe it was better to wonder what her temporary partner might be like in bed than to spend the night obsessing about Lara.

She needed to sleep. She *really* needed to sleep.

She'd just started to drift off again when she heard someone at her door.

Meg bolted to a sitting position, instantly reaching for the sidearm at her bedside. She stared into the shadows left by the night-light.

She could swear that her doorknob had turned.

Leaping out of bed, she flattened herself against the wall, then threw the door open. No one there. She looked cautiously into the hallway. It was empty, as well.

Had a friend tested her door to see if she was sleeping?

She'd lived with her fellow cadets for months now. They didn't try doors to see if they were locked; they rapped loudly. Or they texted. Or called her cell.

Barefoot, she moved silently down the stairs and into the lounge area, but the place was deserted. Everyone who'd been there earlier must have gone out for dinner or drinks. Guards patrolled all of Quantico; it was almost impossible to get in without providing an ID.

She checked the kitchen. No one. Finally, she gave up.

She went to the front door and carefully peered out. But her caution wasn't needed.

There was no one around.

As she turned to head back in, she paused.

She could hear a motor gunning somewhere.

Ridiculous! She was getting paranoid. She lived in one of the safest places in the country. Only military, physicians, cadets, agents, police and other authorized individuals could be here.

And she'd searched everywhere, found no one. She was, quite simply, paranoid. Maybe not a bad way to be out on the streets — but here?

She forced herself to go upstairs and back to bed, locking the door to her room again. She tried to sleep, but couldn't. She was glad she'd received her regulation *real*

Glock and had that to use rather than the red-handled fake they'd had during their training period.

Why would someone take on the dangerous task of stalking her here? Not that she was so dangerous, but this was Quantico.

And really, why would anyone stalk *her*?

What people didn't know seldom hurt them, Slash thought.

But it could kill them!

What Ms. Brand-New-Agent didn't know was that Slash McNeil was the most intelligent and organized serial killer she'd ever face. Every move he made was planned; for every step he took, he had a backup plan. He had access — anywhere he wanted to go.

He could watch her, as he had watched others. Watch, and not make a move until the time was right. He could make her disappear; he could make her reappear — whenever he chose.

Now, Lara Mayhew . . .

The time wasn't right!

But this woman . . .

She annoyed him. She couldn't leave well enough alone. Had to be a cop, had to be an agent. Thought she was tough.

Well, it didn't matter how tough she was.

He had strength and power. Physical strength — and the power of the right people behind him. And power, everyone knew, mattered much more than strength.

He'd watched her as she'd looked around, watched her face, and the emotion she couldn't hide. She was an open book, especially when she didn't know she was observed. She was beginning to doubt her own senses, her own sanity. She was afraid she was letting it all get to her, that she was paranoid.

Slash smiled. He liked paranoid. Paranoid was good.

A scowl replaced his smile. He didn't like Bosworth. He didn't like the "special" unit, the Krewe of Hunters. They were secretive. They had separate offices. They had more security cameras than the damned White House or the Capitol building.

But he knew about Bosworth. He knew some of his weaknesses.

And while the man might be tall and solidly muscled, that didn't really mean anything. A single bullet could bring down a football tackle, a Hulk Hogan, a mixed-arts expert . . .

Slash reminded himself to stay on target.

Right now, *she* was the target, pretty, tall, lithe, with all that raven hair drawn back, indigo eyes still giving so much away.

It was going to be fun taking her down.

He smiled, revved his car and began to mentally plan the things he might do to her.

"We don't know about the second girl yet," Jackson said. "No prints in the system and we haven't been able to find a missing-persons report to match up with her. But the information about Cathy Crighton is interesting. She was tentatively identified by a coworker from a police sketch, and then a DNA match was made. She grew up in foster homes in Kentucky, moved to Los Angeles, worked in a few restaurants there, then moved to New York City, and came to Georgetown about five weeks ago. A friend in Oklahoma — someone she'd met in one of her foster homes — first filed a missing-persons report. She has no known family and was just starting to make friends at the restaurant, Big Fish, where she was working. Police interviewed her old boss and they don't think he was involved. She'd been late for work previously and he'd told her that if she failed to show up for her shift on time again, she was fired. It never occurred to him to call her in missing."

"What was their take on the boss?" Matt asked. He was in Jackson's office in their

Alexandria facility, sitting in one of the handsome oak chairs in front of Jackson's desk while Jackson sat in his swivel chair behind it. The office also included a sofa grouping with a number of chairs by the fire; it was a pleasant place, conducive to group discussions and brainstorming.

Matt's own office was just down the hall. While the four-story row house wasn't furnished with antiques, it still seemed to offer more of an at-home feel than their more modern facilities around the country. At first Matt had been surprised that the Krewe of Hunters chose to be outside the Bureau's main offices. But their tech services here were top-notch, and so, Matt gathered, was their security.

They had access to various labs and nonagent employees, computer whizzes and experts in all kinds of fields. The special agents of the Krewe units, overseen by Adam Harrison and managed by Jackson Crow, occupied the entire second floor with offices that allowed for consultations and a large boardroom with screens and computers and everything they needed for major conferences.

Jackson passed him a file. "It's all emailed to you, as well. But I figured you'd want your own take on the man and that you'd want to interview him right away."

Matt raised a brow. "I thought you wanted me on the trail of our missing woman, Lara Mayhew."

"I do."

"But what you're saying is that we have a bird in the hand?"

"Exactly." Jackson hesitated. "I'm not sure yet what I feel about Lara Mayhew's disappearance. We have nothing solid to link that to the murders of these young women and we certainly have nothing to link Congressman Walker to any of it. But sometimes our work is all about eliminating possibilities. If we can find Lara Mayhew alive, then we'll know she was in hiding and that none of this is related."

"We may be on a wild-goose chase," Matt pointed out.

"We've been on a few. And on more than one occasion, we've caught the goose."

"Meg is convinced that her friend is dead."

"If so, the body may turn up. Until then, let's proceed this way. Meg is due in here within the hour. Angela went over to the academy with a few agents and they're moving Meg out of her quarters and into a town house she's rented. Kat is at Wong's office, and we've arranged to bring the first body to him, as well. You might want to go over there after you've met up with Harvey Legend — boss at the Big Fish — and see what Kat and Wong have to say, although I'm pretty sure we've got a budding serial on the rise."

"When I get back from all of that, we can head out on Ms. Mayhew's trail," Matt said.

"Hey, it's a road trip," Jackson told him, with a smile that offered little humor. "Bring some music. That'll pass the time."

"I know one thing," Matt said.

"What's that?"

"I'm doing the driving. I like being at the wheel, in control."

"Sure. Whatever. Cling to that power, Agent Bosworth."

"I like driving."

"I'm happy for you."

Meg could hardly believe how quickly she could be packed and out of the quarters she'd called home for nearly four months. But that was because she'd had help.

She wasn't against doing the hefting and hauling herself, but she had Angela for organization and four agents for trips to the car with her boxes and gear. When Meg had said she could just hire a moving company, Jackson Crow had shaken his head and told her they could draw on their own manpower.

Of course, it hadn't been that difficult because she didn't have much of anything. When she'd gone into the academy, she'd left most of her own belongings in storage in Richmond; she hadn't arranged to have her bed, sofa, TV, books and other belongings sent to her new town house yet. It would take a phone call and a day of being there to receive them, but at the moment, she thought the place was rather sad. It was empty; it wasn't home yet.

Her room at the academy had been home.

Saying goodbye wasn't easy. Most of her class would be in their rooms for a few more days. The friends she was able to see were both sad and excited; some were headed off to field offices in other states, but they all had encouraging words for one another. "It's the agency. We never know where we'll end up, do we?" Or "It's never goodbye in the agency. We'll meet again somewhere."

And they might. And some of those who'd been with her for the four months might well meet again. But then, they might not. That made every goodbye sad.

Still, everyone was curious. Fascinated that she'd been selected to join the "special" unit that held a certain mystique and seemed almost like a secret society.

Everything had happened quickly; Angela had called her that morning. Since she'd be going off for a few days with Special Agent Bosworth, it might be best to get her moved now. She shouldn't worry about logistics, Angela had said; she'd have all the help she needed.

And she had. She'd been out in a remarkably short time.

"I put your perfume bottles on that side table," Angela told her, looking around the parlor of her small town house. "Makes it seem a little more like home. Jackson and I combined places so we have furniture you might like," she offered. "Do you want to come over and look at it?"

Meg understood that a number of agents in the Krewe were married or living with or seeing one another. The FBI didn't disallow agents from having relationships, but they weren't customarily permitted to work in the same units. Here, it seemed almost par for the course. She'd rather awkwardly mentioned the ease of fraternization within the Krewe.

"Maybe we find it hard enough to develop relationships on the outside. Most people will never really understand us. And then again, the closer we are as partners, lovers, friends, whatever, the more successfully we work together. It's almost as if you begin to get a sense of what the other person is seeing or feeling — or even where he or she might be. We're still exploring, of course. Our special units aren't even a decade old. But for the moment, we're not trying to fix what isn't broken."

That made Meg think about her own life.

About her own problem with relationships. She'd always told herself that her dating life suffered because of her passion for law enforcement. She was young and she had plenty of time to figure out who she was before adding another person to her life. But she'd never really believed that was true.

She might have believed that she was a bit of a freak. And every time she dated someone, it was an act because she could never really make it work. Anyone who understood the truth about her would walk away. And so, she always did so first.

"You okay?" Angela asked her.

"Yes, of course, why?"

"I asked you about needing furniture. You're just staring at me."

Meg flushed. "Sorry. Thanks. And I do own furniture. I have to call the storage and moving people. I'll do that when we're back."

"Well, if you need anything else — or you need stuff before then, let me know," Angela said.

She stood by one of the windows. The town house had come with drapes so she was all right as far as window coverings went.

Angela peered down at the street. "I wonder if that's one of ours," she said.

"One what?"

"There's a black sedan down there . . ." She paused, shrugging as she turned back to Meg. "Government vehicle of some kind. They all seem pretty much identical."

Meg went to look out the window, too. The car in question was just like the black sedans the Bureau — and other government agencies — often used.

It was parked about a block down the street in a legal parking spot, too far away to see if it had any special insignia or some kind of marking.

But before they could take another look, the sedan jerked out of the parking place.

It sped down the quiet street.

As if the driver knew he'd been seen.

"Strange. The license is covered with . . ."

"Mud," Meg finished. "It looked like mud, anyway. As if the driver had spent time out in the woods or something."

141

"Or as if the license plate had been purposely covered. As if someone was watching."

"Watching what?"

"Us," Angela said, pointing at Meg. "Or, more specifically, *you.*"

5

When Matt was a college student, he'd worked at a local pub in Richmond. The owner had been an Irishman and Matt — with Irish in his own background — had been certain he'd have a great time working there.

It didn't happen. He quickly realized that a man's background didn't always mean very much. Some people were good and others were jerks — no matter where they came from.

His boss had been one of the latter. The employees had called him Fat Bastard.

Harvey Legend was that kind of guy. Big, beefy and full of self-importance, he yelled at three of the servers while he was on his way to see Matt. His attitude didn't seem to fit the tone of the place, since the restaurant was elegant — white-clothed tables, wine and water glasses, a selection of flatware at each setting. He recognized public officials at several of the tables, and various people involved with government.

A hostess had gone to get Legend for Matt; he waited in a handsome foyer with a hardwood reception stand and a plush carpeted floor.

Legend arrived, shook hands with Matt and seemed pumped up about the FBI coming to see him. Matt had the feeling that the guy thought Cathy Crighton was finally worth something because she'd brought the FBI to his door.

"When, exactly, did you see her last?" Matt asked.

"Like I told the police, it was about five weeks ago. She showed up late on her last night here and I told her not to come back if she wasn't on time for her next shift. She didn't show, and I figured she knew I meant it. I didn't think about her again," Legend explained to Matt. "I've said all this to the cops who came here, but I don't mind going through it again."

"What about her last paycheck?" Matt asked, ignoring the man's self-righteous manner.

"Still on my desk," he said with a shrug. He frowned, looking past Matt, and shouted at one of the young women heading toward the kitchen. "Sue! There should be water on that table by now!"

"Yes, Mr. Legend," she said, flushing and glancing awkwardly at Matt. He offered her an understanding smile as she hurried on.

Fat Bastard, oh, yeah.

"Her paycheck?" he repeated.

Legend sniffed. "It was only for three hours. She got in late, and her last night was the first night of the pay week. Like I said, it's on my desk."

"It didn't occur to check on her when she didn't come to get it?"

"Hey, I'm not child services for adults," Legend said defensively. "I left her a message, but she never came in. The check's not for a lot of money. Our hourly wage is minimum. The tips here are good, though, and the waitstaff does very well."

"Did you know anything about her personal life?" Matt asked.

"Not me. She wasn't here that long. She was an okay waitress — not great, but okay. She was bad about showing up on schedule. And I never had her close the place. Wasn't sure I trusted her with a bank."

"What about customers? Did you ever see anyone watching her? Did she have any regulars?"

"I don't encourage the same waiters or waitresses to serve the same people all the time. As you can see, we get an elite clientele here, most of 'em political. Better to keep politics out of the kitchen, I say. So, no special customers."

"Is there anyone here who could give me some information about her personal life?"

"Sue. Sue Gaffney." He nodded toward the smiling brunette, who was coming from the kitchen just then.

"Perhaps you'd be so good as to have someone else handle her tables for a few minutes?" Matt asked politely.

"Absolutely." Legend went on to summon Sue and yell at other members of his staff. Maybe his yelling was considered a mark of affection.

Unlikely.

The brunette came rushing from the dining room, looking a little flustered. He realized that her eyes were moist despite the fact that she was distracted.

She offered him her hand and then drew it back, apologizing. "Hollandaise sauce. I'm sorry. And I'm so sorry about Cathy. She really was a sweetheart."

Sue obviously meant it.

She shivered suddenly. "And what happened to her — it's so terrible!"

"Very, and of course we want to put away the person who did this," Matt assured her.

146

"Listen," he added, "I need your help. There's no family to turn to. Was she seeing anyone? Did she say anything to you about anyone bothering her or following her or even looking at her too long?"

Sue shook her head. "Cathy was open and giving and sweet. And yet she was shuffled around like a used sweater when she was a kid. She still had faith in people, and she loved being here. She wasn't seeing anyone. She hadn't been here long and was just getting on her feet. She was going to take part-time college classes. She hadn't decided what she was going to major in, but she was going to learn about government and eventually get involved in some way. She was really wonderful!"

Matt produced a business card and handed it to her. "If you think of anything at all, please call me. You never know what little thing might help. Do you know if there was anyone she waited on exclusively? Did she like any particular customers? Hate any customers?"

"She just loved it that we had lobbyists, senators, campaign heads, congressmen and congresswomen, secret service — you name it! — in here. She liked all of them. I'm telling you, there wasn't a mean bone in her body," Sue said. "I miss her so much!"

Her eyes filled with tears she tried to blink back, and Matt knew she couldn't break down in the restaurant; she wanted to keep her job.

"Please," he said. "Call me with anything."

Sue nodded.

He gave her an encouraging smile. About to leave, he paused. "Does Congressman Walker ever dine here?"

"He's been in once or twice. Oh! Yes! He used to come in with my favorite customer!" She looked around and lowered her voice. "I thought the world of Congressman Garth Hubbard. What a loss, too. Such an intelligent man. And so polite. He could be in the middle of a political argument and yet he never failed to thank his waiter or waitress. First his heart attack, and now Cathy — it's dreadful. They say the good die young. Well, Hubbard wasn't exactly young, but you know what I mean, right?"

"Absolutely. Thank you," Matt told her.

She waved his card in the air. "You should come back here, too. The food is very good. And honestly, it's not overpriced."

He smiled and made his way out.

Maybe there was a connection between the murdered women and Lara Mayhew's disappearance. What it might be he couldn't begin to fathom.

And maybe there was something to the idea of a conspiracy.

But a conspiracy to do what?

Leaving her new not-much-of-a-home-yet town house, Meg discovered that Angela was driving them back to the OCME. The remains of their first victim had been brought there, and Wong and Kat were both going to comment on their findings.

"I don't think there's anything new," Angela told her. "But we'll meet up with Matt and talk to Dr. Wong and Kat." There wouldn't be much they didn't already know, but it was a chance to see the other victim. And to touch her.

And learn if, somehow, Cathy Crighton might still be there, among them.

They didn't expect to find ghosts, the remnants of the human spirit — whatever word you wanted to use — at the morgue. Nor did it seem that spirits liked to hang around in a cemetery. In a situation like this, they were usually seeking a way to tell others what had happened.

Some remained where great or traumatic events had taken place, while some weren't even sure why they lingered. Some merely enjoyed their status. Others were anxious to move on — once justice was done, a loved one helped — or perhaps after seeing a beloved child grow up.

Cathy Crighton wasn't in the morgue — other than in her raggedly damaged human form.

Water, be it from a river, a lake or an ocean, wasn't kind. Creatures lived in water of all types and consumed tissue and flesh.

Discoloration occurred.

When life was gone, a body was an empty shell. And in circumstances like this, the body was barely recognizable as the woman she had been.

Meg would've had the same fear she'd had earlier — that this young woman might have been Lara, had she not died weeks before Lara had gone missing.

"We still haven't been able to identify the young woman recovered this week," Wong said. He glanced over at Kat Sokolov. Apparently, they'd worked together before and Wong got along well with her. "We agree she's between twenty-five and thirty-five, but there's one difference — she's not a natural blonde. As far as we can tell, the murder occurred in exactly the same way. He seems to take them completely unawares. Chloroform — on a handkerchief, napkin, whatever. He knocks them out, and hits them with the stronger drug, strong enough for surgery. Then he slits their throats."

"Would you compare him to any other well-known serial killer?" Matt asked.

Wong shook his head. "No. At least not in the obvious ways. He's not taking pleasure in their pain. Most serial killers enjoy the victim's terror, and sexual killers generally need the power. That's how they get off. But this guy . . . he doesn't rape them. He doesn't need to see their fear — he almost wants to avoid it."

"Methodical," Matt Bosworth said.

Kat nodded. "As for the victims, they were both young. Similar in appearance."

"When we learn this young woman's identity, I believe we'll find that she's from similar circumstances," Matt said.

"Meaning?" Kat asked.

"She'll be someone who could disappear for a day or two without others noticing. She lives alone. She has a job where she wouldn't necessarily be expected in every day. The killer watches them for a long time before he takes them," Matt said.

"I think you're right," Kat said slowly. "Cathy wasn't immediately missed because she was so new to the city and had no close friends or family to watch out for her on a daily basis. Our second victim isn't going to be a homeless drug addict living on the street. But again, she'll be someone who doesn't have family nearby. And she's someone who probably didn't have a boyfriend." Meg was silent. That description didn't fit Lara Mayhew. Lara had an aunt not far away, an aunt who loved her. She had any number of friends.

She'd had Meg, a close friend about to graduate from the FBI.

Meg realized she'd been holding her breath when she was forced to inhale. Despite the cold in which the body had been kept, the smell of decomposition and antibacterial chemicals suddenly seemed overwhelming. She fought hard not to let her near-nausea show.

Matt stepped forward, making a pretense, she thought, of studying the bloated, patchy face. He set a hand on the corpse and looked at her. "Meg, what is this? On her eyes?"

She came closer and touched the corpse and studied the unknown woman's face. The body was so cold and stiff she didn't feel she'd touched a human being at all. She looked at Matt and then over at the others. "Permanent makeup," she said. "It's like tattoo art. She has lip liner and eyeliner."

"Yes, we've noted it," Kat agreed. Wong

152

nodded solemnly.

"Possibly done in the area. We can check into that," Matt said.

Angela stood quietly toward the rear of their group. "I'll get some of our people on it right away. There'll be a number of facilities around here doing that kind of work. We'll also get a good likeness of her on the media. When we ask for help, we're often surprised by where we get it."

"Anything else here?" Kat asked.

"No," Matt said. He gestured at Kat and Angela and then Meg. "Nothing, right?" They shook their heads in unison.

Meg couldn't have been happier to leave. Outside, the DC sun seemed especially brilliant and the sky was a fresh, bright blue.

The air smelled so clean . . .

"Are you okay?" Matt asked.

"Of course," she said. "I did just go —"

"Through the academy. Yes, we all know," he told her. "I'll see you at the office. We'll be driving to Richmond tonight. I'm sure you have places for us to go?"

"Yes," Meg said, staring back at him. She did have places for them to go, based on her history with Lara and the trail of information detailed in Lara's journal.

They'd go to the kind of places they used to love visiting. And, of course, if they found nothing, it would be embarrassing — and she was afraid it could be the end for her with the Krewe of Hunters.

Adam believed in her. Was that going to be enough? Was she really ready to find her friend in the same condition as Cathy Crighton and their Jane Doe?

She'd accepted that Lara was dead. She'd seen her.

And yet, despite that, she was living on hope. Maybe, as Matt had suggested, their connection was strong enough that Lara might have somehow reached out to her for help. One mind connecting with another . . .

She didn't think that Matt Bosworth, unlike Adam, believed in her. He didn't say so, and certainly wouldn't be vocal with his opinion. He'd been skeptical when she'd said she knew Lara was dead. But he was the consummate professional; he'd been told to go with her and he would.

That was all right. She'd do whatever was needed, if she could only find out the truth about Lara.

Jackson would be attending the main task force meeting later on. That meeting was intended to keep local law enforcement up to date on the information they'd obtained thus far.

They held a small meeting of Krewe agents before Matt and Meg were due to go on the road in pursuit of Lara Mayhew.

They were in one of the two large meeting rooms at Krewe headquarters. She wondered when Angela Hawkins had time to manage everything she did; she was the one who tied all the threads together. She already had a board with pictures — Cathy Crighton was pictured as she'd been alive, via photographs from her friend Sue, and as she was now, dead. Their second victim, still unidentified, also had her place on the board — with only one picture, the way she was now, on the gurney at the ME's office.

The time patterns they knew regarding the deaths had been noted; pertinent facts about the victims had been noted as well, down to the fact that Cathy had last dined on meat loaf and potatoes, one of the specialties at the Big Fish — and their Jane Doe had consumed sushi, made with high-grade tuna.

While the tuna itself might have been available at the Big Fish, there was an unusual seasoning in it that was only used by specialty sushi restaurants in the city. Angela stated that she and Kat would be tracking those down, along with facilities that offered permanent makeup.

Meg was wondering again how much sense it made for her and Matt to go off on what could be a total waste of time when there were leads to run down. As soon as Matt gave his report about his meeting with Harvey Legend at the Big Fish, however, she understood that while they might be looking at a far-fetched idea — that of a conspiracy — certain circumstances might prove to be more than coincidental.

"The Big Fish caters to the Washington elite," he told their group. "Our first victim, Cathy Crighton, worked there. Both Congressman Hubbard and Congressman Walker were known to dine there with their retinues. Yes, many restaurants in the area cater to members of government. And the murders of Cathy Crighton and our Jane Doe might have absolutely nothing to do with what's been accepted as the natural death of Congressman Hubbard. But since Lara Mayhew is missing after leaving a strange call, I do think it's highly important that we find her — whether any of these incidents are related or not."

"Your plan is Richmond tonight and moving on tomorrow?" Jackson asked.

Matt turned to her.

Meg nodded. "We'll speak with Lara's aunt and try some local places she loves and figure out if she's been seen or not."

"And then Harpers Ferry?"

"If she left me a message, it's there," Meg said. She hesitated. "There was also a small cabin we used to rent up near the Gettysburg Battlefield. It's unlikely, but the owner is a friend and there wouldn't be a phone trace or internet tracking of any kind if she did go there."

She noted that Matt had gone quiet. He was watching her.

"There's been no movement on her bank account or credit cards," he said.

She swallowed painfully. That might well mean that the apparition she'd seen in the mirror meant what she'd been afraid it did — that Lara was dead and she'd died in DC.

"If she's hiding out somewhere, she'd be smart enough to know she could be traced through cards and numbers," Kat pointed out softly.

Meg didn't hear a phone buzz but Jackson Crow excused himself and left the room. He walked back in almost immediately.

"There's been another death," he said. "And you're heading in the right direction. This girl was found close to Richmond."

Just where was the line between life and death?

Lara realized she could hardly move. Her limbs were heavy and felt stiff. She'd been over every inch of her prison.

She'd sworn that she'd live, that she'd survive. And if she did, there'd be no hesitation. She wouldn't allow anyone to get away with this or anything else. Slander, unemployment, even jail, whatever the repercussions . . .

They were all better than death.

She was tired, exhausted, hungry. She drifted in and out of sleep. She suffered moments when she was sure she was dead. Those were followed by moments when she vowed that she'd live.

She'd learned to monitor the water, but how long could she go without food?

She huddled against the wall.

They would find her. *Someone* would find her. Aunt Nancy would raise the alarm; Meg would never accept that she had just disappeared.

Every hour she wondered if and when the killer was coming back for her.

Would she die by a knife, through

strangulation, a bullet?

Or would she just starve here in the pitch-black darkness . . .

Fade away until . . . she was among the dead?

6

"It isn't Lara," Matt said, glancing over at her. "At least we know it isn't your friend."

He was doing the driving. He'd made that clear from the start. They were in a company car but it wasn't a sedan. It was actually a nice little compact SUV.

The color was still black.

Meg nodded. Dreadful as the situation was, she couldn't help feeling some relief that the body wasn't Lara Mayhew's. The young woman had been quickly identified. A neighbor had called about a howling dog; when police had gone in, the dog had been ravenous and near death from dehydration. Seeing the picture of a blonde woman with two people who appeared to be her parents on the mantel, the Richmond police — aware of the body recently discovered on the banks of the Potomac — had immediately forwarded the image to DC. Subsequent investigation had revealed that she was Genie Gonzales of New Iberia, Louisiana. She'd only recently moved to Richmond and taken a job at a coffee shop. That much Meg and Matt had known before they left the Krewe offices.

They were about ninety miles from Richmond. They'd arrived late, but the detective who'd been called to the site where the body was found would meet them at the morgue, along with the ME on the case.

"I don't understand how this serial killer's working," Meg heard herself say as they headed south down I-95. "Maybe this case isn't connected. Maybe we're grasping at straws. I can see how a serial killer might move on to an area close by, but . . . DC and Richmond? The traffic between the two is horrendous. Plus, there are only a few days between the murders."

"It's quite possible there *is* no connection. It's the human need for a comprehensible narrative. We want a plot, connection, something that reeks of conspiracy. There's one theory that Jack the Ripper was in line for the crown of England. The most recent theory has it that he was a German hairdresser. He could've been a deranged butcher of some kind, someone who could hide in plain sight in Victorian

England because there were so many slaughterhouses in the area and many people walked around covered in entrails and blood. What's scarier, of course, is the Ted Bundy kind of killer — charming, hiding behind an appearance of such normalcy that he was instantly trusted," Matt said.

"Like a congressman," Meg put in.

Matt laughed. "Really? Who trusts Congress these days?"

She smiled at that. "Well, we don't trust them with our taxes anymore, but that's a far cry from murder. And murder like . . . this?"

"Hopefully, this young woman will be the last," Matt said. "And hopefully, we'll find your friend alive and well."

Meg didn't reply.

"It's possible," he said.

"I know you doubt me about seeing her. But I did."

He was quiet for a minute. "I don't doubt you. If you're in the Krewe, you understand that there's another plane between life as we know it and what comes next. Our more scientific members believe that it's a matter of energy. Energy can't be destroyed, it can only find new forms. I'm not that scientific. But maybe this is about science. Maybe seeing that energy is what we do. But I believe that if energy can project itself after death, it could also happen in extreme, life-threatening circumstances. In other words, it's possible that you saw her because she desperately needs your help."

Meg glanced at him, surprised. He'd mentioned the possibility before; now she saw that he really believed it.

He shrugged, then reached forward, flicking a dial on the SUV's sound system.

He cast her a quick look before returning his focus to the road. A slight smile curved his mouth. She suddenly heard Kermit the Frog and Fozzie Bear break into song with "Movin' Right Along."

Meg laughed.

"Well, it is a road trip, isn't it?"

"I just never imagined you as a Muppets fan."

"I love the Muppets, grew up on them. I think Jim Henson was brilliant and he left an impressive legacy," he said.

The Dark Crystal?"

"Love it. Fantasy — and sci-fi."

"And did you enjoy *Sharknado*?" she asked. "You saw it?"

"Every campy minute."

"Well?" she asked.

"I especially liked the part where he broke out of the great white's belly with a chain saw — and rescued the previously consumed young woman," Matt said.

Meg eased back in her seat. Maybe he wasn't going to be quite so bad.

The Muppets were followed by Led Zeppelin and the Animals and a mix that just about incorporated everything out there.

They got to Richmond in no time, and decided to head into the office of the OCME first thing.

"You can move through traffic, Bosworth," Meg said. "I'll give you that. And your choice in music isn't bad, either."

She realized she'd actually relaxed in the car. She knew it because she felt her muscles and stomach knotting again.

"We do this for a living. Of course, this is never just a job. But if we take the monsters out there with us every second, we'd go a little crazy and quit being useful. Glad you liked the mixes!" he told her.

Standing by the passenger's side door, she nodded grimly. "Yeah. Thanks."

"We know this victim's not your friend," he reminded her.

She nodded and turned toward the building. There was hope.

Because if Lara was dead, why hadn't she washed up on a riverbank yet? The way this new victim had appeared on the banks of the James?

Maybe Meg Murray isn't such an incompetent new agent, Matt thought.

She could stand stoically by a corpse without falling apart — and yet there was an empathy in her eyes that meant she did feel the pain. It was necessary to feel, especially for Krewe members.

She'd fallen to pieces the other day, but . . .

How well had he done the first time he'd seen a loved one on a gurney?

Dr. Aubrey Latham, the ME on the case, had a droning voice that might have resulted from years on the job. He went through a rundown of the injuries inflicted on the body, stating that the cause of death had been the slash to the throat, the severing of the carotid artery. All the other injuries had been postmortem. Pieces of her organs were missing — probably loose in the waters of the James or consumed by river life. She'd been blonde, young, pretty, twenty-seven years of age. There was chloroform in her system, along with propofol.

"Of course, the tongue is missing, too," Dr. Aubrey told them. "Pretty similar to the other two women discovered in Maryland and DC."

Matt nodded. He moved forward, making a pretense of studying the woman's face as he set his hand on her cold body. Nothing. He looked into the young woman's face. She hadn't been in the water as long; she wasn't as damaged or bloated as the others. He could envision her the way she'd been in life.

"Was this chopping done with any kind of medical skill?" Matt asked.

"In my opinion, no," Aubrey said. He demonstrated. "The tongue was cut out first. I'd say the guy has some strength. It's harder to cut up a human being than you'd imagine."

"And the slash down the torso — a brutal slash, too?" Meg asked.

"Yes, and sloppy. Stupid, too. He stuffs the body with rocks but doesn't create a decent cavity," Aubrey said. "I don't really understand how you guys classify these things, but he's leaving no DNA that we can gather. And, of course, he's using the river to help him with that, too. He has to be covered in . . . blood and guts when he's done, but no one's seen anything, that I know of."

"No," Meg said. "Not that anyone's reported."

"I guess it's easier to kill undetected than

166

one would think," Aubrey said. "He must knock the women out and transport them before he does his killing. There's no lack of wooded areas during the summer in Virginia. So, he takes them somewhere — kills them, rips them apart and throws them in the river. I read up on the other cases. He may be getting sloppier. This one popped up within hours."

"Maybe he was tired or in a hurry," Meg murmured. "Time of death?"

"Between 2:00 and 4:00 a.m.," Dr. Aubrey told them. "What do you think about the tongues?"

"My theory?" Matt asked. "He means to silence them. Silence them about the murders? About something in his life? Or something he perceives they know? I'm not sure. It could also be that he just wants a signature — and that's his signature."

Detective Wharton, who'd been called to the site where the body had been discovered on the James River, cleared his throat. "We were lucky to get a quick ID," he said. "City cops were called in by Ms. Gonzales's neighbors when her dog barked and cried endlessly. They saw her picture and everything fell into place. Her next of kin in Louisiana has been called, but that was a ninety-year-old grandmother in a nursing home."

"There was no disturbance at her house?"

"Nothing other than that the dog tried to eat shoes and the poor thing had been scratching at the toilet bowl."

"She was working at a coffee shop in Richmond?" Meg asked. "That's been confirmed?"

"Yeah. She'd hardly been there a month. She was a newcomer to the area," Wharton said. He was a man in his early forties, polite enough, but somewhat stiff. He'd greeted them with professional courtesy; in autopsy, he'd let the doctor do the talking. "I was told the feds would be taking the lead on this case and that a few agents would be down in the morning. Then I got another call saying you'd be here tonight. So, are you going to be the lead?"

In Matt's experience, law enforcement agencies generally worked well together. Every once in a while, though, someone felt a jurisdictional urge. He liked to be as deferential as possible — unless someone acted like a dog peeing on a tree to mark his territory. But he didn't feel Wharton was a jerk — just a man concerned about how it was all going to work.

"This is a task force with everyone

needed," Matt said. "Two agents from my office will be down here to work the Richmond angle, but they'll be consulting with you. We're following a couple of other leads and won't be in the city that long. We have DC and Maryland police working it as well, and plan to have a communication system in place so we can all keep in touch. No one knows a given area like the police who work it. But this killer is crossing state and district lines, so we have to be mobile to keep an eye on him."

"We're grateful for how quickly and efficiently you've handled this," Meg told Wharton. "And for your willingness to see us now."

The detective warmed visibly, but Matt suspected that his words, no matter how careful, hadn't been what had changed Wharton's opinion. Meg's sincere appeal seemed to do the trick.

"Of course." Wharton nodded. "What else can I do?"

Matt requested Wharton's report from the scene and assured him he'd be included in the task force meeting the next morning.

Meg told the ME again how much they appreciated his time and help.

Outside the Richmond OCME, Wharton hesitated. "You need help with anything in the city?" he asked.

Matt smiled at him. "I was actually born here."

"And I'm from Harpers Ferry, but I went to college here," Meg said.

Wharton laughed. "Hell, I might ask *you* for help getting around the city. I didn't move here until I was about twenty-five. Okay, have a good night. I'll see you in the morning."

Before he could leave, they heard a loud bark. Matt spun around just in time to see some kind of little terrier mutt running toward them.

"Hey!" Meg said, crouching down to pet the little dog. "What are you doing here, all by yourself in the middle of the city? Did you hop out of a car?"

"I'll be damned!" Wharton swore. "That's the dog — that's Genie Gonzales's dog! They brought it from the house to animal rescue. I don't know how it wound up here."

"You sure that's the same dog?" Matt asked him.

"Positive. We had him at the lab first. We combed him out, looking for trace evidence. We didn't think the killer had been in her apartment, but we try to get backup on everything. I know he was taken to animal rescue. I talked to them afterward. We were

170

still investigating her past, trying to see if there was someone who'd take him," Wharton said.

Meg scooped up the little creature. It was trembling in her arms. Matt couldn't tell what kind of mix it was. The face was terrier. A poof of fur over the eyes suggested Cairn, Skye or even a Yorkie. The legs were too long for any of those breeds. The dog appeared to be a mix of many breeds that shouldn't have been mixing.

"Poor thing," Meg murmured.

"I'll take him. You all don't need to worry," Wharton said.

Meg's arms seemed to tighten around the creature.

"I don't know how the hell he got here," Wharton said again. He shrugged. "I like dogs and I just . . . well, I'd hoped they were going to give him some more time before putting him down." He shrugged. "Genie got him from the shelter. Poor guy."

"Put him down? Why?" Meg demanded. "He didn't hurt anybody! He's remarkable! He followed his mistress here!"

Wharton's expression was awkward — and wistful. "He must've gotten out of an animal control cage somehow. Bright little guy. And found his way here! And I just meant that, you know, if dogs aren't adopted in a certain period of time, well . . . there's no choice."

"Meg," Matt said, "sad to say, animals sometimes have to be put down."

"Yeah, but half the time it's the jackasses who fight them or raise them to kill who should be put down. This guy didn't hurt or kill anyone!" Meg said indignantly.

"Well, no," Wharton agreed. "But here, hand him over. I'll take him back to the shelter."

"I'll hang on to him," Meg said.

"He can't go on a road trip, Meg," Matt said, staring at her incredulously.

Just when he was beginning to think this was going to be okay.

"No, he can't. But I'm seeing a friend in the morning. If the police are done with him and the FBI doesn't have an interest, which I don't think we do, I'll see that he has a home," she said determinedly.

"What if he *is* needed again?" Matt asked. He liked dogs, but they were on an investigation! And never mind that this one happened to be ugly as sin.

"Then I'll know exactly where he is and go get him again."

"All right, well . . . I don't see anything wrong with the idea," Wharton said. "We pick up more strays in the city — if you want more dogs."

"I think we're good for now," Matt remarked drily.

" 'Night, then," Wharton said. "See you tomorrow."

"Wait, do you know his name?" Meg asked.

Wharton smiled ironically. "Killer. That's the name on the tag he had."

"Killer. Great," Matt couldn't help muttering.

Wharton left them, and for a moment, Matt stared at Meg again, still incredulous, and she stared back at him defiantly.

"What? There's a rule about a dog in a company car? If there is, I know how to call a taxi."

"There's no rule against dogs in the car," he said. "As to the hotel or a restaurant, I'm not sure."

"Many hotels are dog-friendly these days," she assured him. "If ours isn't, I can use my own money and check in somewhere that is. Or I'll call Nancy Cooper — that's Lara's aunt — and see if I can bunk with her for the night."

Matt lowered his head. The medium-priced hotels his units used on the road did take animals. He'd seen them with their owners in the lobby. "Let's go," he said, trying not to sound irritated.

He failed.

She ignored him and headed for the car.

His phone rang when he got in. It was Jackson, calling to let him know that Will Chan and Kat Sokolov would be down in the morning for the task force meeting in Richmond. The dog, curled on Meg's lap, looked up and gave a little bark.

"What's that?" Jackson asked him.

"That's just Killer," he said.

"What?"

"The victim's dog. Meg's decided to get him a new home. Or maybe *give* him a home."

"Ah. Nice," Jackson said.

That was because Jackson wasn't sitting in the car with the yappy mutt.

"Anything else on your end?" Matt asked Jackson.

"Not yet, but it's hard to pound as much pavement as we're trying to right now — following various trails, looking into makeup places and so on. But I know that something will break soon. It always does."

"Soon," Matt echoed. "Let's hope it's soon enough."

"Stay in the loop, and make sure we have your schedule on a daily basis."

"Will do," Matt promised, and ended the

call. "What are you — a dog hater?" Meg asked him.

"No. I don't hate dogs."

"Just this one?"

"I don't hate him at all. But he doesn't belong in the middle of an investigation."

"He's not in the middle. We're going to a hotel for the night. He'll be with me. He won't bother you — or anyone else."

"You don't see me throwing him out of the car, do you?"

"I don't intend to give you the chance."

He was hungry but decided to drive straight to the hotel. Remembering the dog, he pulled into the parking lot of a convenience store. She frowned at him. "Why are we stopping here?"

"Weren't you planning to feed the beast?"

She flushed. "Of course." She started to thrust the dog at him so she could go in. He already had his door open.

"I'll get it," he told her.

It took less than a minute to buy a bag of dog food. There wasn't a question of which brand, since the place only carried one. He also purchased the only leash they had.

When he went back to the car, he noted a sedan that had been parked at the edge of the lot; it now turned onto the road.

Government car, he thought. Even in

Richmond, black government cars often seemed to rule the road. He squinted, trying to see the license plate, but the car was too far away.

When he reached his car, the dog was barking.

Meg seemed perplexed.

"What's up with him?" The dog acted as if he were trying to break out of Meg's grasp, jumping and clawing at the window.

"I have no idea. I was just sitting here and he suddenly went crazy," she replied. "Maybe he doesn't like you."

"He's not barking at me," Matt said.

The dog woofed and sneezed. And settled down in Meg's lap again.

"Did anyone come near the car?" he asked.

She shook her head. "Not that I saw. You weren't gone very long."

"I wondered if someone had gotten out of that black sedan."

He was startled by the way she turned to look at him, blue eyes large, forehead creased. "The . . . black sedan?"

"They tend to be very common around here," he said.

"I didn't notice it, but . . ." She straightened, shrugging. "Nothing," she said.

"What?"

"Angela and I saw a black sedan when I was moving today. It was parked — and it seemed to take off when we saw it. I never got the license plate."

"I didn't get it on this one, either. It's probably nothing. These areas are riddled with black sedans." Matt wasn't convinced that a black sedan in the Richmond–DC corridor meant anything at all. They were plentiful to the point of boring.

"Yeah, I know."

"I think you've just decided to adopt a neurotic dog," Matt told her.

That made her smile. "He's not neurotic. He somehow escaped animal control to find his mistress — and managed to get as far as the place where her body was being held. That's pretty remarkable."

"Or it could've been carelessness at the shelter and . . ."

"Who cares how he got out? How did he get to the morgue? How did he *know* to go there?"

"Okay, so he's loyal — and neurotic," Matt said.

He left the convenience store lot and drove to their hotel. As he'd expected, they took the dog, requiring a fifty-dollar deposit for the night. Meg insisted on putting it on her own card. He argued that the Bureau wouldn't care, but rather than make a scene at the desk, he let her have her way.

"You hungry?" he asked her.

"I'll order from room service."

He pointed to a sign. "They stopped room service at ten."

"I don't think I should leave Killer in the room by himself," she said.

"There's a pizza place down the street. I'll run and pick up a couple, okay?"

"That'll be great."

Their rooms weren't next to each other, but they were in the same hall.

"What kind?" he called to her.

"What?"

"Pizza?"

"Cheese. Cheese is fine, thank you."

Matt went ahead and threw his luggage in his room, and then decided to hop in the shower.

He changed into a clean pair of jeans and a polo shirt and hurried back out. He didn't take the car; it was just a short jaunt down the street. He waited about ten minutes for the two pies, then turned to leave the shop. He found himself pausing when he saw a black sedan idling on the street. The same one?

Unlikely, he thought. There were always

black sedans around here. He returned to the hotel, dropped off his own pizza, then went to Meg's room to deliver hers. Before he could knock on her door, he heard Killer growl. For a little dog, Killer could make some noise.

Meg opened the door, one foot holding back the dog. Her hair was gleaming wet, as dark as a raven's wing. She smelled sweetly of soap, and for the first time, he realized what a beautiful woman she was.

He handed her the pizza.

Killer was at his feet, jumping up, begging for attention.

"All right, all right," he told the dog, and stooped down to pet him.

"Were you in the hall a few minutes ago?" Meg asked, setting the pizza box on the foot of the room's one bed.

"I just got back, put my pizza in my room and came here," he said.

"Oh."

"Oh, what?"

"Someone was in the hall a minute ago. Killer was growling."

Matt laughed. They were both getting paranoid. "It's a hotel," he reminded her. "They rent rooms to other people, too."

He felt a little awkward. Maybe it was because he'd just really noticed her looks.

No, of course not; he'd known she was attractive before. But now . . . maybe he was just standing too close to her.

"Good night, Killer," he said to the dog. "Meg, we have our meeting at nine. I think the RPD wanted it earlier, but they're giving Kat and Will time to get here and meet up with our local counterparts, as well. So you can sleep in, but we need to leave at eight-thirty."

"Gotcha."

As he turned to leave, Killer whined.

"I guess he doesn't want you to go," Meg said.

"Hey, buddy." He stooped to pet the dog again. "You can't have us both, you know. And trust me, she's much prettier."

He stood, gave Meg a wave and left the room.

He was tired and ate his pizza quickly, downing it with a bottle of water he found in the room. He switched on the television. There had to be at least six local news stations and every one he turned to was talking about the DC killer who had now branched out into Richmond. He listened to a few of them carefully. The media didn't know about the victims' tongues being cut out, nor had they been given the information about the bodies having been slashed and stuffed with stones.

Tired, he started to drift off.

He wasn't sure how long he'd been asleep but he roused slightly.

There were footsteps in the hallway.

Late-nighters returning? He sat halfway up; the footsteps passed by.

A second later, he heard the dog barking from down the hall.

Matt leaped out of bed, reached for his Glock and ran to the door. He stood to one side of it and threw it open, then stepped out into the hallway.

An elderly woman in a raincoat and a scarf was sliding a key card into a door. She noted Matt, his pajama pants and naked chest — he held the gun behind his back — and offered him a crooked smile and a wave. He waved and slipped back inside his room.

Footsteps in a hotel hallway and black sedans on the road.

Hell, he *was* getting paranoid.

Yet he lay awake and finally got up. It was 2:30 a.m. according to the clock radio beside his bed. He walked down the now-empty hallway, stopped in front of Meg's door and tested the knob.

Killer didn't bark this time. He whined. He knew it was Matt.

Matt started to knock, to make sure that

everything was all right. Dumb idea. He'd just wake her up.

He headed back to his own room. He needed to sleep. This was a rough case, and whatever it took, they had to stop this man. Finding Lara Mayhew, dead or alive, might well be the key.

He locked and bolted his door and put his Glock on the bedside table. He could sleep for another few hours.

He did. When his alarm went off it caught him in a dream, a weird dream in which black sedans had taken on personas, like the friendly little cars in Pixar movies. But these sedans weren't friendly. Their front lights were equipped with large, gleaming knives that went around the bulbs in a macabre fashion. Their grills were filled with sharp-looking teeth. And they were pelting down the street, apparently driverless, while he ran and ran — all the while knowing he couldn't outrun a car.

"Whoa, no more pizza that late at night," he told his tired reflection.

Then he stepped into the shower and forgot his dream, well aware that it was going to be a very long day.

7

The task force meeting was grim. Kat Sokolov, who'd gone to see the body of Genie Gonzales before coming in to the RPD, spoke with them briefly before they got together with the local officers. Matt then took the lead, telling them about the other two women and what they presumed about the killer from what they'd discovered so far.

"We believe the killer is organized, although it seems he's grown more careless with Ms. Gonzales. The odd thing about these murders is that he doesn't seem to get off on the torture inflicted. In each case, the victim was drugged — heavily drugged with a pharmaceutical used in surgery — before her throat was slit and any cutting on the body began. There seems little doubt that we're dealing with the same man, a serial killer. What makes this an all-points alarm is that the first young woman was killed nearly a month ago, the second just a few days ago and now we have Genie Gonzales. We ask that all officers on the case be extremely careful with the media. We need to keep the more gruesome aspects of these murders quiet. We don't want to end up with copycats or other mentally defective individuals out there trying to take credit for the murders."

He went on to take questions, and then Will Chan stepped up to inform them that they'd work on nothing but this case until the killer was brought to justice.

By ten o'clock, they'd finished. There was no additional information they could give, other than the fact that, thus far, the killer had chosen three blonde women — one whose hair had been bleached — and they did seem to be a physical type. Five-five to five-seven in height, age around twenty-seven. Young and pretty.

Matt added, "I also believe that he stalks his victims and knows about them. The two women who've been identified were new to the areas they were living in. They were currently unattached. They didn't have family or friends who'd be checking up on them immediately. If it hadn't been for her dog's barking, Ms. Gonzales might have gone several more days without a name." He

184

paused briefly. "As I suggested earlier, it also seems that her murder might have been rushed. Her body wasn't as carefully weighted with rocks as the first woman."

"And no one saw or knew anything?" an officer asked.

"So far, we have no witnesses. We assume the killer is able to clean up before being seen. In this corridor, it's easy enough to drive into wooded areas near the rivers, perform the deed, dump the body and hop back into a car. I'm guessing he might have clothes in his trunk and that he washes up in the river, then changes his clothes. He's in an isolated area, so he takes the opportunity to do that."

"We figure he's stalking them," another officer began, "but how does he snatch them?"

"I believe he's watching them — and since he stalks them, he knows their schedules, their routines. He plucks these women right from the streets, after work perhaps, out shopping, wherever, but he obviously avoids heavily trafficked parts of the city and he's probably using the cover of darkness. It's important for every patrolman and law enforcement officer to be vigilant and to ask neighborhood groups to keep their eyes open. All information from the centers here and in DC will be continually shared, no matter how minute. Remember, no detail is too small. The go-betweens from this office are Agents Sokolov and Chan."

Matt waited, looking around at his audience. "We're also aware of one missing woman from the DC area. Agent Murray and I are on her trail, hoping to find a living woman and not another victim. It's crucial that we continue looking at missing-persons reports, since we don't know how long the killer keeps his victims sedated before killing them or if he carries out the murders quickly. We owe justice to the dead, but our first priority is always the living." When he finished speaking he heard a little bark and glanced down. Killer was at his feet.

Killer was a big hit at the station. But no matter who had him or where he went, he always came back to sit at Matt's feet.

Hey, go see Meg! She's the one who wants you.

The dog wagged his tail. Shaking his head, Matt reached down to pick him up. The damned dog even had an underbite. He felt far too skinny.

"So damned ugly you're cute, huh?" he asked the dog.

He hadn't noticed that people in the room

186

were still watching him until he heard laughter and a smattering of applause.

Detective Wharton walked over to him, grinning.

"The story's traveled, and the dog is a hero. And it seems he likes you best. Don't know about his judgment, though," Wharton joked. "I'd be sucking up to Agent Murray."

Matt glanced over at Meg. The officers on the task force were splitting up to begin their day, and one of the RPD men was asking her questions. She was answering him in a low, modulated voice. She was going to be a good agent, he thought, then immediately qualified that. She was new and it would take a while to be certain, but . . .

He realized that his reaction had been grudging. He wondered why. He had nothing against female agents; he loved the balance within the Krewe.

Maybe he'd never seen himself training a first-time agent.

Maybe he was afraid he wouldn't be proficient at it.

Or maybe it was something even deeper. He had to accept that they needed to watch each other's backs. Was he worried that she wasn't capable — or that he wasn't capable of trusting her?

He forced his attention back to the matter

at hand. "Detective," he said to Wharton, "we have an appointment to speak with the missing woman's aunt, but if you could give me an hour after that, I'd like to see Genie Gonzales's apartment."

"We did a thorough job searching it," Wharton told him.

"I know you did. I'd just like to get a feel for her."

"Certainly. Say, about one this afternoon?"

"That'll be fine," Matt replied.

Meg was still speaking with the young officer. Matt checked his watch; they should leave. The situation here was covered by Kat and Will.

He walked over to her and gestured that it was time to go.

She nodded and shook hands with the young detective.

Matt paused to let Will know they were leaving, then he and Meg headed out.

"He does walk, you know," she said.

"What?"

"Killer. He walks. You're still carrying him."

"Oh." That was when he realized that he was still holding the dog and had been for quite some time. In his arms, the animal had barely moved.

He set the dog on the ground. Killer fell

into step with him as they made their way to the parking lot. The dog obediently jumped onto Meg's lap in the passenger seat when they reached the car.

"You may be getting too attached, you know," he told her.

She shook her head. "Actually, I'm going to ask Aunt Nancy to keep him for me until I get back."

"Because he's such a beauty?" Matt asked her. "Such a charming little guy?"

She smiled. "Yes. He has the most beautiful soul an animal could have. Have you ever heard of Greyfriars Bobby? When I was a child, my dad told me the story about him. He was a terrier who sat at his master's grave in Edinburgh for years after his death — and he's buried near him now. People fed him and cared for him, but he spent his days at his master's grave. This little guy is a Bobby. So loyal. I knew I wanted a dog when I could, and this is the one. My town house is — Well, it's really empty right now, but I figure even with furniture, it'll feel cold for a while. Killer will fix that."

"Not too fond of the name," Matt said.

"I'll think about it. I'm sure Genie named him Killer ironically, because he's so little and so affectionate. Going against type. But . . . changing his name doesn't seem right. Taking care of him does."

"Whatever you say." *Her dog,* he told himself. *Sort of. Her decision.*

She pointed to a street sign. "Turn here. Nancy has a beautiful old home at the end of this cul-de-sac."

They arrived at the house and Meg paused, touching his arm before he could turn to get out of the car. "I, uh, spent a lot of time here. Nancy is a very dear and old friend. I call her *Aunt,* too, although we aren't related."

He felt her touch. Her eyes seemed oddly intense.

"And you're afraid I'm going to be a jerk and make her cry?"

She frowned. "That's not what I meant . . ."

"That's exactly what you meant. Hey, I'm the one suggesting Lara might be alive, despite the fact that you 'saw' her. But never mind. I'll be on my best behavior."

He got out of the car. As Meg had said, Nancy lived in one of the grand old places that spoke of all that had been good about the Old South — true warmth and hospitality. He smiled. Those were the things he loved about his own home, his own family.

Granted, not everything about the South had been good — certain attitudes, beliefs, behavior.

But kindness and graciousness also abounded.

Yes, he'd be on his best behavior. His mother hadn't sent him to dance lessons for nothing, he thought with amusement.

Once they'd entered the house, Matt wondered why he'd been so certain that Nancy Cooper would be a fragile old lady.

The woman who opened the door was dressed in workout clothing; she had a small but lean, muscled frame. Her hair, iron gray, was cut stylishly short. She wasn't the kind of woman to hide her age, but her age didn't matter — she was lovely. She seemed to glow with energy and intelligence. She welcomed Meg with a warm hug.

She smiled at the dog, taking him from Meg's arms and putting him on the floor, urging him to run about as if he were at home.

Then she looked at Meg with a question in her eyes, one Meg couldn't answer.

They clung together again, and Matt remembered that it was this woman's niece who was missing. She was certainly shaken with worry and dread.

She drew away from Meg at last to shake hands with Matt. She made no pretense of doing anything but assessing him. To her credit, he had no idea what her assessment had been.

"You've been with the Bureau long, Agent Bosworth?" she asked.

"Ten years."

She nodded. "Come into the parlor."

He followed Meg into a handsome room with furnishings from the mid-1800s — all of it polished and well maintained. But this meeting wasn't a cozy sit-down in the parlor; Matt almost felt as if he had arrived at a war summit. Nancy sat at the head of the table, where a service for tea and coffee was already set. Nancy briskly asked them if she might pour and if they preferred coffee or tea.

When that nicety had been observed, she sat back. "I haven't seen Lara in the past few days. Nor have I heard from her. As time goes by, I'm more and more concerned. However, I don't believe she's dead."

Meg bowed her head for a moment.

"I pray you're right," Matt said. "But is there anything in particular that's convinced you she's alive? Has she contacted you in any way?"

"No." Nancy took a deep breath. "I would know. I'm sure of it. You may think this is silly, Agent Bosworth, but I knew the moment my sister — Lara's mother — died. She was my twin. They say that twins intuit these things. And I did. Lara's parents were killed in a horrible car accident more than fifteen years ago when we had that freak blizzard late in the season. At least twenty people in the area were killed in that storm. But I knew. Patricia and I — we often read each other's thoughts. Make fun of me if you will."

"I have no intention of making fun of you," Matt assured her.

"Really?"

"Really," he repeated. "I'm a big believer in intuition."

"Aunt Nancy," Meg said, "I should explain. Matt belongs to a special FBI unit — and so do I, as of yesterday. We're called the Krewe of Hunters. We all have some . . . intuitive abilities, I guess you could call it. We see people, like I saw Mary Elizabeth after she was killed."

Nancy seemed to relax as she studied them both. Then she let out a sigh. "The police are just humoring me, I think. I realize that when a young woman goes missing and she fits the profile of a serial killer's victim, most people would assume there's little hope."

Meg reached across the table and took

Nancy's hand. "Aunt Nancy, I have to tell you — I feared she was dead."

Nancy turned to Meg, meeting her eyes. "You had one of your visions?" she asked.

Meg glanced over at Matt. "Brief. It was very brief. I'd taken a shower and the bathroom was filled with steam. I cleaned the mirror and she was standing behind me. I turned and she was still there — just for a second or two. I gave up hope — well, you know why. But Matt and some of the Krewe members believe I might have seen her in the mirror because she was reaching out to me . . . for help. That she might still be alive."

"She *is* alive," Nancy said. "And that isn't just hope speaking." She looked at Matt. "My husband and I had no children. Even before her parents died, Lara was like my own child. She's an idealist, the same way her father was. George was a columnist, and he wrote political essays that pointed out not only the negative, but how it could be fixed. He also worked tirelessly to petition congressmen for bills to benefit education and health care. Lara is a crusader, as well. She works passionately when she believes in a cause."

"I'm disturbed that, if she did go into hiding, she didn't try to get back to either you

194

or Meg," Matt said.

"If she felt she was in danger, she wouldn't have done so. Lara would never have put me in danger," Nancy said. "There's also the possibility that she's being held somewhere — that she was kidnapped!"

Matt meant to be gentle — but Nancy didn't seem the type who wanted lies.

"We're aware of that possibility," he said. "But I can't figure out why she would've been kidnapped and held," Matt said. "If she was taken, it's because she knows something she shouldn't. She's an idealist, as you've both told me. If she'd learned about a lie or some political scandal, she would've stood up against it. So there'd be no reason for anyone to abduct her — and keep her alive. I could be wrong, but I doubt it."

Matt wasn't sure what else to say. There was very little that could be tracked that the Krewe wasn't capable of tracking. Lara's credit cards hadn't been used. She'd been in Congressman Walker's company, left his office late and was never seen again. She hadn't withdrawn any large sums of money before her disappearance.

He didn't want to tell Nancy that he hoped there was a reason for her to be held; if not, her chances probably weren't good.

"You're going to look for her, right?" Nancy asked, staring at Meg and then Matt. "You'll look until you find her. If she's hiding, no one knows where she'd go better than you do, Meg. You two were like little peas in a pod, loving all the same places. I know she's somewhere, Meg, I can feel it."

"We intend to look — and we *will* find her," Meg promised.

He wished she hadn't made that promise. Despite his fervent hopes to the contrary, he suspected that if they found Lara Mayhew, the odds were that they'd find her dead. Above all, he didn't want to introduce a false sense of confidence about Lara's chances.

Meg stood. "Nancy, when was Lara here last?"

"About two weeks ago," Nancy said. "You didn't know?"

"The academy was pretty intensive. I'd talked to her — but I didn't know she was coming here."

"She surprised me. Just showed up one afternoon and didn't leave until the next morning. Needless to say, I was delighted to see her."

"Did she stay in her room?" Meg asked.

"Yes, and you're always welcome to stay there. I'm sure we could accommodate

Agent Bosworth, too. It's a big house."

"Thanks, but we have to work, and I want to try and go everywhere Lara and I used to go," Meg said. "Would you mind if I went to see whether she left anything in her room?"

"Of course not!" Nancy replied. "You know where it is."

Meg headed for the stairs.

"May I?" Matt asked Nancy.

Nancy grinned at him. "I was assuming you'd *expect* to go up there."

He nodded, smiling. He liked the old girl. "Thanks."

He followed Meg up the stairs. Lara's room was neat and pretty and actually somewhat sophisticated; she'd come here as a child, but if she'd kept posters of rock bands and movie stars on her walls back then, she'd since taken them down. The pictures in her room now were prints of old classics, beautifully framed, many medieval. Her bed was covered in a crimson flower-pattern spread that complemented her drapes. An antique dressing table sat against one wall, while double doors led out to a balcony.

Meg was at the dressing table, carefully opening drawers.

He instantly looked around for a journal

and pulled out the drawer on the bedside table.

He was rewarded. There *was* a journal. He sat and pored through it while Meg continued to search for anything that might give them any clues.

"Listen to this," Matt said, finding Lara's last entry. " 'I really long for the days when we were such believers. When idealism meant everything. I was told that government involves compromise and I believe in compromise. I know that there's no politician who can make everyone happy. What I *want* to believe in is men and women who are passionate — who are so dedicated to their cause that they aren't swayed by money or adulation. Have I found that man? Or does everyone eventually buckle?'

" 'They say *The enemy of my enemy is my friend.* Or wait — *better the devil you know than the devil you don't.* I never knew what a confusing maze I was entering! Meg got it right — Go out there to fight for justice, to right wrongs. Ah, what a discussion the two of us had at Harpers Ferry!' "

For a moment, Meg looked stricken. But she'd learned a lot of self-control at the academy, Matt thought. She quickly regained her composure.

"Lara should run herself. She has strong

convictions," Meg said.

"What was your discussion at Harpers Ferry about?"

Meg shrugged. "I told her that the FBI criminal division was just what I wanted. That I'd go after the bad guys. I also told her that half the time we never really know the truth about someone we voted for until they're in office."

"Sounds as if you felt you were taking the easier route."

"Yes. What do you suppose was going on in DC?" Meg wondered. "I guess I don't follow politics closely enough," she said apologetically. "Even being best friends with Lara."

"Politics — it's pretty damn complicated." Matt held up the journal. "Will Nancy mind if we take this?"

"Not at all, but we'll ask her."

They asked, and she didn't mind. They were welcome to the book, she said. They were welcome to anything they wanted. As they walked to the door, Killer came running up, wagging his tail. He hadn't gone upstairs with them; he'd stayed happily enough with Nancy.

"You're visiting here, little guy," Nancy said. "Right? You're leaving the pup with me? What's his name?"

Meg looked over at Matt.

Apparently, she couldn't bring herself to tell a woman whose niece was missing while a serial murderer was on the loose that the dog's name was Killer.

"Kelly," he said.

"Kelly. Cute." Nancy smiled.

Matt prepared to leave. "Thank you. We'll use all our resources, but if you hear from Lara, please call us immediately."

"Definitely," Nancy said.

"Even if someone tells you not to call the police," Matt added.

"I'm not foolish," Nancy said.

"Many people who aren't foolish want a loved one back so badly they're willing to risk anything. But if she *has* been abducted, you need our help."

Nancy put her arms around Meg and hugged her again. There were suddenly tears in her eyes.

"Find her, please, find her!" Nancy's words were muffled and her voice broke as she began to sob.

"We will find her! We will," Meg vowed.

At their feet, Killer — now Kelly — whined softly.

"Oh, silly me, crying when I'm sure everything's going to be all right!" Nancy said. She eased away from Meg and plucked up the dog. "We're going to be all right, Kelly. And don't you worry. I'd keep you myself, but Meg says she's coming back for you!"

Still holding the dog, she saw the two of them to the door. Matt shook her hand, sorry to see that tears were still brimming in her eyes. Meg hugged her a final time.

"You'll keep in touch?" Nancy asked.

"Daily," Meg replied.

Then they returned to the car.

"You shouldn't have done that," Matt told her.

"What? I shouldn't have said I'd keep in touch?"

"No. That we'd find her."

"Why not?"

"You may not be able to keep that promise," he said.

"But we will find her," she said stubbornly. "Didn't *you* tell me that?"

"Yes, I did tell you we *might* find her. I certainly haven't given up hope. But it's one thing for us to operate on that assumption and another for you to make unwarranted promises to a bereaved relative."

She paused, scowling at him, her hands on her hips.

"Fine. Then *I* will find her."

Matt went around to the driver's side of

the car. "Where are we going?"

"What?"

"Where are we going? This is your hunt, remember?"

She looked at him coolly and slid into the passenger seat. He realized she probably had no real idea. How did you hunt for a missing person who might have been abducted — or who might have gone into hiding?

She dug into her bag while he revved the car but remained parked. She brought out Lara's Richmond journal and read aloud, " 'Sometimes I want to go back. Way back to the days of innocence when we truly believed. Follow the trail as Meg and I did when we were students. Richmond to Sharpsburg, on to Harpers Ferry where we were *home,* and Gettysburg, where we learned that ideals are everything, and that good men may fight for different causes.' "

She turned to him. "Hollywood Cemetery. One of her favorite places. It's on . . ."

"I know where it is," he said curtly. She closed the journal and he drove to the cemetery.

"I don't really think she'd be hiding here, would she?" he asked.

Meg was gazing straight ahead. She didn't reply.

"Did you hear me?"

"Yes." She turned again and looked at him. "No, she won't be hiding there. She won't be there if she's . . . alive. But if she's dead . . ." Her voice trailed off.

Matt wondered what she meant. That if Lara was dead she'd show herself to Meg in a place she loved?

Meg wasn't sure what she was doing. If she was going to give any credence to the words in Lara's journal, she had to think of them as a sort of map. And then, all she could do was follow that map — without really knowing if her friend was dead or alive.

As a native of Richmond, she was proud of the graceful state capitol building with its rotunda statue — claimed to be the only one for which George Washington had actually sat. She loved the Confederate White House and was deeply moved by the sad history of Jefferson Davis's family when they'd lived there, losing a son when he'd fallen from the balcony. She'd once read to Meg from Varina Davis's memoirs about the day she'd lost her little boy. The president of the Confederacy had held his dead child while his generals had begged him for orders. Jefferson Davis, his wife and family were buried at Hollywood Cemetery.

Conceived and created as a "rural garden" cemetery, it had winding trails and beautiful, poignant stones. It truly was a garden with its sloping lawns, little hills and graceful old trees with gentle, shading branches that swayed in the breeze. The monuments included many marble angels — angels in glory and angels weeping, their emotions somehow visible in their stone poses. A great pyramid was a memorial to the Confederate war dead. But Hollywood Cemetery wasn't just a sad reminder of the lost Southern "cause." All manner of men were buried there, some who'd been moved long after their deaths, when other cemeteries had fallen into disrepair or urban progress had forced them to close. Teachers, lawyers, generals from almost every war the nation had ever fought, even the war against itself, were buried here. Long-grieving wives, many of whom had outlived their husbands by twenty to sixty years, now rested beside the men they'd loved.

The cemetery was huge, sprawling and lovely. While there were twenty-two Confederate generals buried there — along with thousands of soldiers — Meg headed first to an area where she knew she'd find one of Lara's favorite graves, that of Varina Davis, first lady of the Confederacy. She was, naturally enough, next to her husband, the one and only president of the ill-fated Confederacy. Monuments and stones and statues honored the men who'd fought for what they believed was a just cause. History — and human decency — had proved them wrong.

But while they stood by the obelisk that marked the graves of Varina and Jefferson Davis and his family, Meg felt nothing.

There was no sign of Lara. No sign of anyone.

She felt Matt watching her, occasionally pausing as if he, too, were searching the area for what most people wouldn't see — but which some might feel.

"It's a beautiful place." He spoke quietly, but she sensed that he was impatient. That he thought they were on an impulsive and ill-conceived mission.

"I'm sorry," she murmured.

"Don't be," he said. "I never mind coming here." He smiled at her suddenly and recited:

"If life and death be things that seem
If death be sleep and life's a dream
May not the everlasting sleep
The dream of life eternal keep?"

She laughed softly. "John Bannister Tabb, Confederate soldier, priest, poet and I don't remember what else," she said.

"Wow. I'm impressed," he told her. "You weren't even born here, steeped in this history."

"Harpers Ferry, not that far, and even more steeped in history," she responded. "When you go downhill toward the national park and the river, you can practically turn back time. Especially on a dark night when the fog is falling."

"I know from everything you've said that Lara loved history — and that she saw it as an important path to what the country is today," he said quietly.

"Yes." Meg sighed. "She's not here."

"You sure? It's a big place. We haven't begun to cover it."

"I'm sure. And I don't know if that's good or bad."

"It's good. I told you before, Meg, she might still be alive. This could be a sign."

Meg realized that he was looking beyond her. She turned, but at first she saw nothing. Then, slowly, she did. There was an older woman sitting on a gravestone not far from them. She wasn't in Victorian attire; her clothing was more recent. Meg recognized the long skirt, the buttoned-up bodice and belted waist of a dress that might have been worn in the 1930s. The woman's hair was in a bun and she wore a knit capelet over her shoulders, despite the fact that it was a bright, warm summer's day.

And Meg realized the woman was sitting on a stone that was part of a Confederate section; many who were buried there were veterans who had survived the conflict and died at a later date.

Matt walked past her. He went straight to the woman — and spoke to her.

Slash had heard that plenty of people were dubious about this so-called "special" unit of the Bureau known as the Krewe of Hunters.

They liked to tease that those agents were a little nuts. That they were the psychic division and that they communed with the dead.

Yeah, yeah. Well, he for one didn't buy it.

Bosworth looked bat-shit crazy, that was for sure. He was just standing there, talking to a gravestone.

Slash chafed at the time he was wasting. Ridiculous, following these two all this way. But he'd seen them at the graveyard.

He knew they were handling the case.

So . . .

Still, this wasn't fun. This wasn't like choosing victims, researching them, watching their movements.

That was enjoyable. The hunt. To his own mind, he resembled the greatest of jungle cats, light on his feet, never moving until he knew that he needed only to run and leap and he'd have his prey, helpless, in his hands, at his mercy.

There was no mercy. A jungle cat had to kill.

So did he.

For a moment, he felt a strange discomfort.

Yes, he enjoyed that kind of kill.

It involved cunning and cleverness and care — and then the pounce.

As to the other kind of killing . . .

That, too, required cunning, he told himself.

It was far more subtle and dangerous and took even greater care and cleverness.

But it was . . .

Business.

These two really had to go, he thought. He formed his fingers into the shape of a gun and aimed it at Bosworth. Then he turned to Agent Meg Murray, still standing just a few feet from him.

Maybe she thought Bosworth was bat-shit crazy, too!

He watched her.

No, he was wrong; she didn't.

Killing her might be business. But business could also bring its own fun.

She had to go.

He didn't want to shoot her.

He wanted a slow kill . . .

He wanted to see her eyes. See her eyes in that last moment — before she knew what had happened, before she knew what was going to happen. See her eyes . . .

When she knew she was going to die.

He'd been worried at first. She carried a gun. She had training. Thing was, nobody would suspect him. No one was ever on guard.

Except she was mostly with the other agent, the big-ass experienced one.

Slash smiled. There could be a way. If only Bosworth could die, too. It all had to look right, though.

That's what it was all about. Optics. An accident could always happen. A fatal accident. But first . . . the girl.

Slash watched. She seemed to be talking to the air now, too.

They were both bat-shit crazy.

They thought they talked to the dead.

Slash almost laughed aloud. And then he sobered. He stepped back behind a memorial obelisk and frowned, startled by how scared he suddenly felt. What if . . . ?

What if there was the slightest possibility that they did talk to the dead?

He needed to get rid of them, just in case. Because . . .

What if?

8

Meg was quiet, watching Matt Bosworth as they left Hollywood Cemetery. She was pleased by his words.

Lara hadn't been there; maybe that meant she wasn't dead.

Then again, cemeteries were filled with the earthly remains of the dead, yet one didn't see many ghosts there.

They'd seen Leticia Clark, though. She was one of those tragic women who'd lost her husband to the Civil War. Henry Clark had been killed at Cold Harbor, but Leticia hadn't died until 1931. She'd mourned him all those years, never remarrying.

In death, she mourned at his grave — as she had in life.

"Think we talked her into moving on?" Meg asked. She was still a little surprised to hear herself saying the words.

She was even more surprised that she'd seen him walk past her to speak to the widow, and that he'd seen Leticia before she had. It was frankly somewhat difficult to accept that his "talent" might exceed hers. She'd thought herself so special, and hadn't realized, despite everything she knew about the Krewe, others might have a depth of vision she did not.

Matt glanced over at her and shrugged. He didn't seem at all fazed that they'd both spoken with a woman who had died in the 1930s about a Confederate soldier who'd died in the 1860s.

"I hope so," Matt said.

"Then again," Meg went on, "do we really know what we're talking them into doing?"

"I believe it's right to go on," he said, smiling at her. "We know that ghosts exist, therefore we know there's more than what we usually see, feel, taste, hear and touch. If that's so, and if there's that beautiful light we've heard about . . . then moving on is exactly what should happen." He paused. "Though I have seen something different."

"What's that?"

"Darkness, horrible darkness that can eclipse the dead. Not fire and brimstone — just darkness. I've tried to study different beliefs across the world, a natural outcome of our special talents, perhaps. Maybe there's a place souls go to get cleansed, the purgatory many Christians believe in. Maybe there *is* a fire-and-brimstone hell. Or hell could be simply an absence of God. Of light, and decency. We don't know — at least, I don't." He gave her another quick smile. "And until they move on, the dead don't know, either. So, there you are."

"I've never seen that darkness you're talking about. Just the light," Meg said. "The light people see in near-death experiences. The light they walk into that leads to peace. Or heaven . . ."

Her phone suddenly rang in her pocket; she almost jumped, but grabbed it from her pocket.

The number was Nancy Cooper's. Meg's heart began to beat too fast.

"Meg, are you still in Richmond?" she asked.

"Yes, about to pull out. We're at Hollywood Cemetery. Why? Did you hear from Lara?" Meg asked anxiously.

"No, I'm sorry. Did you . . . see her? Anywhere?"

"No."

"That's a relief. And I'm positive Lara's still alive."

"We won't stop looking," Meg said.

Matt whispered, "What is it? Any news?"

"No," Meg said, shaking her head. She

covered the mouthpiece. "I'm not sure."

"Nancy," she said, speaking into the phone again. "Is anything wrong?"

"I hate to trouble you — but yes."

"What?" Meg could feel her heart beating even more frantically.

Should she be on this case? *Hell, yes.* She had to be on this case.

"What is it?" she asked.

"Kelly," Nancy said.

For a moment, Meg went blank. *Oh, Kelly — Killer!*

"What's the matter?"

"He's been sitting by the door, crying and then howling, since you left. I'd do anything to help, and I'll deal with this, but . . . that poor little dog. My heart is breaking for him. He was fine with me while you were in the house, but now . . ." Meg looked over at Matt, afraid to say anything.

"That's okay," she said automatically. What was she going to do? Matt was going to tell her she'd made a huge mistake and that Nancy was just going to have to keep the dog — no matter how much he howled and cried.

"What?" Matt persisted.

"The dog," Meg said. "He's, uh, crying a lot."

"Tell her we'll pick him up."

She couldn't have been more stunned. She probably gaped at him.

"Just tell her we'll pick him up," he repeated.

"We're coming for him, Nancy."

By the time she said goodbye, Matt had turned the car around. Meg wasn't sure what to say or do. She felt she should apologize, but the words kept catching in her throat. She finally managed to choke out, "I'm sorry."

"We're not on a time constraint," he said.

Who was she going to leave the dog with in DC? Her friends were all in the process of moving. Lara would have kept him.

But Lara was the reason for this unlikely road trip.

"Washington's on the way, so we'll head up I-95 and then go west," he said.

They were back at Nancy's within ten minutes; she was ready for them, a bag with his dog food and the little bowls they'd gotten him in her hand, Killer/Kelly at her side.

Meg stepped out the car to get the dog.

But Killer/Kelly left Nancy and made bounding leaps toward Matt, trailing his leash behind him.

To his credit, the man stopped. It was rather incongruous. The tall, fit FBI agent in his suit, with his smooth-combed short hair and sunglasses, reaching down for what even Meg had to admit was a dog so ugly it was cute.

"I'm sorry," Nancy said. "You're on a professional and personal quest, and I'm whining about a dog. It's just that I know where he came from and I realize he's so traumatized that even a little more time with you might help. I'll keep him if you need me to, but I'm afraid he's going to die of heartbreak on my watch!"

"It's okay, Nancy, we've got him," Matt told her.

"Maybe he'll be a good companion. He's not much of a guard dog — I mean, he couldn't protect you from the bad guys — but I'll tell you one thing, he can bark!"

Great! Now she had a barking dog with her. Meg briefly doubted her own choices. She was the new kid, fresh out of the academy, barely possessing the needed credentials. And then she'd insisted on keeping a victim's dog . . .

Meg stepped forward again, hugging Nancy, making promises again. Matt gave her assurances that they'd do all they could.

He didn't promise results.

When they were back in the car, Matt slipped Killer over to Meg. He didn't say a word as he started the car and began to drive.

When they reached DC, where should she tell him to go? Oh, yes, she was proving herself to be very professional.

They drove away from Nancy's, toward I-95, and still neither of them spoke. Finally, reaching the highway, he set his phone in a car-carrier and said, "Jackson."

His voice recognition system immediately dialed.

A moment later, Jackson Crow was on the phone. "Anything?" Matt asked.

"An ID on the second victim. Her name was Karen Grant. From Arizona. Same basic lifestyle and background as the other two women. She was new to the DC area. She had a job at a pizza parlor in the Georgetown area. She'd been on the job two weeks — and was looking into working her way through school. Twenty-eight years old, mother dead two years, her dad four. She didn't have a boyfriend. Angela tracked her down through the spa where she had her eyes permanently made up. She'd only been there once."

"So we have identifications on all three women. And their backgrounds are almost as similar as the murders themselves," Matt said.

"Exactly. Any new leads on your end?"

"We're driving to Harpers Ferry. We didn't find Lara." Matt paused. "Any reason we need to stop at the office?"

The dog, maybe, Meg thought.

"No, we've got various agents working here," Jackson informed them. "I think it bodes well for Lara Mayhew that she's nothing like the other victims. She's well-known, has family, friends. These girls — they didn't have time to make friends who'd miss them. Who knows? Maybe the killer thought the bodies would stay submerged longer. But Lara's victimology is entirely different. Keep looking for her. If there *is* a connection to these other killings, finding her is the only way to discover what that connection is — and whether there's a political element. Anything at Lara's home?"

"The aunt is telling the truth, at least according to my radar," Matt said. "She hasn't heard from Lara. We went through the house and found the last journal she'd been working on there."

"She talked about Harpers Ferry and a conversation we had there — about politics and work," Meg put in quickly. She hoped Killer wouldn't bark. "We really think Lara knew something Congressman Walker didn't tell us. She's been bothered for

218

weeks. I could tell because of the things she said when we talked. Of course, I was distracted — the academy," she added ruefully, "and Lara said she'd explain more when we saw each other again."

"We're keeping an eye on Congressman Walker," Jackson assured them. "Still, it's hard to imagine that he could be responsible for these murders. I always thought he was one of the good guys. Now, I'm feeling skeptical. But Lara might've been referring strictly to Walker's politics. It's one thing to be a compromised politician. It's another to rip three women apart. Meg, honestly, with the way the victimology here is panning out, I just can't see Lara being taken by the same man. But . . . I don't know. We have to do our best to catch this person before anyone else is killed — whether or not it's the same person who took Lara. Keep in touch."

"Will do," Matt promised, ending the call.

Meg held the dog in silence. Matt glanced at her, barely taking his eyes from the road.

"It's about two and half hours to Harpers Ferry," Matt said. "You okay till we get there?"

"Fine. And then some," Meg replied, worrying about the dog.

"Your family still there?"

"We own a house, but my parents are

down on Hutchinson Island in Florida now. They got tired of shoveling snow."

"Ah, so we can stay free instead of using taxpayers' money?"

Meg shook her head. "I'm sorry, but it's rented."

"So we need a place that takes dogs."

She hardly dared to breathe.

"I have to think about it for a few minutes," she said. "There are a bunch of lovely little bed-and-breakfasts, as well as chain hotels off the highway."

"There's no shortage of places — and you don't have to think about it at all. Angela will have taken care of it from the office," he said, "I just thought I'd give you a bit of a hard time."

"About the dog, you mean?"

"Yeah."

She didn't respond one way or the other.

"You have a lot of friends in Harpers Ferry?" he asked after a while.

"It's my home."

"People know you — and know you went through the academy?"

"Yes. A lot of friends work at the national park or the concessions around it."

"So we can't pretend to be your run-of-the-mill tourists," Matt said.

"Did we need to?"

220

"No, we'll rely on honesty."

"Meaning?"

"We'll just tell the basic truth. Say we're looking for Lara. And hopefully, she'd be able to get word to us if a friend is hiding her. And since you know lots of people here," he added, "if we need a dog-sitter for an hour or two, we should be all right."

"With the windows down, he can wait in the car while we're busy. I have a feeling that he's a really good little dog."

"Of course you do," Matt said.

She wanted to smack him for being a smart-ass.

She wanted to smack herself, too. *Great entry into the Krewe.*

They continued in silence for a while and then Meg asked, "You haven't been with the Krewe that long, right? Six months?"

He nodded. "A bit longer than that. I've been out on cases in Pennsylvania and Maryland so far. We also have a new office in New York City, and I spent time there last year. Jackson set that up."

"He's great. And you two get along well."

"We're both Native American," he said, grinning.

"No, you're not!"

He laughed. "I am. I'm actually one of thousands of people who trace their ancestry

221

back to Pocahontas. I'm a mix of many nationalities now, while Jackson is half–Native American. But it's a lot of fun to trace your heritage all the way back to someone as noteworthy as Pocahontas."

"Nice. I can't really trace my family history very far at all."

"If you're really interested, there are internet sites that can help."

"I know that one grandparent came from Nova Scotia, one from California, one from North Carolina — and one from Harpers Ferry. That's it," Meg said. "What I was always more concerned with was . . . why? Why certain people? Does it have something to do with background?"

"You mean, why you see the dead?" he asked.

She was quiet for a minute. "Yes."

"I guess some people just do. Some feel a greater . . . sensitivity, for lack of another word, to what you might call the nonmaterial world, while others are so skeptical they'll never experience that feeling of a departed loved one being near. I recognize that I have this ability. And," he added, "for me, it's been a good thing. What about you?"

"Sure, I always loved it when people thought I needed therapy."

He laughed at that. Maybe he wasn't so bad — he was straightforward and didn't stand on ceremony, or pretense.

"When was your first time?" she asked him.

He glanced at her, and she was surprised by the amusement in his eyes. "My first time doing what? That could be taken as a very personal question."

She was sure she blushed a thousand shades of red. Fortunately, he didn't seem to want to torture her any further.

"My first time?" he repeated, shaking his head and smiling awkwardly. "I was a kid with an imaginary friend. We had a home that was built right before the Revolution. During the mid-nineteenth century it was a tavern at one time. It has an association with Thomas Jefferson because he helped a cousin purchase it. As a kid, I thought it would be neat if you woke up at night and found Jefferson sitting in a rocker in front of the giant hearth. I never saw Thomas Jefferson, but I did meet Josiah Thompkin. He was a young guy, barely nineteen, and he was killed at the start of the Revolution. Great attitude — he figured being a ghost for a few hundred years wasn't a bad deal. When the place was a tavern, he liked to douse men's cigars with ale and pull at the ladies' skirts. I talked about him and people smiled. Although I think my mother was a little concerned that Josiah was a real historical person. Later, I was at Arlington for a funeral. My uncle had died and he'd been a marine. I was about ten, and I was standing there in the heat, listening to the priest give a long graveside eulogy. Being a kid, I looked around most of the time. I was staring up at the house, the old mansion that Robert E. Lee had owned before the Civil War, built by Washington's step-grandson and adopted son . . ."

"I know the house," Meg reminded him. "I'm from West Virginia, remember?" She couldn't prevent a certain irony from entering her tone.

"Yes, of course. Anyway . . . we were always interested in Washington and Lee family history. And even as a kid, I felt terrible for Lee. Lincoln offered him a pivotal post leading the Northern army, and Lee had to make a decision. Back then, your first loyalty was to your state. And he was a Virginian. They say the entire household could hear him pacing through the night and day, trying to make that decision. He had to know that the Union would take his house — the Union would have to. Guns up here could have shot right across the

Potomac into the Capitol. And can you imagine him having to tell his wife that they were going to lose a home that had come to them through *her* family? But he had to decline Lincoln's offer because he was a Virginian and Virginia was bound to secede."

"And when the Union took the property, they began to bury their dead, ensuring that he'd never come back. Except now the house is a Lee memorial," Meg said. "And?"

"And I was looking up at it, and I saw Lee."

"As in Robert E.?" Meg asked.

Matt was still wearing his dry smile. "Yeah," he said huskily. "As in Robert E. I saw him standing in his uniform, hands folded behind his back, gazing out over the Potomac. He was some distance from the columns."

"Did it occur to you that it might have been a reenactor?"

"Of course. In fact, my mom was certain that I'd seen a reenactor."

"How do you know it wasn't?"

He smiled. "Because I saw Mary Lee walk up behind him and put her arms around him. Reenactors seldom engage in that kind of intimacy. But everyone said it *was* a reenactor — although the management at the house said there were no reenactments that day. I accepted it. Easier than dealing with the ribbing I got for seeing a ghost. I let it all go."

"And then?" Meg asked.

He turned and looked at her. "A girl in high school. A friend. A great kid. Kerry Sullivan. We weren't a couple, but we'd known each other since grade school, and our parents were friends, too. I was actually away, checking out colleges. I dreamed that she and I were walking along a path in the Blue Ridge. Our parents often rented cabins up in the mountains in the national park. I was in New York, and she was supposedly in Richmond. But in my dream, she took my hand when we sat down and told me to be kind to our parents, to reassure them that she was all right. I teased her. I said no one had ever accused her of being all right. She just smiled and touched my face. She'd done that as long as I'd known her — a funny little way of running her hand down my face, telling me not to be a jerk. I don't remember anything else until I woke up. And when I did, I could still smell the scent of the perfume she always wore. I called home, and my mom was crying. She'd been about to call me, to say that Kerry had died of an aneurysm during the night."

He took a thoughtful breath. "I knew then. Everyone thought I was crazy again because they saw me talking to her at the grave site. She was in a great mood, happy that so many people had come to her funeral. She told me to say good things to her parents and sisters and brothers. Make them feel okay. I promised I'd try. And then she told me . . ."

"What?"

"To use it," he said quietly. "That she could talk to me, that maybe others could, and that . . . I should use it. Bring comfort to the living. And maybe help the dead."

"And that's why you're Krewe," she said.

"I wasn't like you. I didn't know right away that this is what I should be doing, where I should be working. But yeah, I figured a dead girl had talked to me, so I needed to do what she said. First, I went to the Virginia Military Institute in Lexington — a long-standing family tradition — and then did a stint in the service." He paused. "Deployed to Iraq."

She didn't move; he didn't betray any emotion and yet she knew his time in the service must have been very hard. He spoke again.

"Then I joined the FBI. Things have changed, of course, since 9/11. The FBI is much more active overseas now and I was assigned to the Middle East for a while. After that, I went back to school for behavioral science and finally landed at Quantico — and then with Adam."

"He is an incredible man," Meg murmured.

"That he is. I learned how to profile, and to put the results together with what I'd learned about the dead. And from the dead, from those who stayed. I've watched and observed and I discovered that some ghosts won't talk to everyone, and some are better at talking than others. Some are so real you're convinced you can touch them, some can't quite learn to be ghosts — like the way I couldn't learn to ice-skate. They're the hardest to communicate with, these almost-ghosts."

Meg realized that she was smiling.

"What?" he asked warily.

"You really can't ice-skate?"

"Total fool on the ice. I fall all over the place."

"Well, we should be okay," she said.

"Why?"

"It's summer!"

"There you go," he said lightly.

Meg saw that they'd traveled a good distance already; they were headed west now, skirting DC.

Killer sat quietly in her lap, like an angel.

When they came to a rest area, Matt pulled onto the ramp. "We can take him out for a minute," he said, indicating Killer.

"He hasn't barked or whined or anything."

"He's a dog. I'm not taking any chances with this car."

Matt parked near a small lot for dog-walking. Meg got out, setting Killer on the ground and looping his leash around her wrist.

"Need a break? Want coffee?" he asked.

"No. I'm fine."

"Okay. I could use more coffee. I'll leave you two and be right back."

As he headed into the concession area, Meg called to him. "Bosworth."

He turned.

"If you're getting coffee, anyway, I guess I'll have one. Thanks."

He nodded and moved on. He wasn't running or even hurrying; he had a very long gait and naturally moved fast.

Meg took Killer to the dog park. He stayed by her side, sniffed a little and did his business. A Pekingese, seeing him, barked wildly. Killer ignored the other dog and resumed sniffing the grass.

Waiting with him, Meg idly watched the

traffic. She frowned, noticing a black sedan with tinted windows sliding into the rest area. It didn't park.

It merely slowed, then entered the lane that led back to the highway.

She tried to get a look at the license plate as the sedan drove off. There were rows of cars between them, and just when she might have had her chance, the Pekingese and its owner walked right past her. But she suspected that if she *had* seen the license, it would've been encrusted in mud.

Matt returned, carrying two paper cups of coffee. She thanked him as she took hers and then said, "A black sedan just went by, slowed down, then kept going. Tinted windows."

"You think someone is following us in a black sedan?"

"Remember the one outside my town house yesterday? It pulled away when Angela and I saw it."

"Look in the parking lot," he told her.

She turned to see five cars in the lot fitting that description.

"Hmm."

"Maybe they're so popular around here because they're so . . . official. If someone *is* following you — or us — he's hiding in plain sight. Practically everyone around here has a black sedan," Matt commented.

"So you think I'm paranoid or seeing things that don't exist? That I'm trying to create a mystery?"

"Things are what they are, whether you want to create a mystery or not," he said. "And there's nothing wrong with paranoia — sometimes it can save your life. But, of course, you're thinking black sedan because of Congressman Walker's office."

"Yeah. Congressmen tend to be driven around in them. Their aides use them. Lobbyists use them."

"Like I said, just about everyone in Washington uses them. The question is do you really think you're being followed?"

"I — I'm not sure why anyone would follow me."

"Because you're on the hunt for Lara Mayhew," he said. "Anyway, you ready to go?"

They'd only been back in the car for a minute when Matt's phone rang. He said the word "Answer."

It was Angela. She told him they had a reservation at a small local hotel within walking distance of the historic area, a place that accepted dogs.

He said nothing as he hung up. She sat there uncomfortably, holding the dog and sipping her coffee. Finally, she spoke, hoping she sounded nonchalant and business-like but still appreciative.

"Thank you."

"Huh?" He glanced over at her; she realized that he must've been deep in thought.

"The dog. You were right. I shouldn't have taken him."

"As long as you *know* I'm right."

"Why do you do that with everything?" Meg demanded, speaking before she had a chance to weigh her words — and stop them.

"Do what?"

"I said I knew I was wrong. You could've just said, 'Thanks, that's okay.' "

"Doesn't matter. The dog's with us now. That's the way it is. So, we'll accommodate."

Meg fell into silence. Every time she thought he was actually proving to be human, he went and turned it around. Fine.

She finished her coffee, curled her arms around the dog and leaned against the side of the car. She hadn't slept much lately.

"Taking a nap?" he asked.

"You're doing the driving," she said.

She didn't really sleep but she must have dozed. The next thing she knew, they were drawing into Harpers Ferry, her home, a place where the rivers had flooded the land, where George Washington had gone, where John Brown had staged his famous raid and Civil War soldiers had fought time and time again.

Where ghost stories abounded in the often fog-shrouded valley low by the river.

Home. A place where Lara Mayhew might easily have come to hide.

Matt was familiar with Harpers Ferry. He figured it would've been nearly impossible to grow up in Richmond, attend military school and not know Harpers Ferry. The munitions here and the strategic placement of rivers and mountains led to its being valuable in war. Nowadays, it thrived on tourism. There was the history of the Civil War to be experienced; there was rafting and tubing on the river. Visitors could enjoy interesting shops and great stories told by the Rangers; there were reenactments, and all manner of entertainment. He didn't, of course, know the town as well as someone who had lived here. As well as Meg Murray probably did.

Angela had done a wonderful job finding the kind of place they needed. From their hotel, they could ease right down to the John Brown firehouse. A climb up the hill would take them to Harper Cemetery and Jefferson Rock — where you could look down over the valley and the river and see for miles.

And the place allowed dogs.

He liked animals, although he didn't have one because he traveled so frequently. He'd toyed with the idea of an independent cat, but hadn't gotten around to adopting one yet.

Killer . . .

Damn, the mutt was ugly.

Still, there was something about him. Maybe the loyalty that had brought him to the morgue where his owner lay within. Matt figured if they ever encountered Genie's ghost, the dog would come in handy.

He trusted his gut. Intuition was, he thought, akin to his ability to see the dead.

He found it somewhat irritating that Meg had insisted on bringing Killer, but as he'd said himself, the dog was with them now. They had to make it work.

The place they were staying was called the General Fitzhugh Lee Hotel. That was something of an exaggeration; it was more of a bed-and-breakfast, but for their purposes, just about perfect. They were greeted at a counter in the parlor by an older woman who recognized Meg immediately.

"Margaret Murray, child, how are you? When I saw your name I was so pleased. We miss you and your folks around here. I haven't seen you in years!"

"Hi, Mrs. Lafferty," Meg said, returning a hug from the woman, who'd walked around the counter to embrace her.

"Look at you," Mrs. Lafferty exclaimed. "All grown-up and official! I don't mean to ignore you, Mr. Bosworth, but it's been ages since I've seen Meg!"

"Quite all right," Matt assured her. It was totally enjoyable to watch Meg squirm and wonder what he was thinking. Still, the more time he spent with her, the more he admired her — despite the occasional flash of annoyance. She was young, she was new, she was raw. But she was passionate and determined. And undeniably attractive — tall, lithe, with her large blue eyes and generous mouth. He wasn't a fool; he'd immediately responded to the sexual attraction she exuded. And she loved dogs. His grandmother used to say that you could tell who people were by the way they treated animals. Those who were good to animals were usually good human beings — and she always warned him to be careful of those who weren't.

Then why be so hard on Meg? It wasn't the new . . . or the raw.

Maybe it was the way he'd felt when she'd touched him that first day at the morgue. He'd pulled back because she'd been so warm, so filled with life, even with tears in her eyes. And a moment like that wasn't the time to feel anything but empathy for another human being.

Meg immediately asked Mrs. Lafferty if she'd seen Lara Mayhew lately.

Mrs. Lafferty had not.

They were given rooms next to each other on the ground floor; that made it easy with the dog.

Mrs. Lafferty loved Killer right off the bat.

Matt realized that they were again using the dog's original name. Killer.

They didn't have far to go from the parlor to their rooms. He was glad to see that Meg traveled as lightly as he did — one overnight carry-on and an over-the-shoulder bag.

When Killer started to follow him, Meg urged the dog into her own room.

The "hotel" predated the Civil War by three decades; it was furnished with period pieces. Matt found a wall plaque in his room informing him that it had been inhabited by generals from both sides of the "Great

Conflict" and, since then, all kinds of ambassadors, attachés and visiting military. When he'd set his bag on the rack, Matt looked out the window onto the Shenandoah. The view was spectacular, even by night. A full moon had risen. And from his vantage point, he could see the river, brilliant and shimmering in the moonlight. He caught glimpses of the old houses and shops perched at an angle along the slope of the hill, and he knew where the park was, as well as the firehouse where John Brown had staged his famous — and infamous — raid.

A fog was settling low at the base of the hill. Even the greatest skeptic might imagine that the dead walked, that history came alive, in such a place.

"Nice," he murmured aloud. He had to remember to thank Angela for her diligence.

There was a knock on his door and he opened it to find Meg there. "I thought you might be hungry," she said. "I sure am. We've got time to grab a bite and latch on to a ghost tour. Seems like a good way to start."

"And you'll know the guide, I assume?" he asked.

Meg shrugged. "The population here is under three hundred — as far as the town itself goes. I've been gone awhile, but everyone knew my parents, and they come back every once in a while. So do I, although it's been a couple of years."

"Everyone knew Lara, too?"

"I wouldn't want to say everyone, but, yes . . ." She hesitated. "I'd really like to get up to Harper Cemetery. We'll join whatever tour is in session, then go off on our own."

"I'm at your command," Matt said.

A slight sniff as she turned around told him she didn't believe that for a second. He smiled and followed her.

The mist was already rising as they headed out.

Yes, it was going to be an exceptional night for a ghost tour — especially in a cemetery.

9

Killer, it seemed, was coming with them. Even though Mrs. Lafferty offered to watch the little dog, Meg wanted him on their walk. And she knew a charming place up on a hill where they could dine outside with the dog. The food was excellent; the waitress, the busboy, the bartender and the manager all came out to talk to Meg. She'd gone to school with the waitress, and it was with her that Meg spoke the most after introducing Matt.

"So you're home — in Harpers Ferry, of all places — on your first official job with the FBI?" Meg's friend marveled. She laughed delightedly, but then sobered. "Because Lara is missing?" The young woman, Melody Jennings, was deeply distressed by that. "You didn't know Lara?" she asked Matt.

"No, I'm sorry to say," he replied.

"She's so smart, funny, beautiful, and so

239

nice! You *have* to find her."

"She didn't come through here? You're sure?" Meg asked.

"You know how tiny this place is!" Melody said. "If Lara had been here and anyone had seen her at all, everyone would've been talking about it. But, hey, if anyone can find her, it's you. You two had that mind thing going on. Remember when you were kids and Raif Sanderson took her hostage?"

Melody paused to look at Matt again and smile broadly. "It wasn't a situation that called for the FBI. Raif had a huge crush on Lara. I think we were all about twelve or thirteen. He surprised her up at the cemetery one day — she'd gone for a walk by herself. Then he managed to tie her to one of the gravestones. But when the grown-ups all started going crazy, Meg somehow knew to go to the cemetery." She laughed. "Raif didn't sit for a week after that, poor guy. He said he was willing to suffer it all for love. He eventually married an accountant and they moved to Baltimore, by the way," she told Meg.

"Pure logic that time, I'm afraid. I knew how much Raif loved the cemetery — and how fascinated Lara was by a couple of the stories up there," Meg said.

Matt thought, however, that she looked

contemplative.

He was almost certain there'd been something else that had led her to her friend.

"It's terrifying, isn't it?" Melody went on. "She's missing, and that horrible killer is on the loose. You don't think . . . ?"

"We're praying not," Meg said.

Melody shivered visibly. "That case is on the news constantly. They're always warning us not to be alone, to be careful. I mean, we're pretty remote here, in comparison to DC and Richmond, but still . . ."

"It never hurts to be vigilant," Matt said. "Be extra careful."

He'd been thinking that Meg might not be paranoid — that maybe a black sedan *was* following her. And if so . . .

Was it someone from Walker's office, afraid they might find Lara? Or was it someone who knew they were also on the trail of a killer?

"Trust me. I'm a coward. I'm making Billy walk me home — I live two blocks from here! — every night," Melody told them. She shivered again and said, "Well, we're glad to meet you and glad to have the FBI here, Agent Bosworth." She turned to Meg. "Are you really going to take the ghost tour? You could give it in your sleep."

"But it's fun to go," Meg said. "Years ago, when I was very young, it was led by a wonderful woman named Shirley Dougherty. She also wrote the book about the tales. I think back then it was called *Harpers Ferry Myths and Legends.* Anytime I went on a ghost tour after that, the guides had high standards to live up to. Shirley would be in period dress, holding her lantern. She taught history — and then told us what people claimed to have experienced that had to do with that history. She was the best."

"And," Matt added, "you could go on her ghost tour on Saturday night and find her saying the Rosary at the Catholic church the next morning."

Meg grinned. "You went on her tour."

"I did. I agree — she was the best. I heard she died in 2011."

"Yes," Melody said. "And we still miss her."

Matt tried to pay the check, but Melody informed them that the manager had insisted she wasn't to let them do so. Everyone was so thrilled with Meg's graduation and her being there.

They thanked Melody, and Killer licked her fingers and wagged his tail in appreciation, because Melody had seen to it that he'd gotten some scraps of beef.

They walked downhill to the meeting point. Jenny, the guide that night, also greeted Meg with a hug and seemed pleased to meet Matt. "You being here makes me a little nervous," she told Meg. "Makes me feel I'd better get it right!"

"You always have everything right," Meg assured her.

Matt tried to pay for the tour, but Jenny, too, refused to accept any money.

There were few places in the world quite like Harpers Ferry. Darkness had settled over the valleys between the mountains like a cloak. Historic buildings crouched together, and while there were night-lights along the historic trails, the atmosphere seemed to whisper of the past, of ghosts.

Jenny started by pointing out Harper House, explaining that in 1747 Robert Harper had come to the beautiful spot that had then been known as "the hole." An architect and millwright, he'd fallen in love with the place where the Shenandoah and Potomac rivers met, where water was such a tremendous power. He'd purchased the land from a man who had squatter's rights — Peter Stephens, who was running a ferry — under Lord Fairfax, and from Lord Fairfax himself. And thus, Harpers Ferry was born.

Jefferson would call it one of the most beautiful spots on earth; Washington would arrive and assess the potential.

It would become an effective place for munitions and, later, a battleground that was fiercely contested in the Civil War.

"And now . . ." Jenny told the tour that people often saw Mrs. Harper in the windows. Harper had died before the house was finished; he'd asked his wife to look after their gold, and it was assumed that when she died, she remained behind to keep vigil over it.

The John Brown Raid was next on the agenda. But while Jenny talked about John Brown and told everyone about his desire to begin a slave revolt, Matt noted a boy of about ten hovering on the outskirts of the group of twelve.

"Dangerfield Newby, one of Brown's men, was the first to be killed in the action. Sadly, by friendly fire from Brown's own party. His was a sorry tale. His white father had freed him, but when he'd tried to buy his wife and children from a slave-owner, he was told — as soon as he'd earned the required money — that the price had gone up. Angry and desperate, he'd joined with John Brown. The people here, terrified of a slave revolt, had torn the poor man's body to shreds and fed it to the hogs, which is why we still have Hog Alley."

As Jenny talked, going on to tell the crowd how the ghost of Dangerfield Newby was often seen on a foggy night, Matt noticed that the boy was watching Meg.

The boy seemed determined to come around and reach her.

Matt shifted his own position. The kid wasn't trying to interrupt the guide and he didn't seem to intend any harm.

Nonetheless, Matt stayed nearby. When Jenny said the group was moving on, the young boy walked up to Meg.

Meg obviously realized he was coming and turned around. A smile lit her face; Matt was startled by the way that smile touched him. He felt something tugging at him; he wasn't sure whether it was about his emotions — or his libido.

"Joey," Meg said softly, although they were approaching the steps to the upper level — the cemetery, the ruins of one church and the beautiful Catholic church that had survived the war because its canny priest had continued to hoist the British flag, which stopped both sides from firing on it.

She knew the boy. So they weren't seeing a ghost who might help, but maybe this child could.

"Meg." The boy started to speak. Then, seeing Matt, he hesitated. He reached out to pet Killer, who was in Meg's arms.

"It's okay, Joey, Matt's with me," Meg told the boy. "This is Matt Bosworth. He's a federal agent — like me." She turned to Matt. "Joey's family and my family are friends. His house is near my parents' house." She glanced around. "Um, are your mom and dad here, Joey?"

The boy was reluctant to answer, and Matt assumed that Meg would address this later, when they had a little more privacy.

"Hi, Joey, nice to meet you," he said.

Joey stared up at him, still a little wary.

"Maybe I should follow the tour and let you two catch up," Matt said.

"He's really okay," Meg told Joey.

"Oh, you're, like, friends, right?" Joey asked.

"Good friends," Matt said.

"Oh." Joey nodded wisely, as if he'd determined they were actually *more* than friends — as in a romantic pair.

He seemed to like that concept, and neither of them corrected him.

"Have you seen Lara?" Joey asked worriedly.

"No, in fact, I'm looking for her," Meg told him. "Have *you* seen her?"

Joey nodded again.

"Recently?" Meg asked.

Joey shook his head. "But it wasn't that long ago. I can't remember exactly. She was here a couple weeks ago."

"I'm so glad you saw her," Meg said. "Do you know where she was staying?"

"She didn't stay. She said she'd just come for the day."

"Where did you see her?" Matt asked him.

He waved toward the car lot. "She parked, and then she came up the steps." He paused to look at Matt. "You know her — she's so nice. She and Meg . . ." He paused again with a slightly embarrassed smile. "Well, they're nice. They like kids. So I ran after her when she went up the steps. I wanted to say hi."

"That was very sweet," Meg said. "Where did she go?"

"She stopped in the church and she was kneeling, so I thought maybe something bad happened, or maybe she didn't want to be disturbed. But then she walked up to Harper Cemetery. I followed her there." He grinned at Matt. "First we stopped at the *other* John Brown's grave. All the kids know about John Brown's head."

Matt was anxious for whatever information Joey had, but he was ten or so. At that age, kids would keep talking as long as you let them.

"Yeah, it's a creepy story," he said. "It happened years later, and it wasn't *the* John Brown, but *a* John Brown, who had himself buried standing up, with his head in glass. He paid a guy to watch for seven days to see if he'd come back to life."

"And then," Meg continued, "the glass broke and the head came off and rolled around and kids thought it was a toy. They played kickball with it, until someone rescued it. He sent it to the widow, who assured him that she had *her* John Brown's head. John Brown is a fairly common name, except that in Harpers Ferry, everyone immediately assumes it means only one John Brown."

Joey nodded enthusiastically. "Kids still like to play in the cemetery," he said, grinning up at Matt.

"I love cemeteries, too," he told Joey with a smile.

"Hey, you guys coming?" Jenny called to them.

Meg raised a hand. "We'll catch up!" she called back.

Jenny went on with her tour.

"So what else did Lara do at the cemetery?" Meg asked.

248

"Well, she walked around looking at graves," Joey said. "She seemed okay. I went up to her and she hugged me, but she acted kind of . . . weird, so I asked her if she was okay. She smiled and said she was fine. She was glad to see me, she wanted to know about Little League and all . . . But before she left, we walked to Jefferson Rock. We were looking out over the river and she talked about the great legends and how much she loves it here, even if bad things happened a long time ago. They were a lesson to us all," he added breathlessly. "That's what she said — a lesson to us all. We sat on the rock for a while and then she had to go back to work. But she told me if I saw you, I was supposed to say you should go to the cemetery. She said you'd understand what that means. I didn't know when I'd see you again, but I heard my mom talking about how you were in town. So I — I came out to find you."

"We'll walk you home," Meg insisted.

"I'm not supposed to be out. I'll just sneak back in."

"How about this," Matt suggested. "We'll walk you back to where we can see you get inside your house."

Joey shrugged. "Sure. It's a lot of walking, though."

"That's okay. We need the exercise." Meg flashed him a glance like nothing he'd seen from her yet. It was appreciation. She might actually like him a little bit for this. Or, at least, not dislike him quite so much.

They walked back up the hill with Joey. Killer trotted beside the child, happy to be in his company.

They passed a house with a plaque announcing that it had been Stonewall Jackson's headquarters when he was in Harpers Ferry. A block later, Joey paused and knelt down to stroke Killer.

"We'll watch from here," Meg said. "And thanks so much, Joey. I guess no one else knew she was here because she just went to the church and then the cemetery — and left."

Joey nodded.

Meg asked, "She was okay, though, right?"

"She seemed really . . . thoughtful, I don't know, like my mom sometimes gets."

"Hurry into your house. We'll watch until you go inside," Matt said.

Joey gave Meg an impulsive hug and Matt a wave, then ran toward his house. They waited until he'd slipped through a side door.

"Which one does your family own?" Matt asked.

"Opposite side." Meg pointed out a house just behind Joey's, built in the colonial style.

"Nice place."

"My folks will never let it go. But they're both retired. My mom worked for the park service and my dad was a teacher."

"No siblings?"

"No. That's why Lara was like a sister. She was an only child, too, and had lost her parents, as you know. My parents adored her and her aunt, Nancy, and so did my grandfather. We all spent lots of time together." She turned and looked at Matt. "Let's get to the cemetery."

"Thank God for moonlight," Matt said. "You have a flashlight?"

She reached into her pocket. "Of course. Do you have yours?"

"Of course," he said, mimicking her. "I've been out in the field a long time. And I've been through another academy besides the FBI."

"What's that?" she asked.

"Life," he told her.

Slash had left his car in a parking lot in Bolivar — abutting Harpers Ferry — and rented a flashy little sports car, easier to maneuver on mountains and hilly roads, instead. But Harpers Ferry was such a small, tight-knit town, plus the main drive down the hill was a tourist mecca, so he'd parked it, too. Why attract unnecessary attention?

For the past hour, he'd been walking. Uphill, downhill, following these wretched people.

Now they were going downhill again.

He had to make sure he couldn't be seen. There was no explanation for him to be in Harpers Ferry, other than that he was hoping to find Lara, too, and then he'd be on their radar, a definite suspect.

They should have been huffing and puffing. Slash had to admit that fitness training at the academy had to be good. The two ahead of him didn't even seem winded.

He stayed some distance back. As he waited, he saw the kid go through the side door. Curious, he made his way over to the house.

He could move well. He didn't seem to have the wind or the ease of the agents, but he had learned to move like a spirit in the night. It was too bright out for him — the damned moon just had to be full — but what was he going to do?

Be careful. Be very careful.

He got closer to the house. He hadn't

been able to hear what the kid had told the agents.

At the house, he slunk against the wall and peered through the window. There was no sign of the kid. A pretty woman — a blonde — was at the kitchen window washing dishes. A man came in and slid his arms around her waist.

He listened the best he could to their conversation, watching their lips move. He'd gotten pretty good at lip-reading through the years. The conversation was boring.

The husband said he'd had a long day at work. She'd been busy with the PTA.

She was very pretty.

Long, wavy blonde hair. About five-six. He studied her and smiled.

Maybe . . .

But for now, the agents were getting a little too far ahead of him.

And he *had* to find out what the hell they were doing here.

What they knew. And what they might discover.

The cemetery sat at the top of the hill. When Robert Harper died, there'd only been three houses in the area, but Harper had set the four acres aside for a cemetery.

In the moonlight, the gravestones were

beautifully, hauntingly opaque. The night's fog was swirling around the graves.

Killer was oddly calm and quiet, staying close to Meg's feet. It was almost as if the dog sensed that they were in a sacred place, that they walked among the dead.

If the tour group had come to the cemetery, they'd already moved on. While the puffs of fog hugging the graves might have been spooky to some, they were reassuring to her. As a child, she, like Joey, had played here.

She never saw the dead at the Harper Cemetery. They didn't seem to linger. There was talk that Father Michael Costello could be seen walking the heights, still protecting the church he'd presided over during the Civil War — raising his British flag to prevent the opposing forces from firing upon it. She'd never seen him, but she didn't mind believing the legend that he still walked these steep paths.

The cemetery seemed to sit in the midst of a haunted atmosphere.

Matt stood by her side. "And now?" he asked.

"I think I have to find Mary Wager," Meg said.

"Mary Wager. Her stone, you mean?"

"Yes, her stone. There are Wagers all over

the cemetery," Meg began. "I'm sure you know that Robert Harper left no children, but his niece married a Wager, so . . . through the generations, there were many of them. Lara and I were both crazy about her grave marker. It has the most beautiful poem . . . but the marker was falling apart and we shored it up with stones."

She lifted her flashlight higher as she looked around the cemetery. Being here reminded her so much of days gone by, back when she and Lara were young, when they slipped out at night — just as Joey had — to hover on the outskirts of a ghost tour or scamper up the steps to the cemetery. Tonight she barely needed the flashlight; they were on the hilltop and the moon was dazzling.

"Mary Wager." Matt moved ahead of her.

"It's more or less in the center," Meg told him.

He nodded. "I vaguely remember . . ."

The cemetery was somewhat overgrown with haphazard trails. She was accustomed to it; she knew her way through it and took the lead. She came to a stop when she reached the grave. Matt joined her there, his long strides bringing him close to her in a matter of seconds.

She shone her light on the marker and

recited the poem, mostly from memory.

" 'Tis better to have loved than lost,
No matter what the cost.
I died for him, and he for me,
The war the game, the end the same.
I waited for love, did not return,
And then the pain, the bitter burn.
So I loved and lost and lingered here,
In death, I know, my love be there."

"Poetic, and quite sad," Matt said. "So you two, you and Lara, came here and dreamed about Mary's great romance?"

Meg shrugged and glanced at him. He didn't seem to be mocking her.

"There's no record in the archives that we could find, so we made up a story for her. She was a Southern girl and he was a Southern boy, but he fought for the Union. When he died, she couldn't even bury him. So she lived on. She was a good Christian, we'd decided, so no thought of suicide. We imagined her watching the years go by, always believing that she'd see him again once she died."

She realized he was smiling.

"Hey, we were kids."

"Pretty impressive that you were doing this kind of research — in the archives —

when you were that young."

"We learned from my parents."

"A teacher and a mom who worked for the park service — makes sense."

As he spoke, Meg knelt down, holding her flashlight, Killer beside her, and moved her fingers around the old monument. She found the crack and pushed one finger through to the hollowed-out point at the base.

There might be nothing there. This might just be wishful thinking. But . . .

"You know, you could hit a snake or spider doing that. You want more light?" Matt asked. "Let me hold yours, too."

He knelt close beside her. She felt the strength and heat of his body, felt whatever it was that made him so alive, so forceful and charismatic.

The scent of his cologne or aftershave wasn't bad, either.

"Thanks," she murmured as he trained dual lights on the marker.

The crack that led to the little hollow in the stone was low against the ground, hidden by overgrown tufts of grass and weeds.

"Want me to try?" Matt asked.

"No, no, I'm fine. And my fingers are smaller," she said.

They were. Of course, they'd been smaller

still when she and Lara were young and left notes for each other there.

But her fingers touched paper. She stared at Matt; his face was practically touching hers. She flushed and said softly, "There's something here!"

A moment later, she pulled it out — a piece of paper rolled in a tube. She gasped as she almost tore it; there'd been rain since the note was left and the paper was fragile.

"Careful. We can get it back and dry it. Might be good to have the lab look at it, too," Matt said.

He was, she had to admit, always prepared. He'd put down one of the flashlights and had an evidence bag in his hand. As she placed the paper inside the bag, she frowned up at him. "Matt, we have to read it now. What if she's in danger? What if she's in hiding? What if she's alive and she needs us?"

"Let's get out of the cemetery and off this hill first, huh? At least get to where we can open it carefully? It's no good if it's ruined."

He was right and she knew it.

"Okay, we'll go back to the B and B," she said.

Suddenly Killer, who'd been at her feet, quiet and obedient, began to bark.

He stared at the trees, his body rigid and

258

his posture fierce.

"Killer, hey!" Meg whispered.

She saw that Matt had already reached for his Glock. Startled, she did the same.

There was movement in the trees along the massive rock across from them. Meg thought she heard the sound of footsteps receding on the trail down.

Someone had been there, someone who was gone now.

The dog continued to growl.

"Stay as low as you can!" Matt ordered. He crouched down, level with the gravestones, then crept toward the trees. She followed, and they rose to a standing position when they reached the trees, walking furtively through the dark shadows. But they found no one.

"We *are* being followed," Matt said slowly. He pointed to a broken branch. "Someone was watching us from these trees."

"People are up here all day," Meg said.

"This is a fresh break," he told her. "See?" It appeared to be; Meg didn't argue. She'd never considered herself much of a tracker. The situation hadn't arisen for her before.

He set his hand on her back. "Let's go to the hotel. I want to read what this note says."

At his touch, she suddenly felt close to

him; maybe it was natural. The two of them against the world as they stood high above the town, surrounded by graves.

"All right." Killer stayed at her heels as they hurried down. At the top of the steps, Matt paused. He kept very still.

"Whoever it was is gone," Matt said. He dropped down by the dog. "You know what, Killer? You weren't such a bad idea, after all. Go figure."

He started down the stone steps, Meg right behind him. Then they headed back up the hill to the General Fitzhugh Lee.

When they reached it, everything was quiet. Meg used her house key to let them in. Matt followed her to her room.

Killer hopped up on her bed and curled up to sleep. He seemed to believe that his work for the night was done.

Matt took the rolled note out of the evidence bag and set it on the television stand. "You have tweezers?" he asked her. "And a pen or something that's not sharp?"

She found her tweezers and an eyeliner pencil with a soft end for smudging color.

Matt very cautiously began to use the tools to open the damp paper. Meg watched it unfold.

As she saw Lara's writing emerge, her heart seemed to beat harder. Then she felt it sink to her stomach as she saw how much the ink had bled and run.

"We're never going to be able to read it," she murmured.

"You know her handwriting. See what you can figure out," Matt said.

He was standing close to her again. They were nearly touching as they both scrutinized the paper. She felt an instinctive and almost overwhelming desire to turn to him, to gaze into his eyes and pretend this letter didn't exist, that her friend wasn't missing. She wanted him to hold her.

She gritted her teeth, appalled that she could suddenly want a man so much.

Especially this man.

Especially since she was now officially FBI. Officially Krewe . . .

She blinked and stared hard at the paper. She saw her name at the top.

" 'Meg,' " she read. " 'Silly, huh? You'll probably never . . .' Never what?"

" 'Find this.' It says, 'find this.' "

"Yes, yes, you're right," Meg said. " 'You'll probably never find this, but . . .' "

Matt kept trying to read. " 'But if you do — if I haven't retrieved it myself — then I'm in trouble. I'm doing this because I don't know what's really going on. I don't want to falsely accuse, but this has something to do with . . .' "

He stopped reading. "To do with what?" he demanded.

Meg tried to study the paper again. "I can't tell — I just can't tell! The ink ran right there."

Matt said softly, "I can make out the letters *b-a-r-d.* Does that mean anything to you?"

"The bard. Shakespeare." Meg shrugged. "I don't think she'd leave me a note about Shakespeare."

"Seems unlikely," he agreed. "Any ideas at all?"

She shook her head. "We used to leave notes when we were bothered by something. One semester she knew about cheating going on at college. She didn't want to say anything. She felt it wasn't her place. But it wasn't right. She left me a note about it."

"And what happened?" Matt asked.

"Easily solved. The girl doing the cheating dropped out. She was actually a good kid who had some problems. She admitted everything, so Lara never had to do anything. Nor did I."

"Let's leave this here," Matt said. "It'll be dryer by morning. If we still can't read anything, we'll bring it to the lab. I know Gettysburg is on our tour list, but we're about an hour and half from DC and maybe an hour and a half on to Gettysburg from there." He gave her a questioning look. "I know you're really worried and that you won't be happy until we've followed the trail you and Lara used to take, but as you said earlier, the note may tell us something important. It could be too far gone for even our best techs, but I think it's important to try."

Meg nodded and sat on the foot of the bed. She didn't move as Matt walked to the door.

"Hey," he said, his hand on the knob.

"Yeah?"

"Lock this. Lock it when I go out."

"Yes, of course." She stood and met him at the door.

"You're okay?"

"Of course," she repeated.

"If I hear that dog barking, I'll be right back in here."

"I graduated —"

"Yes, from the academy. If you hear me screaming, I'll expect you to have my back, too, okay?"

He was smiling, and she nodded, feeling a little foolish. The door closed, and she thought he was gone. Then she heard his voice from the other side. "Lock it *now!*" he barked.

She did.

Twenty minutes later, she was in a long T-shirt. Her regulation-issue Glock was at her bedside. She didn't turn the television on; instead, she thought about the night. Matt believed that someone had been watching them at the cemetery. He believed that a black sedan might be following them. He wasn't certain, but he was willing to consider the possibilities.

She smiled. He wasn't so bad, after all.

She started to drift off, Killer curled at her feet. She did sleep for a while, but it was a light sleep. Suddenly she found herself wide-awake, hoping it wasn't time to get up for the day. From the dim light easing through the drapes, she thought it must be very early in the morning. She could rest her eyes a few more minutes. She drifted in comfort, but then began to picture Lara's note: *b-a-r-d.*

She jumped out of bed, startling the dog, who gave a worried "Woof!"

"It's okay, Killer," she said.

She hurried over to the TV stand and turned on the light, then stared at the note again. She still couldn't read that part, but the *b-a-r-d* was the end of a word — the beginning of which had smudged.

She ran to her door, ready to tear over to the next bedroom. But when she opened it, Matt Bosworth was already there. He wore just his trousers, bare chest and hair damp from the shower.

"Bard," he said. "I know . . ."

"Me, too. Bard. *Hubbard.*"

"Yes, Hubbard. Lara's note to you is about Congressman Hubbard. I'm pretty sure that your friend suspected something about his death wasn't right."

"And," Meg said, "it has to do with Congressman Walker!"

He nodded, then stepped back. She realized that her hair was tangled around her face and she was inappropriately dressed in her giant sleep tee.

"Sorry, didn't mean to wake you," he said. "It's still early. Not quite six."

"I was awake. I can be ready to go in about ten minutes."

"Good. Great. I'd like to get that note in, see what our experts can tell us. They have lights that can detect what's faded, trace the slightest indentation on paper."

"I know," she said. "That's perfect."

"Perfect," he echoed.

They stood awkwardly for a moment, and then he spun around to return to his room.

Killer followed him.

"Hey, you!" Meg called to the dog.

The animal ignored her.

"It's all right," Matt said. He disappeared into his room with Killer trotting behind him. She ran into the shower, anxious to be as good as her word.

When she stepped out of her room, he was waiting for her. There was a somber look on his face.

"Has something happened?" she asked.

He nodded. "We have another one," he said grimly.

"Another . . ."

"Dead woman."

Meg's heart leaped to her throat. "Not — not Lara?" she asked.

10

Slash was tired as all hell. For once in his life, he wished he didn't work alone.

He'd spent part of the night trying to determine how to break in on the agents. But they had the damned dog. The stupid creature had barked at him when he'd been quite a distance away, hidden in the trees. What would it do if he tried to get into that ramshackle inn with the agents sleeping? Not only that, Slash knew that agents slept with their firearms by their beds, always within reach.

He'd given up watching the old bed-and-breakfast and headed out in the early-morning hours. He was tired and irritated, but he'd worked out his next moves carefully. First, where to grab someone. Second, where to leave her. This latest killing would change the focus yet again.

It would have every law enforcement agent in the tristate and District area fixated on one thing and only one thing.

The killings. *These* killings. The dead women. Eventually, he'd know what he needed to know. Eventually, it would work out. This spate of serial killings would end as swiftly as it had begun. As swiftly as it had ended years before. Once again, the killer would disappear into the annals of crime history.

That was too bad. He realized he'd acquired a taste for what he did. Maybe Slash would remain active; the persona of Slash was so alive and so real now. Sometimes he woke up believing he was Slash McNeil. Sometimes it was difficult to pull back, to remember who he really was.

Last night hadn't been easy. She'd been a fighter and a squirmer. He'd chosen her differently. But in the end, it didn't matter. And in the end, the river would be his salvation, washing away any trace of what had happened.

None of the women mattered. They were nothing — nothing at all. The end result was everything.

Except of course . . .

The agents. He wanted them dead. But that would create a disruption that would cause an even more intense kind of manhunt, would change the dynamics, could ruin everything.

Perhaps, though . . .

He thought about the one he'd been ordered not to kill, at least not yet. Made no sense. A hole in the ground was a hole in the ground.

Maybe she was already dead. Maybe he could find the time to go and watch her beg and plead, let her know exactly who had done this to her, let her see his face before he watched her die. Maybe that would calm his soul, stop this terrible craving to find a way to kill the agents.

But killing a man wouldn't fit Slash's profile, he told himself.

Killing her, though . . .

He ached, longing to kill them, to see them die.

His phone rang. "Hey, up and at 'em — boss wants you!"

Slash silently gritted his teeth.

Some people — who weren't women — deserved to die, too.

And Slash imagined a different kind of killing as he rose to face the day.

Meg stood at the autopsy in Dr. Wong's OCME, trying not to shake. She knew that the victim wasn't Lara. And yet she'd felt that terrible dread when she first heard the news. It was painful to stand where she was, completely still and listening, as stoically professional as possible.

When they'd driven here that morning, she'd tried to reassure herself that it wasn't going to be Lara. Lara had been in Harpers Ferry; she'd left the note. She'd known something — about Hubbard, about Walker — and that was why she'd disappeared. Not because she was dead.

"The victim was killed early this morning, probably about 2:00 or 3:00 a.m.," Wong said. "The throat is slashed, the body was ripped from throat to groin and stones were stuffed into the resulting cavity. We've rushed tests. She was drugged in exactly the same manner as the previous victims. She was found in the Potomac River. What I believe is different about this woman is that she'll prove to be a prostitute. She was sexually active previous to her murder, but there's no sign that it was forced."

"That makes her a prostitute?" Matt asked, puzzled.

Wong shook his head. "She's got a tattoo on her inner right wrist. A rose. It signifies a loosely organized group of working girls who keep tabs on one another. Kind of a sisterhood. I know that because a john went crazy and killed a member of the group about six months ago. He was familiar to some of the other girls. The victim was seen leaving him, he was identified and arrested and he confessed to the crime. But it was nothing like this. I believe this one has our serial killer's signature."

"The tongue is missing?" Meg heard herself ask.

"It is. I'm not an investigator on the case," Wong said, "but I'd like to point out that I believe this to be a rush job. The cuts are more jagged. The body was poorly stuffed — she floated almost immediately. Unless, of course, the killer needs a faster kick — needs the body to be discovered more quickly."

"Let me know when you get an ID," Matt said.

"You bet. Jackson Crow had an artist in, one of your people, Jane Everett. We've got her sketch going out in the media."

"You have any idea where we'll find other girls belonging to this sisterhood?"

Wong gave them an address and the two of them thanked him and then left. Outside, Meg was startled when she felt Matt's hands on her shoulders, turning her to face him. He pulled her gently into his arms.

"We're going to find her alive," he whispered.

Maybe it was the unexpectedness of his action, or maybe it was because she'd become more and more aware with each passing hour of the physical attraction between them. But she was suddenly more afraid of his touch than even the bad news that might be coming. She couldn't explain it to herself — other than to suspect that she feared losing control. Losing independence. And yet . . . she stayed in his arms for a moment, feeling the heat of his chest and breathing in his clean scent.

Then he stepped back and looked at her, searching her eyes. "You okay? Really?"

"Yes, I'm okay."

"We've got to get to the office," he said. "Then we'll go see what our newest victim's friends have to say."

They returned to the car, where Killer was waiting for them; the windows were down far enough to allow him plenty of air. Meg had been afraid to leave him alone in the car on such a hot day, but Matt had taken care of it. He'd parked in a shady spot, and also made a purchase in a convenience store on the way here — a cloth water bowl that could be folded to fit into a pocket. They could fill it from a water bottle and empty it when they had to drive again.

Meg dumped the water, then slid into the

passenger seat.

"Another murder. Here. And we might have been followed in Harpers Ferry. Maybe these murders and Lara's disappearance *aren't* related," Meg said.

Matt glanced over at her. "But we're both pretty sure that Lara wrote something about Walker having a connection with Garth Hubbard's death."

"That's what I don't understand. Hubbard wasn't murdered. He died of a heart attack."

"There was no autopsy. His private physician signed his death certificate. He had a heart condition, so there was no reason to suspect anything . . . untoward. Or anything in the way of a cover-up."

"He was in his own home," Meg said. "These women who are being murdered . . . The killer watches them and takes them off the street."

"But now a prostitute. None of the other women were prostitutes. They were all new to the area from which they disappeared. Why change his choice of victim?"

"Because . . . he needed a kill last night or early this morning. He hadn't chosen a new target yet. Could be that his desire to kill has escalated, that he's not getting the same fix. And a prostitute is easily picked up on the street."

"The timing would fit — if the killer is also our stalker. It's only an hour and a half back to DC from Harpers Ferry," Matt said.

They arrived at the Krewe headquarters and went directly into Jackson's office where he was waiting with Will Chan, Angela and Kat Sokolov.

Kat had been to the OCME already; she'd gone in as soon as the body had been discovered. She told them she was as certain as Wong that the killer was the same man who'd perpetrated the previous crimes and she was equally certain that the time of death had been early morning.

Matt described their visit with Nancy Cooper in Richmond and how Meg believed that someone in a black sedan had watched them at a rest stop. He also mentioned the black sedan seen at her new town house, which Angela corroborated. Then he went on to tell them about Joey finding Meg — and their recovery of the note from the gravestone marker. He produced the note; Angela said she'd get it down to tech support right away.

"We believe that it's all connected somehow — although we're not sure why," Matt said. "But Lara's note seems to imply something about the death of Congressman

Hubbard." He paused, looking at Jackson. "Somehow, we have to get an autopsy done on Congressman Hubbard. I can't help thinking that he was, shall we say, helped to die — and that it had to do with his political stand. Perhaps it was an assassination. If he'd lived to run for the presidency, there's a good chance he would've been elected."

"These women are being killed because of a government conspiracy?" Jackson asked incredulously.

"I know it's far-fetched," Matt said.

Jackson drummed his fingers on the wooden surface of his desk. "It sure is," he agreed. "Unless . . ."

"Yeah, it's far-fetched — unless Lara turns out to be one of his victims," Matt said flatly, looking at Meg, sympathy in his eyes. "Here's my theory. Lara is supposed to show up as a victim of this crazed serial killer. The thing is, if she was the only one dead, the investigation would fall on Congressman Walker and his team. But if a number of women die, then the suspicion falls on someone who's a sociopathic killer."

Meg knew that what they were saying was true. It was what she'd feared all along, even if she hadn't actually voiced it aloud. Even if Lara's body hadn't been found. "Can Adam get Congressman Hubbard exhumed

— and arrange for an autopsy?"

"We have no evidence against Ian Walker," Jackson said. "We have no evidence at all, really. I don't think there's a judge in the world who'd allow Hubbard to be exhumed. But there's one person who can do it — his widow. I'll call Adam now, see what he can work out. Will, go down to tech and see if you can be of assistance. The rest of you — we have copies of Jane Everett's sketch of the last victim. Get out on the streets and see if you can find someone who can identify her — and who she was with last night."

They all rose, everyone taking a moment to pat Killer on the head. Meg smiled as she watched and wondered what it was about a dog . . .

"What?" Matt said, and she realized he was watching her.

"Killer," she replied. "What a name — but he makes people smile."

"Hmpff," he muttered.

He was full of it, she thought. Matt liked the dog.

Did he actually like her, too?

She stepped away, wondering how she'd come to feel so drawn to the man. She was just a fledgling agent to him. He could be decent, but the work always came first. And yet, if she was honest, she'd have to admit she'd been attracted to him from the start — frightening though that attraction could be. He had a certain magnetism. Was it because of his strength? Because she wasn't as strong as she wanted to be and needed that strength?

No, she was dangerously attracted to the man. And she had to stop feeling that way. If she could . . .

Supplied with copies of the sketch Jane Everett had drawn, the two of them headed to the address where the latest victim had been working, at the intersection Wong had given them. For the first few hours, they could find no one who claimed to recognize the dead woman.

They had Killer with them, and he was an invaluable asset. While the women they wanted to talk to tended to scurry away from anyone who looked official, they were captivated by the ugly little dog and stopped to pet him.

Finally, a tall brunette in very short shorts and a leopard halter top glanced at the picture — and her face crumpled.

"It's Marci," she said. "Marci Henning."

"You're certain, and she was your friend?" Matt asked.

The woman nodded, big tears appearing in her eyes, rolling down her face. "Of course I'm certain, and yes, she was my friend. Such a good kid. She came here with stars in her eyes and then she drank too much one night, got into drugs . . . and wound up with an arrest record. After that, she couldn't even get a job in a coffee shop. Me, I'm out here because I'd rather be doing this than dealing with jerks in a crappy, low-paid job in the service industry. Marci . . . she wanted something more."

"I'm sorry," Meg said. "But . . . this is important. We desperately want to catch her killer. Justice for her, and for the other victims. What can you tell us? Did you see anything? Do you know anything about her last customer?"

"I wasn't with her. I was at the bar over there. Drunks are easily seduced," the woman said. She offered her hand. "I'm Ollie. Olive Warner. And I do know who was with Marci around the corner. Hold on. I'll find her."

"Thank you."

"Now no one can work the street," Ollie muttered as she started walking.

She was headed toward a seedy bar, and they followed her in.

The place fell silent, except for the old jukebox wheezing out a country tune as they entered. Meg could feel the distrust all around them.

Matt stepped forward, holding up his badge. "We're not here to bust anyone for anything. We're searching for a murderer, someone who gets off on chopping up women. We need your help."

Killer let out a woof that sounded almost like the word *please.* Meg lifted him in her arms, not at all sure about bringing the dog into a dive bar. Later, she wondered whether it was Matt's request, Ollie's plea or Killer's woof that changed things.

There was silence for another moment and then Ollie Warner spoke up. "Marci is dead. This horrible killer is attacking *us* now. I know one of you was with her — one of you saw something."

The bartender, a grizzled man who looked as if he hadn't seen water or soap in a week, was the first to respond. "Marci was here until about one in the morning."

"Thank you," Meg said.

A slim woman in a skintight blouse rose from a bar stool. "I saw her after that. We were . . . we were on the same block. I saw her get into a car."

"What kind of car?" Matt asked.

"I'm not sure of the make, but it was black," the woman said.

"A black sedan?"

"Yeah, you know. They're all over the city," the woman said. "Everybody uses them." She sniffed. "And you'd be surprised just how many we see trolling the streets around here."

"Did you see who was in the car?" Meg asked hopefully. "Can you describe the driver?"

The woman shook her head. "Sorry, no, I can't. But . . ."

"But what?"

"I saw it drive away and I noticed that the license plate was all . . . covered in mud."

Before they'd driven away with their witness reports, Matt was on the phone with Jackson, who was going to plan a press conference to make sure women were on the alert for a black sedan, even though they knew that if he saw the news, the killer might change his vehicle. At the very least, they'd force his hand. It was a small victory — with the dead piling up and Lara still missing.

But before Matt ended the call, he received further instructions from Jackson. They were to stop by the office for Adam. Killer would stay with Jackson; the rest of them were on their way to speak with Martha Hubbard, widow of the recently deceased congressman.

He looked over at Meg. "We have to be at our most persuasive. This could be our most important move, a way we can finally get to the truth."

"I'll beg and plead as soulfully as I can," she promised.

Her tone was sarcastic but he knew she actually meant what she'd said. Matt looked straight ahead again as he drove and wondered if she realized just how far her sincerity went. She was definitely the right one to be on this mission.

Angela was waiting with Adam Harrison in front of the office. She scooped up Killer while Adam slid into the car.

"Press conference is in thirty minutes. Jackson will do the speaking," she told them.

Matt waved and moved back into the traffic.

Meg turned around to speak to Adam. "Do you know Mrs. Hubbard?" she asked.

"Yes. We're old friends. I was a huge supporter of Congressman Hubbard. He had a platform that was socially inclusive and fiscally smart. He was . . . political magic, and he never reneged on a promise he made to his constituents," Adam said.

"Maybe you should've gone to see Mrs. Hubbard alone," Meg murmured.

"Oh, no, my dear. You're going to be an asset, I'm certain." Glancing in the rearview mirror, Matt saw that Adam was impeccable as always in a soft gray suit, blue shirt and darker tie.

As he neared Congressman Hubbard's home, Matt saw something that made him slow and then pull over.

"What are you doing?" Meg asked. He pointed down the street. The congressman's house was in a neighborhood of sweeping lawns and they had a decent view of the horseshoe drive in front of the house.

"Someone's just leaving," Matt said.

A large party was about to drive off in two black sedans. Matt saw that it was Congressman Walker, his wife and his retinue. Ian and Kendra were getting into a black limo driven by Joe Brighton, his ex-marine campaign manager. The other two men — handsome and charismatic Ellery Manheim and Nathan Oliver — were entering a second car. Peering closely, Matt saw that the two little granddaughters were already in the car that Ian and Kendra Walker were stepping into, which explained the need for two cars.

"Company who got here before us," Adam said thoughtfully. "How interesting — or maybe not." He went on to say, "The families have been close for years. Walker and Hubbard were on a number of committees together."

"Still, what timing," Matt said. "We'll wait a minute."

"And hope they drive in the other direction," Meg added.

They did. Matt wondered if he let out an audible sigh of relief. A few minutes later, he drove down the street and into the horseshoe drive.

The Hubbard house wasn't as big or as opulent as the Walker house, Matt observed. Not that he knew much about interior design. It was homey, simple. Martha Hubbard was as warm and welcoming as her home.

She greeted them herself when she opened the door, stepping into Adam's arms and hugging him warmly, tears filling her eyes. "So good of you to come, Adam. I've been trying to catch up — to reach everyone — since the funeral. But the children were here, and I'm in the middle of making various decisions. I have to decide whether to keep this home or not . . . So many details that must be handled."

"Maddie, Maddie," Adam said soothingly. "I wouldn't be bothering you now if I didn't think it was important. May we?"

They were still standing in the foyer.

"Of course, forgive me!" Maddie Hubbard looked past Adam and tried to smile brightly at Matt and Meg. "Come in!"

The parlor was in the front of the house. There was an inviting hearth, the mantel covered with family pictures. A throw over the sofa might have been knitted by the widow herself.

Adam introduced them. "Agents Matthew Bosworth and Margaret Murray."

"And I'm Martha Hubbard, although I'm better known as Maddie," she said. "Sit down. The Walkers were just here with their little ones, so I'm in a bit of disarray."

Meg laughed softly. "What a lovely home, Mrs. Hubbard. I only wish I had one as warm and charming as this."

"Well, thank you, dear, and please, I'm just Maddie."

They sat down; Adam looked at Matt and he knew that meant he was to begin.

He folded his hands as he faced her. "We're sorry to bother you today," he said. "I've been a fan of your husband and your family for years. I can only imagine how painful your husband's loss is to you. But we're here to ask for a favor that will be very hard to give. And while we can't tell you the particulars, we have good reason to believe that your husband's death might not have been . . . natural."

She was a plump woman with a beautiful smile and naturally graying hair. She stared back at him in such shock that he was afraid that he might have caused her to have a stroke or a heart attack herself.

"Maddie, we don't mean to upset you," Meg said, reaching over to pat Maddie's hand. "It's just that . . . if something like that happened, it was a crime not just against your husband, you and your family, but against the American people."

"But — but . . . how?" Maddie gasped out the words. "He was here. He was at home. I was making apple pie. He was in the bedroom. And when I went to get him . . ." She broke off, covering her face.

"He took digitalis, right?" Adam asked. "He didn't have a severe condition, but he took digitalis."

Maddie nodded. "There's no reason to believe . . . Like I said, we were both at home. It had been a long day. He kept his pills in his pocket. But why would you think . . . ?"

"Maddie, what I'm about to say must remain in this room," Adam told her. "A young congressional employee is missing. She left a note for a friend that referred to your husband's death. She was suspicious. We don't know what she might have heard, but under the circumstances . . ."

"The woman Adam mentioned is my oldest friend, and she's still missing, Maddie," Meg said. "She adored your husband. She's an idealist and a wonderful person and . . . she may still be alive."

"I know we're asking a lot," Matt put in.

"Garth is dead and gone," Maddie said softly. "He wouldn't care what was done with his body. It's nothing but a shell now." She paused. "I still wish I could understand."

"Can you tell me a little more about the day he died?" Matt asked.

Maddie lifted her hands. "It was a busy day. He'd worked on Capitol Hill in the morning, and there was a special picnic with disabled children in the afternoon. He was tired when he came home — which added to the stress on his heart, or so we all assumed. We had dinner. We used no salt, and he ate only fish and chicken, no red meat. He was careful. Such a good, sweet man, the best husband and father and . . . Why? Why would someone have killed him?"

"What if someone disagreed with him?" Adam asked.

"Good Lord, Adam Harrison. We're in

politics. Everyone disagrees with everyone else!" Maddie said. "But he knew how to compromise. He also knew how to say, 'This is what I believe. It's up to the voters.' "

Meg touched her hand again. "He'd been out all day, he came home and died. Did he take his pills?"

"I believe he did, but it was too late. The bottle was in his hand, and the pills were strewn across the floor."

"Do you still have those pills?" Matt asked.

"Oh, no, of course not," Maddie said. "I've heard it stressed far too many times, the importance of getting rid of someone else's pills. So many people reminded me of that. They went down the toilet immediately."

Meg and Adam both turned to Matt. "Who stressed this to you?" he asked carefully.

"My daughter, for one. And a number of the congressional wives who were here after the funeral. Ada Cutler, Kendra Walker, Leona Thomas — many of the women."

"Any of the men?" Meg asked.

"Men?" Maddie repeated, sitting back. "I suppose so, but . . . I don't really remember. I was upset. We were talking in the living room. My daughter is a physician. She asked if I'd made sure to get rid of all her father's pills."

Meg glanced at him and Matt knew they were thinking the same thing. They'd get nothing else along these lines, and even if they did, it wouldn't matter. The pills were gone. They couldn't be tested. The only truth regarding what might have been in his stomach or bloodstream lay in Congressman Hubbard being exhumed — and autopsied.

"I just don't see how my husband could have been murdered," Maddie said, not for the first time. She was going to refuse them, Matt thought. Despite her earlier remark about his remains being "nothing but a shell."

But she didn't.

"Garth is dead. I truly believe that his soul is in heaven. If anyone deserved paradise, it's my husband. If you think the removal of his corpse might help someone else, I'm happy to sign whatever papers you need," she said with finality.

She and Meg were looking at each other. They seemed to be sharing something.

"Thank you," Meg said simply.

Adam rose. "Maddie, Garth loved you deeply. I believe he'd be very proud of you now."

"Won't you stay for coffee, tea, a drink . . . a bite to eat?" Maddie asked.

"You seem tired," Adam said.

"I am a bit weary. No matter how darling children are, I'm only good with them for so long, but still . . ."

"Another time, Maddie, I shall be delighted to take you up on your offer," Adam said.

Matt rose and Meg did the same. Maddie Hubbard smiled at him and slipped an arm around Meg. "And you must bring your agents back when they're not working on a case like this. I may no longer be a power on the Hill, but I still enjoy good company."

"I'd love to come back," Meg said, and Matt quickly agreed.

Maddie escorted them to the door. She and Adam embraced again and he stepped out. Matt paused to shake her hand; she stood up on her toes and kissed his cheek. He smiled, liking her very much.

As he and Adam started for the car, he noticed that Maddie had pulled Meg back. She whispered something to her. Meg nodded, and in the light from the old-fashioned porch lamp, he could see her blush. A moment later, she hurried after him.

Maddie waved to them from the door, and they waved in return. They talked about the obvious on the way back — the fact that Hubbard's pills might have been switched. They'd find out when the autopsy was done. Adam wanted to head straight to his office to get Jackson started on the paperwork. He told the two of them to go home and get some rest.

"We have to pick up Killer," Meg reminded him.

"Just go home. I'll enjoy a night with the pup, if you don't mind," Adam said.

"I . . ." Meg wanted to protest. She was already attached to the dog. But there was no reason not to let Adam have him for the night. "Okay," she said.

As he pulled into traffic, Matt asked, "Do you have a bed at your place yet?"

"I'm fine. Don't worry," she told him.

"And nothing in the kitchen yet, right?"

"I'm fine," she insisted.

"Let's get some dinner, since we missed lunch."

"That sounds good," she said.

Matt took them to a place he knew along the way, a restaurant that had an excellent assortment of Mediterranean food, from lasagna to lamb kabobs. He waited until they were seated and had ordered their drinks and their food before he asked,

"What did she say? When she called you back?"

"You mean Mrs. Hubbard?"

"Yes."

"Oh. Um, well . . . it was personal."

"Personal? I didn't think you knew her that well."

"Apparently, she knows us," Meg said wryly.

"Oh?"

She shook her head, blushing again. Her eyes were a brilliant deep blue, sparkling with a rare beauty, when she replied. "She said you were as gorgeous as a TV gladiator. She has no idea if the real ones were gorgeous or not. And that I shouldn't let you go."

Stunned, Matt stared at her, and then he began to laugh. He couldn't help asking her, "And?"

"And what?"

"What did you say to her?"

Watching them sent his blood boiling. Slash was so agitated he could barely keep his position in the driver's seat of his car.

His car. He'd had to resort to the use of his own because of *them.* He'd rushed last night; he'd rushed by grabbing a prostitute. He should've taken someone he'd observed and studied. And he should've taken that woman, his chosen victim, when he knew she'd be alone on an empty street.

But what he did last night — it had seemed so important at the time. He'd felt a desperate fever; he'd had to make a move. He blamed it on them, on those two agents; if it weren't for that foolish woman, Meg Murray, the police would've dropped it. They'd have pursued a killer and nothing more. And now . . .

Still, they knew nothing. They hadn't charged anyone. They hadn't even brought anyone in for questioning.

They were like idiot dogs, dogs with bones . . . chewing, slavering, not about to let go. And now, while he sat in the car, they were in there, laughing, smiling, talking to each other as if they hadn't a care in the world.

It made him angry. But he had to lie low. He needed to remember the timetable — what was important and what wasn't.

And yet . . .

He watched the two of them. And all he wanted to do was . . .

Kill.

11

Meg was startled, not at all sure what to say.

Should she tell him the truth? About what she'd said — or what she felt?

"I said you were a good partner."

"Oh, now, that would be a lie," he said, obviously amused. "You think I'm high-handed, chauvinistic and intolerable."

"That's not true," Meg protested. "Not the intolerable part. You're bearable. Just bearable."

"Ah, thank you for that!" he said, lifting his coffee cup to her and smiling.

"Well, let's be frank. You feel I'm too young, too emotional and not nearly as capable as you are. You'd rather have an experienced man at your back."

His smile deepened. "You're young, yes," he said.

"That means better reflexes," she told him.

"And you're emotional, yes," he went on as if she hadn't responded.

"Well, yes, I was emotional when we met."

He eased forward again, running his finger around the edge of his coffee cup. "I didn't mind."

"You could've fooled me."

"I wasn't rude, was I?"

Meg waved a hand in the air, astonished by this whole conversation. They were almost flirting.

And she liked it. Liked him. How many times in the past few hours had she thought she'd like to take a moment *not* to be an agent, and to turn back into his arms?

"Am I more capable?" he asked. "I hope so. I've been out of the academy for years. A decade. So I hope I've gained something from my experience."

"That's fair," Meg said. "Or fair enough."

"Would I rather have a man at my back?" He shook his head. "No. I want someone I trust. I believe in you, kid." He raised his cup to her again. He turned as their waitress arrived to deliver their meals.

"I'm not a kid," she informed him when their waitress had gone.

"No, I guess you're not," he said. "Ketchup?"

She burst into laughter.

"Ketchup is funny?"

"I can't read you. I can't read you at all. One minute, I feel as if you're . . . well, as if we're almost on the same wavelength — and the next, ketchup."

"It's good on a burger."

She gazed down at her plate and wondered if she was a fool. She thought about her past, her previous relationships. Nothing recently. A great romance in high school that ended the minute she'd gone to college. There'd been lots of flirting with male cops at the police academy. Then she'd dated a lawyer until he'd begun to look at her too oddly, uncomfortable with her "hunches." Then more flirting, this time with the male cadets at the academy. All kinds of innuendo — and yet nothing that she chose to pursue, not with the goal ahead of her. And now . . .

She looked up. Matt was watching her, hazel eyes like broken shards of crystal, his expression as charming as she'd ever seen.

"What is it, Agent Murray? There are things we can't learn at the academy, aren't there? So, you want the truth — without condiments? You're a stunning woman, but surely you know that. I'd love to sweep you into my arms, and never let you go. Of course, basic decency, not to mention social rules, keep me from doing that, especially when we're searching for someone near and dear to you. So . . . if I'm moving too far in what might not be an acceptable direction, I move on to ketchup. It does go well with burgers. Should I have suggested mayonnaise?"

Meg stared at him blankly in bewilderment — and then she slowly smiled. "I do like ketchup," she told him.

"Good," he said. "Perhaps I could pass the salt or pepper?"

"Salt and pepper can certainly add flavor."

"Ask for anything you'd like." He lowered his head as he turned his attention to the food in front of him. Meg felt frozen — and on fire. She knew she should focus on her burger — and the ketchup — as well.

Or she could act. Act on her feelings. And she suddenly wanted to.

She reached across the table and placed her fingers lightly on his hand. "Want to know what I saw when we first met?"

"What?"

"Arrogance — which I've discovered is another word for the confidence needed in this work. And let's see . . . A man who looks like a television gladiator, just like Maddie said. And most important, I saw someone who had my back even when I felt

I was being judged."

"Well, you *were* being judged."

"And?"

"I've already laid it all out quite nicely," he said, his eyes meeting hers.

"So have I."

He studied her a moment longer. Then he asked, "Did you want anything else?"

"Pardon?"

"Anything else to eat. More coffee, dessert?"

"No, no, thank you. I'm done."

He caught the eye of their waitress and quickly paid the check. "Let's go," he said, once his card had been returned.

He held her elbow lightly as he led her to the car. She slipped around to get into the passenger seat. When he began to drive, she asked him, "Where are we going?"

He glanced at her, his smile endearingly crooked. "My place."

"Okay. There is mine."

"Ah, but I have furniture."

She eased back in the seat, realizing that they were headed to his house for the direct purpose of having sex.

It seemed remarkable, but she was glad, and the anticipation was warm and exhilarating. She refused to even wonder if she was committing professional suicide.

The days had been hard and frantic, and now . . .

Evidently, foreplay had taken place at dinner. They'd barely stepped into his foyer before she was in his arms. His hold was more sensual than she'd ever imagined. They tore at each other's jackets and shirt buttons, then paused.

The guns were awkward.

"Upstairs. Bedroom," Matt said.

"You're good with words, Agent Bosworth!" She laughed, but she took his hand and raced up the stairs with him. Soft night-lights lit the way. Their Glocks went on the bedside tables.

He paused again, looking at her in the shadowy light as he slipped her tailored shirt from her shoulders. She nodded in answer to his unspoken question as she returned the gesture. Moonlight played through a slit in the drapes, falling on the sleek, tightly muscled, bronzed expanse of his chest. She leaned against it as her bra fell away. She felt the electric delight of touching so gently, and as he tilted her head, he stared into her eyes one last time, and kissed her.

He was everything she could have hoped for — a practiced lover with the ability to tease with his lips and tongue, to awaken hunger and longing with every brush of his fingers. His kiss was deep and compelling, his touch purely sensual and erotic.

She wasn't even sure exactly how and when they lost the rest of their clothing. She just knew that they were entwined on the bed. She felt the stroke of his fingers and the caress of his tongue and returned both.

Only the foreplay with words had ended. The sweep of his touch continued; his kisses roamed the length of her, brought her near climax and then drew back, again and again. They were in a tangle of kisses and strokes and whispered utterances of pleasure and encouragement. He took the time to look after the necessary precautions, then he was on top of her and within her, and she felt she'd never had such an experience before. Maybe it was the longing, the loneliness she hadn't known she felt, or maybe it was just the magic of this man.

Climax was explosive and sweet, and it occurred again and again. Eventually she slept; it was sheer exhaustion that led her to it at last. At times, she woke, and felt the cool air in the room and saw the moonbeams filtering through, and she basked in the comfort.

She knew that when daylight came, she'd worry again; she would doggedly follow any chance of finding Lara.

And she knew she'd be helped. By Matt.

She closed her eyes and couldn't believe what it felt like to sleep in his arms, surrounded by his warmth.

Slash had watched many people over the years; it was necessary in his business.

He'd never felt like a voyeur before. He didn't like the feeling. And yet . . .

He couldn't quite turn away. The drapes had been closed. There'd been just that narrow little window. And what he hadn't seen, he'd envisioned in his mind's eye.

The two of them, beautiful people, naked in each other's arms. Her long shapely legs, the curve of her back. And him . . . holding her, touching her, feeling her, breathing her in . . .

Slash had felt the fury inside him become something terrible. He'd smashed his fists on the dashboard — almost broken it, but then remembered it was his own car. He'd stared at the slit in the drapes again. He'd been so upset he'd gotten out and walked the open pavement. It was late, so no one saw him.

He realized they wouldn't be leaving and he imagined them in bed. He imagined her hands on the other man, her long elegant fingers moving over his body . . .

And finally he'd realized that he had to control himself.

He also had to sleep. It was difficult being two people — one who appeared by day.

And one who killed by night.

He forced himself to drive away.

He could not force himself to forget.

Matt woke to the sound of his cell phone ringing. He saw that it was Jackson and answered immediately. They'd be at the cemetery, ready to exhume the body of Congressman Hubbard in an hour, Jackson said. He'd meet them at Arlington, along with Adam and Kat Sokolov.

Matt glanced at Meg, who was just beginning to stir. She could look so cool and efficient when they were working. Lying there, with her hair a dark and tempting halo around her face, she managed to look like a provocative vixen, even asleep.

He didn't have time to wonder if what they'd done was a mistake, whether it was right or wrong; it had felt natural, and he could never regret the night.

Neither could he linger.

She was blinking at the daylight coming through the drapes. He couldn't resist a tap on her backside. "Hey, new girl, no hot morning sex. We have to be at Arlington in an hour."

In case he was tempted himself, he hurried to the shower and came out moments later, draped in a towel. He tossed one to her, trying not to look her way.

They hadn't bothered bringing in her bag last night.

"I'll run and get your things while you're in the shower," he told her. "Extra toothbrushes, soap, shampoo — in the cabinet over the sink."

He dressed as she fled into the shower. Downstairs, he set the coffeemaker in motion, then went out to the car to grab Meg's bag.

He paused. Something had been written on the car. He could hardly make it out because the car wasn't dirty. But someone had written on the hood. He leaned closer to study the barely discernible scrawl.

It was just one word. *DIE.*

He hesitated, not wanting Meg to see it, but not wanting to remove it until he'd had the forensic team examine the car. There could be a fingerprint; of course, it might just be that of a neighborhood tough who knew it was a company vehicle.

It might also belong to the murderer — or at least the person who'd been following them, whether or not he was the murderer. Whether or not he'd taken Lara . . .

Matt dashed upstairs with Meg's bag, calling out to her as he left it by the bathroom door. Downstairs again, he poured coffee.

Meg was down as soon as he finished. She'd gotten ready in ten minutes and yet looked as if she'd spent an hour securing her wealth of hair in a shimmering bun. He wasn't sure if she was wearing makeup; her blue eyes were so darkly fringed with lashes she didn't need much.

Although he didn't *want* to tell Meg what someone had written on the car, he also realized that if she were any other partner, he would. "I think we had someone watching us last night," he said. "Either that, or some juvenile delinquents were out writing on cars."

"Oh?" she said, taking a sip of her coffee. "What did they write?"

" 'Die.' "

" 'Die' — as in . . . die?"

He nodded.

"You really think someone's following us, then?" she asked. "Are they afraid we're getting too close?"

"It's possible. So we need to be extra vigilant," he said. "Ready?"

"Yes, of course," she said, all business now.

And he meant to be, too. But as she set her cup in the sink and rinsed it, then walked to the door, he caught her by the shoulders and pulled her back. He kissed her, inhaling her clean sweet scent. "Quickie?" he whispered against her lips.

"No," she returned, smiling into his eyes. "But one day, remind me — and I'll show you a real quickie."

"Wow, you wicked woman!" he teased, locking the door behind them.

In less than thirty minutes, they were standing at the grave site at Arlington. The cemetery workers had already broken concrete and were ready to extract the coffin. They waited for Adam Harrison, Katya Sokolov and Dr. Wong, as the official presiding medical examiner. The three arrived shortly after, greeting them beneath the blue sky of the beautiful summer morning.

Arlington always seemed solemn and yet beautiful to Matt. He had many relatives buried there, all of whom had served in the military at different stages of history.

He'd never seen any of those ancestors walking the grounds, and he saw no one that morning. Even looking up the hill to Arlington House, Matt saw no sign of the dead — that is, of the departed appearing, in some form, in the present. The Krewe always hoped the dead would speak, that they'd solve things simply by saying, "He did it!" or "She did it!" But too often, the dead themselves didn't know. They remained behind because of what they might suspect or because they needed justice in order to move on.

They all stood silent as they watched the workers, perhaps because there was something so sad, something that felt *wrong,* about digging up the dead. Another car drove in to join them.

Matt was disheartened to see that the arrival was Maddie Hubbard, driven by a chauffeur. He went to the car to greet her as the chauffeur helped her out of the backseat. "Mrs. Hubbard, you didn't need to be here," he said.

"My boy, you're as nice as they come," she said with a wink, "but rather slow. I distinctly remember asking you to call me Maddie."

He had to smile at that. "I'm sorry — Maddie," he said. "This isn't easy for you." He shook his head. "You really don't need to be here."

Adam came over and repeated his words, but Maddie hugged him and told him she was fine. Matt introduced her to Dr. Wong, and after that she greeted Meg, who gave her a warm hug. She then took her place with the small group watching as the men worked.

Her voice just above a whisper, Maddie said, "Adam, I know what your people do."

"We find the truth," Adam whispered back. "That's all."

Maddie shrugged and turned to Meg. "Is he here? Is my Garth here with us?"

Matt saw the struggle on Meg's face as she sought the right answer. "No, Maddie. I believe that he's gone on. I didn't know him — but I know of him. And no man has such a sterling reputation without good reason. He was renowned for his brilliance, his passion, his kindness. I'm sure he watches over you with love."

Maddie took her hand and squeezed it. Meg squeezed back. And soon, the coffin was in the hearse to be brought to the OCME.

"Will you be going to the autopsy?" Maddie asked them.

"Dr. Wong, his assistant and I will be there," Kat told her. "And I can promise you, we'll be careful and very thorough."

Maddie nodded and looked at Meg. "Perhaps you and Adam and Matt could join me for an hour or so? I promise I won't cry on your shoulders all morning, but I could use a little company right now." She lowered her voice and indicated her chauffeur. "Sweet boy, but I don't really know him."

"We're at your service, Maddie," Adam said.

"I'll ride with Maddie," Meg offered.

"I came in Kat's car. I can go with Matt and follow you to Maddie's," Adam suggested.

As Wong and Kat prepared to leave, Kat turned to Matt and mouthed the words, "I'll call you when I know something."

He raised his hand in acknowledgment. Then he suddenly looked up the hill. Bright sunlight danced across his eyes for a moment, but he could swear that a strange cloud sat around Arlington House. He didn't know if it was because of his talent, or merely something he wished to see, but there was Robert E. Lee, sitting on a rocking chair, and Mary, his beloved wife, at his side.

"What is it?" Adam asked quietly.

Matt turned to him and smiled. "I like to think that Lee's up there," he said.

"He was one of the most brilliant generals America ever produced — and sadly that genius probably prolonged the war."

"But when it was over, no one worked

harder for reconciliation and peace. Maybe he's up there now and then, in the house he used to own, grateful that the country mended," Matt said.

Adam shrugged, a wry smile on his weathered face. "And maybe he's praying that politicians don't mess it up again!"

Matt nodded.

He slid into the driver's seat and followed Maddie's chauffeur out of the cemetery.

Maddie gazed out the window, studying the cemetery as they left. She reached for Meg's hand and clung to it.

"You've all gotten me thinking. I blamed myself for Garth's death, you know. Oh, I didn't let on to my children what I was feeling, but . . . I was in the house. I was humming away and baking, with salt-free salt and sugar-free sugar, thinking it was going to be such a treat for us both! And there he was upstairs — dying on the floor. In agony."

"You two were truly a love match. Through all the years, the children — and politics!" Meg said. "That's really beautiful."

"It was," Maddie agreed softly. "But . . . if you're right, if his pills were switched . . . The thing is, he was with various members of congress all day. Not to mention aides, attachés, ambassadors and so on." She turned to Meg. "If there's some kind of drug in his system that shouldn't be . . . will they ever figure out how it got there?"

"Maddie, there'll be clues. The ME and Kat — they know what they're doing. And I can't help feeling that my missing friend might be able to tell us something — if only we can find her. She might point us in the right direction."

Maddie frowned. "Am I in danger, Meg?"

"No. At least, I don't think you are."

Maddie looked out the window again. "I've been invited to accompany Ian and Kendra Walker to Gettysburg in a couple of days. Ian is due to give a speech — and he wants to use it as an occasion to honor Garth."

"I'm sure they're planning excellent security, Maddie. And actually, Matt and I were about to go up to Gettysburg. We're following a . . . sort of trail my friend Lara and I used to take. When we were in college, we liked the usual nearby places — Busch Gardens, Colonial Williamsburg, Kings Dominion — but we were also broke a lot and loved to go to battle reenactments, old churches, historic homes, that kind of thing. She's from Richmond and I'm from

Harpers Ferry, so we'd often go to those two cities, and then Gettysburg, as well. Lara studied the events leading up to the Civil War, and during reconstruction. She maintains that politics lead to politics, that our country's history influences our lives today."

Maddie smiled. "You speak of her in the present tense. You obviously believe your friend is alive. And so do I."

"I lose faith sometimes. In fact, for a while, I was sure she was dead. If she's in hiding, I don't understand why she hasn't found a way to contact me yet. And if she's been taken . . . well, why would she still be alive when so many other women are dead?" Meg asked.

Maddie patted her hand. "That's why we have agencies like yours. To find out who, what, when, where and, above all, why. Have faith — until you can't have faith anymore."

"Okay." Meg smiled at her.

"If I do go to Getttysburg, which I should, since the Walkers are dear friends, will you be there for me? I know I can clear it with Adam," Maddie said.

"I'll be there for you and with you," Meg promised.

"Thank you, Meg."

"My pleasure."

They'd pulled up to Maddie's house and into the horseshoe-shaped drive. Adam and Matt parked right behind them.

"Coffee and tea and tea cakes!" Maddie announced. She wagged her finger at Matt. "And don't you worry that my tea cakes are delicate little lady things. I also have a lovely spread of sandwiches, and you'll be quite full before we finish. I guarantee it!"

"I have no doubt whatsoever," Matt said.

Maddie slipped her arm through Meg's as they walked to the house. She drew her close and whispered, "I love to tease that one. I like him. He's a keeper. That's just my opinion, but I'm a good judge of people."

"I'll remember that," Meg whispered back.

In the house, Maddie's housekeeper, a middle-aged woman named Agatha, greeted them and ushered them into the dining room, where food had been laid out.

"And don't worry that I spent taxpayers' money on this!" Maddie told them as they sat down. "Garth was a smart man, and we invested in the right places. This home is mine free and clear, and my dear husband and I worked hard all our lives — I taught grade school until I retired." They passed around sandwiches and tea cakes, and Meg suggested that Maddie tell Adam and Matt about Ian Walker's upcoming speech.

"He's honoring my husband," Maddie said. "And I'm sure it's going to be an impressive speech to attract followers for his presidential bid." Maddie sighed. "Ian is a good man, with good ideas and a passion to serve. But he's not Garth. My husband — you know, he never had a speechwriter. He wrote every one of his own speeches and they came from the heart. He had the ability to bring right and left together, a moderate everyone could accept."

"Meg and I are leaving for Gettysburg next," Matt said.

"She knows," Meg told him.

Maddie turned to Adam. "You'll see that they're there for me, won't you?"

"Thank the Lord that what you want is in my power. Of course."

Agatha made an appearance in the doorway just then. "Maddie, you and your guests might want to see this," she said.

They all stood and followed her to the back porch, now enclosed as a family room with a large-screen television. A reporter at Arlington Cemetery was saying that the body of Garth Hubbard had been exhumed and his widow had been spotted at the cemetery along with "District representatives."

"Well," Adam said, "I guess in a place like Arlington, there's no way to avoid being seen. At least we — and Garth's coffin — were gone before the media arrived."

The reporter voiced her own curiosity about the event, stating that they were seeking an explanation from law enforcement.

The roving reporter was replaced by a handsome anchor sitting at the station's news desk. He announced that there were no new findings in the River Ripper murders and that the public needed to stay on high alert. Police and FBI were reporting that various details indicated that the latest victim had been killed by the same murderer. While this victim was a known prostitute, he went on to say, the previous victims had not been. He stressed the need for safety precautions with a murderer in the vicinity. While the killer might have changed his vehicle, young women were warned to be wary of any black sedans that approached them.

Watching, Maddie brought her hand to her mouth, obviously dismayed.

"It just can't be," she said. She turned to stare at them all. "I can't believe your friend is missing and that my husband might have been murdered and that all these women are dead. I know you told me it might all be a cover-up for . . . for some political reason. It's all too horrible."

Meg stood silent. She wanted to walk across to the older woman and hold her. Comfort her.

But Maddie was suddenly very straight and fierce. "If so, I promise you I will do anything in my power to stop them! Let me call that news station right now. I'll give them a story to run with!"

"Maddie, what are you doing?" Adam asked her.

"Trust me!" Maddie said.

She dialed Information to get through to the station. A reporter was immediately available to speak with her. Maddie was charming as she said, "There's no mystery about this, I'm afraid. I've had Garth exhumed because my children and I made a decision. Garth was a proud navy man in his youth and later a congressman, but he was a family man first, and he'll be reinterred in our family plot. That's all. Please let the public know they needn't waste time speculating, and please stop your people from expressing their morbid curiosity." She listened, thanked whoever was on the line and hung up. "Well?"

They all smiled.

"Excellent, Maddie, excellent!" Adam

said. He gestured at Matt and Meg. "My agents should be getting back to the field. No matter how quickly Dr. Wong and Kat work, we won't have results for a while, but I thought perhaps you'd want to go back to the morgue and see how they're doing. Tomorrow, I'll have the two of you head out, check out the speech venue in Gettysburg and settle in where Maddie will be staying. In the meantime, I'll move a couple of agents in here with Maddie, as a precaution."

"Yes, sir," Matt said.

"Yes, sir," Meg echoed. She hesitated, looking at Adam.

"What is it?" he asked.

"Could I possibly have the dog back before we go?"

Adam smiled. "As you wish." He turned to Maddie. "You good with all of this?"

"I am, Adam. Except don't you leave me until your other agents get here! I have to admit that although I love my husband, I'm not quite ready to meet him on the other side."

Smiling, he nodded and turned back to Matt and Meg. "You two can go straight to the morgue. Killer's at the office with Angela. By the time you finish at the OCME, you can pick him up and, by then,

Angela will be able to give you the information about where you're staying. This speech . . . it's Walker's first bid for the presidency. He could be in danger, too."

What he didn't say in front of Maddie was *If Walker's not in on it.*

Meg didn't argue. But she didn't agree. If Walker wasn't in on it, someone in his retinue was. They'd learn who that person was if they could just find Lara.

And find her . . . *alive.*

Meg was getting accustomed to the morgue, Matt thought. Regardless of how often he'd been at autopsies, it was always difficult. Probably because all mortals knew that they were destined for cremation or earthworms . . .

Then there were the philosophical questions about the essence of life itself. Matt knew that when death came, the body was no more than organic waste. In the morgue, and by the time of burial or cremation, the body was no more human than a side of beef in a freezer.

What a terrible way to think.

But maybe not. He wasn't an atheist or even an agnostic. He'd seen — and he believed. He knew that the human soul or essence — the quality that made every man and woman unique — moved on. Rarely, very rarely, agents had seen the dead at an autopsy or in a morgue. It was definitely an unusual occurrence. Perhaps the dead could bear it no more than the living.

As Kat explained that the body had been compromised by embalming and she wasn't sure what they'd find, he was glad to see that Meg's eyes were still somewhat wide and misty. Yet she had what it took to be here — even though she didn't want to be. What she had was not only a sensitivity to human tragedy, but the strength to face it.

"What we're really looking for is the absence of digitalis, yes?" Matt asked Kat.

"We'll do all kinds of toxicology tests — including some not normally done," Kat replied.

"Have you felt anything?" he asked her next.

Kat shrugged lightly. "No. But that doesn't mean one of you won't sense . . . something."

Wong joined them in the room where Congressman Hubbard now lay.

"I have all the victims of the, uh, River Ripper here," he told them, a look of distaste on his face. "They're in the next room. I've been searching for anything they might have had in common, other than their size, their coloring, their age. Anything that might tell us more about why they were chosen. Do you want to make comparisons yourselves?"

"Of course." Matt nodded. He shared Wong's aversion to the "River Ripper" label, but he knew the media just couldn't resist.

Meg fell into step with him as he followed the ME to the next room. Toe tags identified each of the victims. Cathy Crighton, the first to die, had been very badly cut by stones in the river and mauled by the creatures — beyond the brutality done by her killer. The second victim, the first one he'd seen, the woman Meg had feared might be Lara, was next. Her tag read Karen Grant. Genie Gonzales had been transported from Richmond and now, the last young woman, the prostitute Marci Henning, lay on the fourth stainless-steel table.

Matt viewed the four of them and realized that from a distance they really were remarkably alike. Just as he'd expected. But when he moved closer, he noted that the fourth was somewhat different.

"How tall was she, Dr. Wong?"

"Five-four," Wong said, "approximately."

"The cuts seem more jagged — as if they were done quickly," Meg commented. He turned and saw that she was pale, but still right by his side.

"Good observation. Especially consider-ing the condition of the corpse," Wong said.

"But you still believe it's the same killer?" Matt asked.

"Definitely. The kind of drugs found in the system and the amount of each, the way the first slash was made, the fact that the tongue is missing and the way the body cav-ity was torn open. Yes, I'd say the same man — right-handed, and following his method consistently. The difference is . . . he was either in a hurry on Ms. Henning, or . . . he was tired."

"Interesting. If you're a serial killer, why go after someone when you're exhausted?" Meg wondered.

"Maybe he has a timetable," Matt said. "Which is a very frightening idea." He let out a sigh. "I'll go over the morgue photos tonight and see if there's anything else, anything at all that I can discover. So far, we know that Cathy Crighton left work and was probably taken off the street. It was likely the same with Genie Gonzales. We don't know about Karen Grant, and we know that Marci Henning was working the street — and left in a black sedan." He found himself gently touching Marci's hair. A life never really lived, a life of broken dreams. And then death.

"All right," he said. "Thank you, Dr. Wong."

On the way out, he stopped at the table where the ME's assistant was midway through Congressman Hubbard's autopsy. He touched Garth's shoulder and looked up at Meg; she needed to do the same. But he felt nothing except the coldness of death. Meg reached out, letting one hand rest briefly on the same shoulder, then shook her head. As they stepped into the hallway, Matt felt his phone ringing. It was Jackson.

"Meet me at the Walker house. We've had a strange development," Jackson said.

"What is it?"

"A delivery was made to Congressman Walker."

"Delivery of what?"

"A human tongue, Matt. A human tongue."

12

Despite the fact that no law enforcement personnel other than the FBI had been called in, it seemed like mass confusion at the Walker house.

The congressman's wife was lying on the sofa in the living room, having been sedated already. Ginger was sitting nearby, holding Kendra's cup of tea. Walker was pacing and his aides — Joe Brighton, Ellery Manheim and the very tall, brick-solid Nathan Oliver — moved throughout the house, trying to keep everyone calm.

"There was talk," Walker was saying. "There's always talk. But when I heard that Maddie Hubbard had her husband dug up — I knew! There's a suspicion that someone killed him and now, whoever did it, they're after me. This is insane! The political parties don't get along, the independents don't get along, we all fight among ourselves, but this is ridiculous. But they're not going to get me down!"

"Agent Sokolov just came and took the tongue. We don't know for sure that it was human," Ellery Manheim offered.

"Agent Sokolov isn't a liar!" Walker stopped his pacing for a moment. "She said 'judging by its appearance, it is, but there's a degree of decomposition and degradation.' She was pretty damned sure it was human."

"You have to drop out. You have to! It's as simple as that!" Kendra Walker wailed from the sofa.

Nathan Oliver slammed one giant fist into his palm.

"I will not give them that satisfaction. I will not!" Walker swore. He'd resumed his pacing. He stopped again, staring from Jackson to Matt and then Meg. He pointed a finger at her. "You! You and your friend Lara. Is this her? Is this her way of hurting me for some supposed slight of mine?"

She was in a congressman's house. She was a public servant. But that was too much. "Lara Mayhew may well be dead, Congressman Walker. And if she's alive, she's staying as far from this . . . this mess as possible. How *dare* you accuse an innocent woman who isn't here to defend herself?"

"There was a human tongue on my

doorstep!" Kendra snapped.

"You have cameras and a gated yard. Have you checked your security footage?" Matt asked.

Walker paused; obviously, the idea hadn't occurred to him, odd as that was. "Nathan!" he yelled at the big man. "Get on that. Get on it immediately."

The big man abruptly left the room.

"My home. It showed up at my home!" Congressman Walker said. He turned to Jackson. "And what the hell are you people doing about it?"

Meg noted that when the congressman spoke to Jackson, he had the look of a man who wished he hadn't said those words. But Jackson didn't respond with anger; he just stood there, towering over the man, his features perfectly controlled.

"Everything that's humanly possible, Congressman. That's what we're doing. Perhaps the mystery will be solved when we see your home security tapes."

"A tongue," Kendra moaned. "A human tongue." She managed to sit up, struggling a bit, and gestured at Meg. "You'll be with us, right? In Gettysburg? If Ian insists on going through with the speech, you'll be there? I mean, in the same house, on the same floor? Maddie Hubbard said you would. I don't care what police and agents they put around the house, but I want someone who's a known factor with me."

"Yes, Mrs. Walker, I'll be there," Meg said. She was surprised that this seemed to calm the woman. Maybe Kendra had heard that she'd been an officer in Richmond before applying to the academy. Or maybe she simply wanted someone she'd met before.

But wouldn't her own people be there, as well? Meg wondered.

As if in answer to her silent question, Ellery Manheim cleared his throat. "Kendra, you realize that Joe, Nathan and I will be there, too."

"Yes," Kendra said in scathing tones. "And you were all here today, too, when a tongue appeared on our doorstep!" Kendra groaned. "I'm sorry. No one was in the house at the time. It's just that I'll be with Maddie, and Ian will have to practice his speech and shake hands and pet dogs and kiss babies, and you'll have to be vigilant for him . . . I want Agent Murray nearby."

Meg wanted to say that she'd actually promised to be there for Maddie, and Adam had agreed, but as far as security for Kendra Walker was concerned, it wasn't really up to her. Still, wherever Kendra was, Maddie was sure to be, too.

"I'll check on that outside footage with Mr. Oliver," Matt said.

"No need."

Nathan Oliver had come back into the room, looking pale and sickly.

"There is no footage. The main computer was off," he said.

"What?" Walker demanded.

"Oh, God!" Once more Kendra sat up, putting her head in her hands. Meg thought she was going to berate the household again, that she'd accuse them of either an atrocious crime or atrocious negligence.

"My fault!" she whispered. "The children were here earlier that day . . . I forgot that my computer's connected with the cameras. The kids were playing some kind of game. I didn't check . . . It didn't occur to me that . . ."

She started to cry softly. Her husband crouched beside her. "Kendra, Kendra, we'll find out what's going on!" he vowed. "But, baby, I can't be intimidated by this. We have to stand up to whoever is doing these things, can't you see?"

Kendra gazed into her husband's eyes. "I do see," she said. "I do. And we will prevail, Ian, yes, we will!"

Meg looked over at Jackson and Matt. Despite what had happened here today, they weren't sharing the information about the tongues of the River Ripper victims.

She had to pray that if the tongue proved to be human, it would match one of the victims.

And that it wouldn't belong to Lara Mayhew.

She wouldn't allow herself to think that way. She just hoped they were leaving the congressman's house soon.

"We have the box that was left on your doorstep and the, uh, item inside it," Jackson said. "Forensic units are dusting the porch and the gate and trying to discover how someone slipped in. The box is a white carton like the ones used for takeout at Chinese restaurants around the city. We'll still see what prints, if any, are on it. Mrs. Walker, we can't offer any guarantees, but we have the best men and women working this investigation, with some of the best equipment in the country. The Capitol police are stationed outside. You have your own people in the house and I intend to send agents to be here around the clock. You'll be safe."

Unless the danger is inside your house! Meg thought.

"Thank you, Special Agent Crow," Kendra said. "Yes . . . and I . . . I'm going to bed. I'll have Ginger sit with me. I'll be fine. After some sleep, I'll be okay."

But when she tried to stand, she stumbled. Her husband was instantly at her side.

"I'll see you upstairs, Mrs. Walker," Ellery said, nodding to Ian, who nodded in return.

"Thanks, Ellery."

Ellery began to walk her toward the stairs, but she pulled back. "Nathan, you're sure the security cameras are running now?"

"Yes, ma'am." Once she'd gone upstairs, Jackson turned to Walker. "One of my agents is on his way now. Will Chan. If anything can be extracted from your cameras, he'll do it."

"I'm glad," Walker said distractedly. He walked over to a cherrywood table with a bar service and poured himself a drink. "Gentlemen — and Agent Murray? Would you join me in a Scotch? No, wait, sorry, you're working. Lord forgive me, I need this." He swallowed down the shot, throwing back his head.

"We'll take our leave now, Congressman, and give you some peace. As I said, Will Chan will be here soon, along with two agents who'll stay for the next twelve hours."

"Thank you — and forgive me. I didn't mean to be rude or abusive," Walker said. "Neither did my wife. I can't tell you how shattering it is to open your door and find . . . what we found."

"We understand," Jackson murmured.

"I'll see you out." Joe Brighton headed to the front door; Jackson, Matt and Meg followed.

"He really is a good guy and Kendra is great," Joe told them. "It's very upsetting. The Hubbards have always been close friends, and now Garth is gone and Maddie's digging him up — and there's a tongue on the Walkers' doorstep."

"Perhaps it wasn't human," Meg suggested.

"I'd know a cow tongue — and that was no cow tongue. It was human," Brighton declared. "But you people are doing your jobs, and we appreciate it."

"That we are," Matt said. "However, it would've helped if there'd been security footage."

"I'll take it upon myself to see that it's up continuously now. I'll check it every hour, even when the kids aren't here." They said their goodbyes.

At the cars, Jackson paused with them. "Go home. You two need to drive to Gettysburg tomorrow. The forensic unit has the box and Kat's taken the tongue to the morgue. We'll see if it fits one of our victims.

We'll pray that it does — and that there isn't a fifth one out there."

"It was convenient that the security camera was down, don't you think?" Meg asked.

"Beyond a doubt," Jackson replied.

Matt squinted back at the house. "I'm convinced there's something not right here."

"I feel the same way — but at least we have an in now. We have plenty of reason to be around, which will give us a chance to discover what's going on. I'll call the minute we know anything. You need to get up north."

"I agree," Matt said. "We still have no idea what the hell's going on and how it all connects, but if anyone's planning anything big, it'll be at Gettysburg. A speech on hallowed ground? What better place to strike?"

Matt drove straight to his house, not even thinking to ask Meg if the plan he'd settled on was all right with her. When she asked where they were going and he told her, she just nodded. "I packed for a week, so I'm fine. But I do want to get Killer."

Killer jumped all over Meg when they collected him from the office and he also lavished his affection on Matt. In fact, the little dog seemed so gratified to see him that it was almost embarrassing. "Hey, mutt," he whispered. "I called you ugly — I guess you've forgiven me. Or you don't care."

As soon as they reached his house, Matt dug in his refrigerator; he'd hoped his place would be decent, and it was. He had Mrs. Briar clean for him once a week, and she did his shopping, too. He was pleased to find a good selection of groceries and offered Meg her choice.

He felt her standing behind him as he studied the refrigerator, felt her arms come around him, and he turned to face her.

"I think you're showing your age, Special Agent Bosworth," she teased. "I thought you were considering another activity before dining."

He smiled and kissed her, glad she'd initiated the contact. He'd been afraid she'd obsess about the object left on the Walkers' doorstep, afraid she'd worry that it belonged to her missing friend.

"Showing my age, eh? Well, I suppose I'll have to totter around and prove myself!"

He pulled her hard against him, his hands sliding along her body.

Killer barked.

"Upstairs," she whispered against his lips.

"He is a dog, you know."

"Yes, and he's watching!"

She freed herself from his arms and headed for the stairs, warning Killer, "You behave, young man, and we'll have something delicious very soon — although I'm sure they were giving you treats all day!"

Matt recognized that she could be as determined as he was. Following her into bedroom, he closed the door. Apparently, Killer knew the rules; there was no more barking.

He looked at Meg; she looked back at him. All admissions were out in the open, and they were ready for this. Ready for each other.

The Glocks had to go first, and then they removed their own clothing and each other's.

It had been a long day. Naked, they fell together on the sheets, entwined like a pair of desperate teenagers.

He loved it when she moved beneath him. Loved the sounds she made.

"Showing my age?" he whispered. "Old?"

"Yeah, but you're managing," she teased in return.

They were soon spent, breathing hard. He glanced over to find her huge blue eyes on him.

"A little late for this question, but . . . is there someone in your life?"

He shook his head. "No. And I figured the same for you. Or we wouldn't be here."

She smiled. "What faith you have in me."

"I think I'm a good judge of people."

"Me, too, but . . . your cabinet is supplied with everything." *Including condoms.*

"I'm not involved, though. That doesn't mean I haven't had a woman stay on occasion," he said.

"Ah," she murmured. She smiled and curled against him. He stroked her face and then kissed her, and they made love again, more slowly, more thoroughly, sensuously and seductively . . . Then Meg pulled away from him and rose. "You have a robe somewhere?" she asked.

"I do indeed. Closet. Seemed like a good place for it."

She grinned and took his terry robe from the closet. He liked the way it looked on her. She told him, "I'm going to dive into your fridge and see what you've got. I'm starving. In fact, I'm going to find something to munch on while I'm cooking!"

"Right behind you," he said, and he was. Rolling off the bed, he reached into a drawer for a pair of sweatpants, dragged them on, then started down the stairs. He almost called out to her, some joking remark about her cooking, but the words froze in his mouth as he hit the first-floor landing.

There was . . . someone in the house. They were not alone.

Meg stood, completely still, in the parlor, staring at Killer — who sat at the feet of an apparition.

Matt presumed that the pretty blonde in the white halter dress had to be Genie Gonzales. She was barely there, her presence little more than a trick of the lights against the dying day. And yet he could see her.

She bent down toward the dog, and he could've sworn that Killer felt her and saw her as she stroked the top of his head. Then she looked up at Meg and spoke, her voice merely a whisper on the air.

"Thank you," she said.

Before Meg could utter a word in response, the apparition faded and was gone.

13

"She made it this far. We'll see her again," Meg said, pouring iced tea from a pitcher into glasses. "They always say love is the strongest and greatest emotion in the world. That it transcends time and space. She loved that little dog, and he proved he loved her. She's stayed because of him — and I'm positive that she'll gain strength and come back because he's here. She'll help us."

He smiled, catching her hand and kissing it. "Yes, I believe she'll come back, and yes, she loved Killer. Still loves him. It would've been nice if she'd already learned how to stay around long enough to tell us something."

"We'll have to be patient with her. What I'm afraid of is that the people like Genie — her ghost, I mean — won't know what happened to them. Imagine this. The killer sneaks up on them, and before they can see him, he has the chloroform ready and knocks them out."

"That's possible, but with four victims, maybe one of them *will* know something. And tonight, we've seen that there's hope of reaching at least one."

Matt heard his phone ringing upstairs. He swore softly and set down the frying pan filled with omelets Meg had started and he had finished.

"I've got it." She turned to race up the stairs. She came running back, the phone still ringing. "It's Kat," she said, breathless. "According to call display."

He answered quickly, curious as to why Meg hadn't just answered it.

"Hey, Kat, what's up?" he asked. "Hang on. I'll put you on speaker."

He did, and they both heard Kat say, "The good news is that no new bodies have been pulled from any rivers. The other news is that the tongue delivered to the Walkers belonged to Cathy Crighton."

Matt glanced at Meg. He wondered if she'd been afraid to answer the phone, afraid of what they'd find out.

"Will's here with me," Kat told them.

"Hey, guys," Will greeted them.

"Anything on the surveillance videos?" Matt asked.

"Not really. Only the fact that the camera

was turned off inside the house, which we knew. But whatever's going on, we should have control of the situation. Malachi, who's another agent, and Logan are at the house. They'll be spelled in the morning."

Two agents on twelve-hour shifts, neither sleeping.

"Kendra Walker seems pleased, and I've confirmed that the surveillance is on now. The Capitol police have a patrol car out in front and the DC police are on watch, as well. It's about as safe as it can be."

"I don't think anything's going to happen there — not tonight, anyway," Matt said.

"I agree," Kat added promptly.

Meg spoke up, a little tentatively. "We — we've made a contact. Brief, but . . . a contact."

"Yeah? Tell us about it," Kat encouraged.

Meg described the seconds-long appearance of Genie Gonzales.

"That's great! Wonderful," Will said.

"Next time, I guarantee she'll have more strength," Kat promised.

"I hope!" Meg said.

"I'll fill in Adam and Jackson and the rest of the Krewe," Kat told them. "We'll say good-night now, okay?"

"Hey!" Matt said. "What about Congressman Hubbard?"

"We rushed everything, but these tests can take a while. I should know something in the morning," Kat said.

When he'd finished the call, Matt smiled at Meg. "You could've just answered it."

"But it was your phone."

"When we're on a case, always answer a phone. Doesn't matter whose it is. The Krewe is a team in the deepest meaning of the word. You're part of that team."

She lowered her head and nodded, and he felt the heat of being with her streak through him again. She could be an absolutely wicked lover, and yet there was still a shyness about her. He recalled the affairs he'd had, some short, some only one night — and a few that had lasted several months, even close to a year. But his work had always come first. And when it came to his work, there was a lot he couldn't share with many people — certainly not his special talent. His grandfather had once told him that things happened when they were meant to, when the time was right.

Maybe it was true. And maybe that time was now. Because they had the same talent, because they'd been thrown together on this case — because they both needed someone.

Was he enamored with the light in her eyes, her faint flush . . . or the way she'd stood straight up and defied — politely, mind you — a United States congressman?

"Let's eat," he said huskily.

They did, Killer at their feet. Meg fed him scraps of egg, which he seemed to thoroughly enjoy.

They talked about the case, reviewing the facts and theories. Later, they went to clean up, and somehow, she splashed soapy water on him. That demanded a turnabout — in the interests of fair play. Before either of them knew it, they were in a full-fledged water fight and then they were racing upstairs and it was a while before they slept.

This had been a long day — and a satisfying night — but he had a feeling the longest days were still before them.

Matt was already up and out of the room when Meg woke. She showered quickly, relieved that her things — her clothes and toiletries — were in the house.

Downstairs, a cup of coffee was waiting for her. Matt was on the phone, as he often was, and she assumed he was speaking to a member of the Krewe, but she sipped her coffee until he'd finished his call.

"Good morning." He grinned as he put down his cell. "The day's starting early. We've got a meeting at Congressman

Walker's office on Rayburn," he told her. "Jackson will be there, along with other members of the Krewe, not all of whom you've met. Capitol police will be there, too, as well as people from other security forces. We'll drive to Gettysburg right after."

"Can we stop by the house first?" she asked.

"We can, but why?"

"I don't think we should take Killer to the meeting."

"Good point. Sure."

Long as she had known Lara, Meg had never really familiarized herself with a congressman's routine. She'd had no idea until she arrived just how big the man's staff was.

The office was frantically busy. She met a number of tech staff, more advisers, although she didn't entirely understand what all of them did. Approximately half the twenty people would go on to Gettysburg, but only Walker's personal retinue and security would be at the house he'd rented; the others would be nearby. During the meeting, they discussed the open-air speech, determined where various people would be stationed during that speech and who would be responsible for the safety of whom. She was specifically as-

signed to Kendra Walker and to Congressman Hubbard's widow. She'd be onstage
with them during the speech — basically
ready to throw herself on Kendra Walker
should any trouble arise.

Once the meeting broke up, most of the
protective officers left and the staff returned
to their jobs.

The Krewe retired to Ellery Manheim's
office. There, the group — which included
Jackson, Angela, Will, Kat, Malachi, Logan
Raintree and the artist Jane Everett —
agreed that Logan and Jane would back up
Meg.

"Personally, I think he should cancel the
speech," Ellery Manheim said.

"That's crazy," Joe Brighton argued. "You
have to think about the ramifications. Right
now, his appearance before the public is
more important than ever."

"And I'll never let anything happen to
Walker," Nathan Oliver said, nodding
toward the Krewe members. "We have the
elite among us, not to mention scores of
other security people."

Ellery Manheim shook his head and
absently opened one of his desk drawers.

Meg happened to be standing almost
behind the desk, which gave her a perfect
view into the drawer. She saw something

there that made her gasp.

At first, she didn't even know what it was. A lump of some kind, a red lump that resembled a badly cut piece of meat at the butcher's. Chills shot through her. The object was just lying there between a calculator and a box of paper clips.

"Mr. Manheim!" she said, shocked by the hard note of authority in her voice. "What is that in your desk drawer?"

Her question quickly brought others in the room around.

Manheim stared down at it, first with bewilderment and then with shock. "I — I don't know! I have no idea, it wasn't there earlier! I swear, I . . . It can't be!"

Matt moved forward. "I think this meeting is over. Kat, will you get Dr. Wong and a photographer brought in, please? We're going to need everything documented before this is removed. Mr. Manheim, we'll need to speak with you at our offices."

"What?" Manheim said. "Oh, no. No, this was planted. I didn't put that there. I've never seen it before . . . Good God, I'm a neat freak and practically a germophobe! I didn't . . . I'd never . . . I'd . . ." His voice trailed off. Shoulders slumped, he said, "I'm happy to speak with you wherever you like."

Less than an hour later, Meg stood outside

an interrogation room with Adam, Jackson and Kat, plus Carl Hunter of the DC police, as well as members of the Capitol force. Matt Bosworth was questioning Ellery Manheim.

A search warrant had immediately been requested and signed; other members of the Krewe and police were at the Walker residence, searching Manheim's rooms in the house. Manheim also kept an apartment in Arlington. That, too, was being searched.

Meg wondered, watching the man, if Manheim was telling the truth. He kept running his fingers through his wavy dark hair and shaking his head.

"Congressman Walker finds a tongue on his doorstep and we're all rushing around to make sure that he's not upset and that poor Kendra is sedated!" he said. "I'm attacked in the same way — and I'm under arrest!"

"You're not under arrest," Matt said calmly. "You're in here so we can talk to you privately." He paused, letting his words sink in, then asked, "Who had access to your desk?"

"The entire staff! And Congressman Walker takes appointments. Someone could've wandered around the place. I just know I didn't do it!"

"Mr. Manheim, you have access to the black sedans at Congressman Walker's house."

"Oh, no, you're not going to get me on that! Half this city has access to a black sedan! God, it doesn't matter. I'm ruined. But I didn't do this!"

"You have to understand, Mr. Manheim. A young woman is missing, four women have been brutally murdered and a tongue was left at a home where you frequently spend time. And now . . . one's been found in your desk drawer."

"Yes! And like I said, it was obviously planted there! This could be a conspiracy. Someone wants to bring the congressman down. And they're trying to make it look like he's involved — or his staff is — in these awful murders."

"They're doing a good job," Matt pointed out.

"This is ridiculous! I never killed anyone. I love Congressman Walker and I loved Congressman Hubbard and . . . and I sure as hell have no interest in killing women or cutting them up. I love women — in the right way! And you have nothing on me — well, except a tongue in my desk drawer. But I didn't put it there! Oh, and you've got a fingerprint on the box the tongue came in, but hey! I took the box from Kendra when she started to scream!"

"Mr. Manheim, where is Lara Mayhew?"

"I don't know! We were at a meeting and she left angry. She quit! She quit — and she walked out. Oh, God! I don't believe this!"

Meg turned when the door opened and Logan Raintree entered the room, motioning to Jackson, who went out and through the door to the interrogation room.

He leaned over the table and said, "Two more tongues have been discovered at your personal residence, Mr. Manheim."

Manheim stared at Jackson in what looked like total disbelief. "No! No! I didn't commit these murders. I'm being framed for all this!"

"In your desk, Mr. Manheim, and in the drawer of a bedside table at your private residence. How did the tongues get there? Don't you lock your doors, Mr. Manheim? If so, how did someone else do this?"

Manheim was suddenly angry. "Why ask me? You're the FBI. You know how to break in anywhere!"

Jackson stood back. "Mr. Manheim, you're under arrest."

They had their man, or so it appeared, but Matt didn't believe they did. While Man-

344

heim was being processed, he and Meg went to speak with Congressman Walker. Kendra was with her husband at his office, and while Walker seemed to be devastated, Kendra's demeanor was one of relief.

"We finally know. We know the truth," she said grimly. "I'm horrified that this came so close to us and that such a terrible man had our trust. Oh, God! We slept in that house with him there. My grandchildren were around him. But now . . . now we have to move on. This is going to hurt Ian badly, but . . . but at least we know the truth. We don't have to be afraid anymore. It's going to be all right."

"It will never be all right, Kendra," Walker said. "I'm going to resign."

"You're not going to resign. You can rise to become the greatest president this nation has seen since Lincoln. If you resign, you're giving in! The other day you said you refused to do that. I know I've wanted you out of public service at times, but I also know it's where you should be. You can't resign. You'd be handing the opposition exactly what they want. Manheim wasn't working alone, and we may never find out what really happened, but . . . he was a . . . a spy in your office, secretly working for one of your enemies," she said wildly. "Someone on the far right or the far left. You can't let them win!" Kendra told him. She nodded at the two agents. "We're having a press conference in ten minutes. You're welcome to be there. We can thank you publicly for your good work."

"We prefer staying behind the scenes, Mrs. Walker," Matt said. He found it interesting that Walker and his wife had apparently reversed their positions; now *he* was talking about resigning, and she was urging him not to. Curiouser and curiouser, as *Alice in Wonderland* said.

He saw that Meg was trying hard to contain herself — and then, apparently, she couldn't. She moved forward slightly, looking taller, almost regal in her dignity.

"Congressman Walker, there's still a missing woman out there. And she disappeared after being in your office. What happened that night? Why did Lara Mayhew leave? Why did she quit?"

Walker looked like a beaten man. He shook his head. "I loved Garth Hubbard," he said quietly. "But we disagreed on a few fundamental issues. He was the one with the power — the chance. So I went along with him. It was that simple. When he died, I changed the platform. Lara Mayhew couldn't accept the changes I wanted to make. She said I'd made certain bills so convoluted that no one knew what they were anymore and wouldn't vote for them. She begged me to keep my promise. I told her I *was* keeping my promise — to myself. That was it."

"Then where's Lara? Why would she be in hiding?" Meg demanded.

"I don't know," Walker said. "I just don't . . ."

"You should speak with Manheim, that monster!" Kendra broke in. "Oh, Lord, and to think I turned to him when I found the . . . the tongue on our doorstep!"

One of Walker's office staff walked in to say that the press had assembled for his conference.

Walker stood and took a deep breath. Kendra straightened his jacket.

When he was gone, she turned to Matt and Meg, tears in her eyes. "You'll stay with us? I need him to get through that speech in Gettysburg. We have to rally around him. He's a good man. Maybe even a great one. *Please,* help me. Help him. He's devastated by all this, devastated for the poor women who've been killed. He *has* to make that speech in Gettysburg and I'm afraid of his enemies, afraid of what they might do. They hope he'll resign. As I said to my husband,

347

don't let them win."

"We're public servants, Mrs. Walker," Matt said. "We go where our special agent in charge tells us to go."

She seemed to accept that. She smiled. "Thank you. My husband believes in you both. And so do I."

Meg didn't waste any time. As soon as they were out of the office, she said to Matt, "We have to talk to Ellery Manheim again. Everyone seems to think this is over — that Manheim is like a Ted Bundy, the charming fellow next door, political campaigner by day, mad monster by night. They think the killing's stopped. But you're the one who convinced me Lara could be alive. I'm new to all this. Do what you need to so I can get in to see Manheim."

He didn't care that it was daylight. He placed his arm around her shoulders and met her eyes. "The Krewe is a team, Meg. You know the magic we have. Yours is the same as mine."

"And what's the magic?"

"We speak with Adam Harrison."

It was Meg's turn to sit across the table from Ellery Manheim. They were alone; he was waiting on the attorney he'd hired but had agreed to speak with her as long as anything he said was off the record. She was grateful that he was willing to see her at all. She had, after all, been the first to see the tongue in his desk.

Of course, he started the interview with "I didn't do it. I didn't kill any women!"

"Mr. Manheim, what I'm hoping you'll help me with is a living woman — or, at least, one I pray is still alive. I've spoken with Congressman Walker. He says Lara Mayhew left because he wasn't going to adhere to amendments to a bill he was working on with Congressman Hubbard. Is that true?"

"Yes, it's true. Lara thought he was changing course and compromising in totally the wrong direction. That he wasn't willing to stand up for his principles. She was upset and angry. She said he'd do anything to have his way." Manheim hesitated. "I have a feeling that she suspected he was glad Congressman Hubbard was dead — and that Ian might even have argued with him or something, tried to provoke him to instigate the heart attack."

"Did he?"

He shrugged, a rueful smile lifting his weary features. "You should know. You dug him up."

"I didn't personally dig him up, Mr.

Manheim. And I'm asking you, what do you think?"

"I wish I could say I thought Walker did do something. I wish I could say he's a murderer. But to the best of my knowledge, Walker argued with Hubbard but in the mildest, most civil terms. And to the best of my knowledge, he's done nothing evil in his life."

"What about your closest associates? Joe Brighton and Nathan Oliver?"

"You think a man as big as Oliver could've snuck into Congressman Walker's house without being seen? I doubt it."

"Do you suppose he could have hurt someone? Could Oliver have done something to Lara Mayhew or to these other women?"

"No, he's a gentle giant," Manheim said. "He really is."

"What about Joe Brighton?"

"Joe's a good guy, too."

"So, on the night Lara disappeared, did you all split up when she left?"

"I think we talked for another little while. Joe was afraid she'd start bad publicity, a campaign to say that Walker was a liar and a traitor to his ideals." He brightened suddenly. "I had nothing to do with your friend's disappearance and I can prove it!

I'm the one who drove Walker home that night."

"So you can vouch for him?"

"Absolutely. First Joe Brighton left. He said he'd spoken his mind and was washing his hands of the whole thing. Then Walker said it was late and he was tired and that it's a free country, so Lara had the right to speak out if she wanted. Nathan Oliver kept pacing, saying he had to get going with the communications he'd need to issue if she did make some kind of statement. Walker said that was it for the night, we all needed to sleep."

"Thank you for trying to help me," she said.

As she sat there, the door opened. Matt came in with a small, slim man carrying a briefcase. "This is over," the other man said. "Ellery, we're getting you processed out. You're free to go."

Ellery Manheim looked almost as stunned as he had when he'd first seen the tongue in his drawer.

Meg glanced at Matt, who nodded.

The attorney came forward and dropped a stack of papers on the table between Manheim and Meg.

"Affidavits," the attorney said. "Sworn statements from eye witnesses showing that

Ellery Manheim couldn't possibly have committed the murders. He has positive and proven alibis for the nights Genie Gonzales and Karen Grant disappeared. Ellery, you've been framed. And we don't even have to go to court to prove your innocence. All charges are being dropped."

The rest of the afternoon was crammed with press conferences.

Matt was required to take part in one; he and other officers spoke with the DC mayor, telling the press that yes, the tongues had been sliced from the mouths of the dead women and all of them had now been found. Yes, Ellery Manheim had been arrested — and then cleared. What had originally appeared to be the case of a deranged serial killer might actually be a campaign to oust Congressman Walker. Police and federal agencies had withheld the information about the tongues to prevent that knowledge from compromising the investigation. It continued to be an active case that was being pursued by every law officer on the northeastern coast.

Matt was satisfied with the conference; he believed in honesty with the public, only holding back when it mattered. But once information got out — as it did after the arrest and release of Ellery Manheim — it was best to make sure that it was fact and not rumor.

He and Meg watched as Walker held a press conference himself that day. He proclaimed that he'd still be speaking in Gettysburg. He was all the more determined, he said, to see that his platform, so similar to the moderate platform put forward by the late Congressman Hubbard, was heard and understood by the American people.

Later that afternoon, Krewe members gathered around the table in the large meeting room at their office. Everything had changed so swiftly. Matt reflected that he'd predicted a long day, but nothing like this.

Meg sat beside him, and they listened as Angela used her whiteboard to point out where they were with the case. "We know that Ellery Manheim couldn't have killed two of the women. His lawyer was smart enough to provide sworn statements and videotaped interviews. The surveillance at Congressman Walker's house proved that Ellery was still in the house at five o'clock every night. Will Chan has gone over the surveillance footage himself. It wasn't tampered with in any way. We don't know exactly what day and time Cathy Crighton disappeared, so we can't prove who was where when. But considering the fact that Dr. Wong has stated the murders are all by the same killer — and Kat has corroborated this — there was no reason for the judge to do anything other than clear Ellery Manheim."

"I do agree with Dr. Wong's findings," Kat said. "Same killer."

"That leaves us with two theories to follow," Matt began. "The first is that someone with training in espionage and assassination is trying to oust Congressman Walker. Or, and more likely in my opinion, someone — or more than one someone — in Congressman Walker's retinue is responsible. Some kind of conspiracy, perhaps. But Walker's given the authorities complete freedom to search his home, his offices and everywhere else imaginable. Including his cars," he added.

"The techs still have the cars," Logan Raintree said. "So far, no sign of blood or any indication that any of them was used in a kidnapping or murder. We're working every angle, we're investigating every argument Walker's had in Congress, every person who might have a grievance against him. They're handling a lot of that from the main offices at Quantico. We'll be doing some of that, too, but we're concentrating on Walker's circle. We're not alone on this case. We have the assistance and cooperation of the Capitol police."

There was silence for a minute; they all knew that Walker had enemies. But Lara Mayhew had disappeared after a meeting with Walker and his aides, not with any of his known enemies.

"We saw Genie Gonzales . . . briefly." Meg flushed slightly, as if saying such a thing out loud was still foreign to her. It probably was.

"In the Krewe, we always maintain hope that the dead will help," Jackson said.

"Yes, but it *has* to be someone involved with Congressman Walker. At least when it comes to Lara. Why would she have disappeared if it weren't for whatever happened in his office the night she left that message?"

"We have to look at all possibilities," Jackson responded.

"And what about the letter Lara left me?" Meg asked.

"They're still trying various methods to restore the writing," Angela assured her. She went to the table and leafed through her papers and attached another one to the board. "This is their latest attempt. The first sentence is easy enough to read.

355

Unfortunately, the words that explain why she wrote the letter remain blurred. The *bard* is visible, so we can assume she was writing *Hubbard.* They've cleared another partial word, as you can see here — *s-b-u.*"

Matt leaned forward. *"G-e-t-t-y-s-b-u-r-g,"* he spelled.

"Well, there's reason to believe that something is bound to happen there," Jackson said. "The rest of us will continue the investigation and protection detail. We'll accompany the Walker party and Mrs. Hubbard. As we planned, Matt, you and Meg need to get up there now. Continue your search for Lara Mayhew. She may well be the key to the truth."

14

Meg was eager to resume their search, so she was glad when the meeting ended. Jackson said they should go by instinct in Gettysburg that night and to get some rest for the days to come. They should do whatever Meg thought they needed to that might lead them to the whereabouts of Lara Mayhew.

When they stopped at his house to pick up Killer, Matt took her by the shoulders before she could walk inside. "This is going to be difficult. Concentrate on Lara. We'll be stuck with the Walker camp soon enough, so tonight is the time to let Gettysburg talk to us. Remember everything you two loved there. We'll do some of those things — and figure out why she wrote what she did in her note to you."

Meg smiled at that. "Okay. Road trip. Remember to play the Muppets, and I'll be okay."

"It's a deal."

And he did play Muppet music as they started out. Killer barked with excitement at the first song.

"Dog isn't so bad," Matt muttered.

Congressman Ian Walker and his party had rented the old MacAndrew farmhouse, not far from the national park visitor center. Both Matt and Meg knew the place, although neither had stayed there before. Angela had called to tell them that they wouldn't be able to get in until the following night, however; the remaining room was rented to another family.

Meg suggested they go to a nearby bed-and-breakfast where she'd often stayed with Lara, and Angela took care of the booking.

Meg was friendly with the people who owned it; one of them, Charlene Sayers, wouldn't have a problem keeping Killer there. And if they encountered a problem after that, she knew of a doggy day care in town.

They didn't arrive until eight — although eight that evening felt like two in the morning.

Peter Sayers, who owned the bed-and-breakfast and ran it with his niece, Charlene, greeted them when they came in. Peter had lived in the area his entire life and had purchased the bed-and-breakfast when the previous owner had died. He'd added baths to every room, air-conditioning, and glassed in the back porch to allow for a sunny breakfast room.

Their host was a jovial man of about fifty, a widower with no children but a fondness for his college-age niece, a young woman just as enthusiastic about local history as her uncle.

Peter was a reenactor, glad to take on the role of his own Confederate ancestor for numerous reenactments, from Sharpsburg to Cold Harbor and on to the North.

"Meg, I was delighted to hear your name when the young woman called for your reservations tonight!" Peter said, greeting her with a hug. "But two rooms — and you're not here with Lara?" he asked. "Ah, I see you're traveling with a new friend?"

"Actually, Peter, Lara's gone missing. And we're hoping maybe we'll find her here or come up with some idea as to where she might be."

"Is this her dog?" Charlene asked, coming around to meet Killer.

"No, he's — he's my dog," Meg said. She realized that yes, he *was* her dog now.

"He's adorable!" Charlene crouched

down to pet him.

Matt laughed. "*Adorable* might be stretching it."

"I say he's adorable," Charlene insisted.

"I'm so sorry to hear about Lara," Peter told them. "Are you afraid she's — well, it sounds odd or clichéd, but — met some kind of foul play? We've seen the news up here. Horrible what's going on in the DC and Richmond areas with all those murders."

"Yes, it is. And I pray she's all right — and that we'll find her soon," Meg said. "So I'm trying to follow some of our past footsteps, and then, tomorrow night, we're moving on to help with security for Congressman Walker."

"He's bringing in a crowd that's even bigger than the customary summer hordes!" Peter said. "Oh, my God! After the news from Washington today, the phone didn't stop ringing. People can't wait to hear him speak. In fact, it's pretty splendid that you happened to come here for tonight. I'm sold out after this until the middle of fall. But tonight, it's just us and Mr. and Mrs. Avery — fellow reenactors, except the old buzzard plays a lieutenant in Pickett's division. His ancestor was in on Pickett's Charge . . . and survived. Go figure. I'm really glad that tonight worked out. I'd have hated to turn you away, Meg. And you, too, Mr. Bosworth," he added politely. "But . . . security. Are you still a cop, Meg?"

She shook her head. "I'm with the FBI now, Peter. So is Matt."

"Ah, I'm sorry!" Peter said. "So you're Agent Bosworth or . . ."

"Matt is fine," Matt assured him. "And we're thrilled to be here."

"You have the two ground-floor connecting rooms. You know them, Meg. It's where we always put you and Lara."

"Great," Meg said, smiling.

"Would you mind suggesting a place for dinner where Killer would be welcome?" Matt asked.

"I think you should go to the Dobbin House Tavern." Charlene turned to Meg. "You and Lara took me once, remember? Meanwhile, I'll be happy to keep this little scamp with me. He *is* adorable — no matter what you say!" she told Matt.

"Up to you," Matt murmured to Meg. "It's still your search."

"That's lovely, then," Meg said. "Thank you."

The Dobbin House Tavern was beautiful and far older than the great deciding battle in American history that most people came

361

to Gettysburg to relive or understand. The Reverend Alexander Dobbin had come to the area to start his new life during the Revolutionary era, and built his house to stand the test of time. The tavern offered all modes of dining, from elegant to casual. Matt said he'd never been before and he listened to the waitress when she explained just how old the house was and how wonderful it was to work there.

"Nice," he told Meg when they'd placed their order. "So you came here a lot?"

She nodded. "We both loved it — and my parents love the place, too. It was a stop on the Underground Railroad, you know. There's a crawl space where runaway slaves could hide. This area had a lot of nonviolent protesters before the war. There's a rich Quaker heritage, part of William Penn's legacy. There are so many layers of history here, although of course Gettysburg is most commonly associated with the Civil War and that pivotal battle."

"I haven't been here recently, but I have seen reenactments," he said.

"My parents would approve. They think everyone should come to Gettysburg and see a battle reenactment — although now, of course, we see men fighting and dying on battlefields in our news coverage. But it's still astounding to see guns pointing right at the men — and to watch them walk into the fire, anyway. That, combined with Lincoln's speech . . . well, it reminds us all what it means to be an American and how we need to preserve that dream so many of our forefathers believed in. And fought for."

"I understand their feelings," Matt said. "There really is something hallowed about these fields, about knowing what happened there in July 1863 — on the very ground where you're standing."

"When we leave here, can we drive around the parts of the battlefield that are open at night?" Meg asked.

"You lead, I follow," Matt said.

"Somehow, I doubt that's the way you usually feel," she told him drily.

"Hey, I'm an excellent team player." He rested his fingers on hers. "Don't you agree?" There was mischief in his eyes, and she found herself wondering if it was right that he could make her smile and laugh — and more — when everything in their world seemed to be at such a critical point. And yet, for a moment, she was tempted to suggest they head back to their beautiful old bed-and-breakfast and start their search in the morning.

But she also felt an urge to go out that

night. To — as Matt had said — see what this place had to say to them. Gates at the national park were closed after dusk, but it was still possible to stand by the fences surrounding many of the sites.

Some of the bloodiest sites.

In the end, they went down West Confederate Avenue. Meg asked Matt to stop, and they both got out of the car. The moon was just beginning to wane; it hadn't been a foggy night, but mist seemed to spread across the field beyond the picket fence.

"I remember reading that the battle waged through the town and beyond," Matt said, "with the Confederates pushing the Union back the first day. And then reinforcements poured in from the south and the east. By day two, the Confederates were struggling. And by day three, Pickett's Charge proved to be catastrophic for the Rebels. It was the first major battle Lee had to fight without Stonewall Jackson."

As Matt spoke about the war, Meg wondered if a place actually could speak to someone. She thought she saw shapes, figures in the mist. She hadn't noticed them before. These days, the field was lovely, green and sweeping; she knew that during the battle, there'd been trees, brush, scraggly rocks. She imagined soldiers, silent and grimed and bloodied, moving through, weary from the fighting.

Then a man stopped and looked right at her. She'd seen him before, years ago.

"Private Murphy," she whispered.

"You know him?" Matt asked quietly.

"Yes," she answered. "When we were about sixteen . . . We haven't talked about it since. Lara and I were here, and we were discussing the battle and the fact that so many of the men, and especially the generals, had been friends before the war. It was late on a gloomy fall afternoon and we wondered if what we were seeing was real. You hear about 'residual' hauntings, people reliving a great trauma over and over again. We were just lying on the grass, and this soldier stopped — and it was him. Private Murphy. He could tell that we'd seen him. And he asked that I bring flowers to his little girl's grave. She died in Richmond and is buried at Hollywood Cemetery. Of course, the first thing we did back in Richmond was look for her grave. I never knew whether it was really his daughter's or not, but we found a grave for a Rosy Murphy, who'd died at the age of three in 1862. We didn't see Private Murphy again — and there are dozens of graves with the name Murphy in

Richmond."

Matt took her arm and they moved a short distance. Private Murphy came to the fence; he hardly seemed aware of Matt. His face was seamed with dirt and sweat, but his smile was as sweet and sad as it had been a decade earlier. She'd thought him old when she'd originally met him. Now she knew he couldn't have been more than twenty-five or twenty-six when he died.

"You're all grown up, miss," he said.

"Private Murphy." Her voice was barely a whisper.

He'd been a handsome young man, strong and fit — and brought down by war.

"We brought the flowers to Rosy," she told him.

"I knew you would," he said. "You've come to find your friend."

"She's . . . here? You've seen her?" Meg asked. Her heart sank. It had to mean Lara was no longer alive.

But Private Murphy shook his head. "I've felt her near . . . but not among the dead. I feel her, as if she is calling for help. And now you're here. I pray that you find her." He glanced over his shoulder. "Thank you," he said. "My company is moving on."

He reached out to touch her face. Meg didn't know quite what she felt, whether it was something cold, or something so warm that it stretched across time and life and death. And then he turned and began to trudge wearily with the others, marching on to fight again — perhaps his last battle.

Matt pulled her back into his arms. "We need to get some rest. Now. Maybe tomorrow, we'll understand what he was saying."

"He was real," she said urgently. "You saw him. You heard him, too."

"I did. And I think we need to look at this another way now, too."

"What do you mean?"

"I mean we need to consider the possibility that she's being held somewhere. And because of what happened yesterday, she could be in real danger. We have to find her before Congressman Walker gives his speech — and we're going to need help."

"What kind of help?" Meg asked.

"Angela Hawkins help. Krewe help. If she's being held, it's someplace where there are no windows, where she has no chance of getting out. Where she has no way of communicating. Except through the power of her mind, which may be how you saw her. But we'll be no good to anyone if we don't get some sleep. Time to go back," he said, leading her to the car.

Meg wondered how she was ever going to

sleep with so many thoughts — and fears — rushing through her mind. Matt was quiet, too, as they returned to the bed-and-breakfast. When they entered, they could hear Killer barking excitedly. Charlene met them at the door, smiling, a book in her hand.

"Boy, that dog knew you two were here the minute the car pulled into the drive!" she said. "Did you have a nice dinner?"

"Yes, very. I love the tavern," Meg said.

"Well, I guess I'll head off to bed. You locked the main door?" Charlene asked.

"I did," Matt replied.

They went down the hall toward their bedrooms. Killer trotted beside them, and as Matt started to go in one door and Meg in the other, he stood there, confused.

Matt laughed. "I think he wants us together. Clever little thing. Even if he *is* ugly."

"Stop that. He can hear you."

Matt bent down. "But you're wonderful," he told the dog.

Meg smiled, then escaped into her room; Killer apparently made up his mind and followed her.

She had to shower. All she could remember for a moment was the horror of the dried-out tongue, still bearing dried-out blood, and the muck and blood of the ethereal soldiers as they trooped back across the war-torn fields.

She showered quickly. She was so tired and yet, everything, all her emotions, felt . . . so new. She'd never experienced this intense need to be held.

She was so deep in her thoughts that she didn't expect to see anything, and yet when she came out of the shower, with the mist steaming from the bathroom, she did.

Genie Gonzales was back . . . seated on the foot of her bed, Killer curled up beside her, gazing up at her adoringly.

"Genie, please try . . . Can you tell me what happened to you?"

The apparition faded and flared — like a bad hologram. And then grew more solid again.

"It was a man," she said finally. "I never saw his face. He was in a black sedan. He had a map in his hands and he called out . . . asking for help. I bent down to the driver's door . . . and then . . . nothing. I could see around me, but I knew I was dead. And I saw Killer coming to the morgue . . . and I saw your kindness to my dog."

"A map? So he asked you for directions? He lured you to the car?" Meg asked.

Genie stared at her, eyes huge and luminous, as if they were about to shed ghostly tears.

"Stop him, please, stop him . . ."

Then she was gone, and that time, when the image wavered, it didn't return.

Meg was in a towel, so she couldn't go rushing into the hallway. Then she remembered that she was on the ground floor and the rooms connected. She hurried to the door and twisted both locks on her side, and flung open the first door to pound on Matt's.

He opened it, wearing a towel, as well. For once, she hardly noticed.

"She was here again. I think she can break through because of Killer," Meg said breathlessly. "She doesn't know who killed her, but it was definitely a man, and he lured her to the car. He had a map, and he was pretending to be lost. A black sedan — he was driving a black sedan. They need to do more than just search Congressman Walker's cars — they need to tear them apart. They should be looking for hairs and fibers and anything else that could possibly be in there."

Matt nodded. Then he drew her into his arms. "We'll get them going on that in the morning," he promised. "But I believe the killer was very careful. No struggle. He knocked his victims out. He didn't kill them in the cars — he killed them somewhere he couldn't be seen, and always by a body of water." He pulled back and said, "We *have* to find Lara."

"Yes."

He took her in his arms again then and held her. But a minute later, she became aware that all he was wearing was that towel. She eased far enough away to hold his face in her hands and kiss him.

And that let her forget the rigors of the day.

Later, as they lay together, she said, "You really do have a way with words, Agent Bosworth."

"I like to think I'm good with my hands, too," he said with a laugh. "Sometimes words aren't necessary. But . . . I can come up with a few good ones, if you wish," he said. And with his lips against her bare skin, he began to whisper a few of them, until she was laughing, too, and in his arms again . . .

Finally, she started to drift off. He was right; they needed sleep.

She was going to find Lara — and she was going to find the monster who had killed Genie Gonzales and the other women. They

371

deserved justice.

And she was going to see that they received it.

She had some distance to go as an agent, Meg decided when she opened her eyes the next morning. Matt woke at the slightest sound, but when she fell into a deep sleep, he could shower, dress and be out of the room — without her noticing a thing. Maybe his ability to wake up so quickly had to do with his military experience. Or maybe it was just another talent that some people had and some didn't — and she was a "didn't."

She rose and slipped back through the connecting door to her own room. She expected to find Killer waiting for her, jumping around with joy at her arrival. But he wasn't there and she knew that Matt must've taken him out for a walk.

Dressed and ready in ten minutes, she held still for a moment and closed her eyes, then opened them again. No ghosts appeared before her. Soon after, she went into the breakfast room. Both Peter and Charlene were there; breakfast was ready in chafing dishes, and Matt was carrying on a conversation with their hosts and the other guests, Mr. and Mrs. Avery.

Peter introduced her to the pair — Jordan and Sylvia. They were in costume, Jordan in his butternut-and-gray uniform and Sylvia in a Victorian day dress.

Killer was sitting obediently by Matt's chair.

"We're a bit early for the annual reenactment," Sylvia said, indicating her elaborate garb. "But Jordan's company has a special luncheon today. The men under General Armistead at Pickett's Charge have a get-together with the men who reenact General Hancock's Irish Brigade. Always breaks my heart. Armistead's mortal wounding was somewhat romanticized in that wonderful book by Michael Shaara, *The Killer Angels,* but the emotion behind it was so real. Armistead and Hancock both served as quartermasters in California before the war, and when Armistead chose to go with his state and the Confederacy, he said to Hancock, 'You can never know what this has cost me.' "

"I suppose this is one of the reasons we remember," Jordan said. "Best friends, sons and fathers, brothers — all torn apart. It should teach us today to listen to one another, to establish real equality for everyone and do whatever we can to keep such a tragedy from happening again." He

373

sniffed. "Members of Congress should be made to take part in one of these reenactments. Maybe they'd quit name-calling and do what they swear they're going to do — serve the country!"

"Now, now, dear, these are government agents," Sylvia said.

Matt laughed. "Hey, we're American citizens, too. And we'd love to see congress get along."

"You're here with Walker's party?" Jordan asked. When Matt nodded, he said, "Well, he isn't a bad guy. Not as good as Hubbard — that man was a shoo-in. But Walker's all right. But what if you were asked to protect a politician you didn't like?"

"We'd still watch over him. Our personal opinions don't enter into it," Matt said. "Our vow is to protect our country and our people, whether we like them or agree with them — or not."

Sylvia grinned. "Well, I think *you* should run for congress, Matt!"

"No way!" Matt vowed, and they all laughed.

"Have you been here for a reenactment?" Jordan asked.

"Many times," Meg said, and Matt nodded.

"Visit us at the camp if you get a chance,"

Sylvia said. "My great-great-great-grandfather was a surgeon in the Civil War. Jordan's ancestor was a Rebel, mine was a Yankee. I switch around at the camps."

"If the war was happening now, we would've been in opposite camps," Jordan said.

"But I'd have followed you anywhere," Sylvia said.

"You're the best, babe," her husband teased. "You know, Mary Lincoln had to turn her back on her family because of her husband."

"I'd do that, too, if I had to," Sylvia insisted.

"Aww." Charlene rolled her eyes to more laughter. "How sweet."

Matt looked over at Meg. "We should pack up and get going," he said. "You ready?"

Meg had managed to down a cup of coffee and an egg-and-cheese croissant as they talked. They couldn't get into the MacAndrew until later in the afternoon but they told Jordan and Sylvia Avery that they hoped to see them again. Sylvia scratched out some notes for them.

"If you want to check out some Civil War surgery, this is where I'll be 'assisting,' " she explained. "Not everything is allowed on park service property, but we rent from a farmer every year and we can do full-scale theatrical work. I'm hoping we'll be able to continue to do that. We're next to the ruins of the Brewer mansion, and the property has just been purchased. I don't know who bought it — hopefully, an historian — and that he or she won't object to our goings-on every year. Anyway . . . stop by if you can."

Meg thanked her. Normally, she loved to go to the reenactment camps, but doubted she'd have the opportunity during this trip. They left soon after, Killer at their heels.

"Where are we off to? Any ideas?" Meg asked Matt.

"You're supposed to call the shots."

"But I'm not sure how. So . . . any ideas?" she repeated.

"How about a drive around the park, which will take us some time," Matt replied. "The problem is that we don't have a lot of time. There are museums everywhere, as well as the cemeteries and battlefields. I'm sure you and Lara went to all of them at one time or other. But hopefully, we'll be able to narrow things down when Angela gets back to me."

"Oh? What did you ask her to do? And what about Congressman Hubbard? Do we have any results from his autopsy yet?"

He nodded grimly. "We know there was no sign of digitalis in his system. Of course, embalming has taken its toll. But Kat and Dr. Wong agree that the death is suspicious. Maddie Hubbard found him with his pills strewn around. He probably went for his digitalis. But what he took was probably some kind of placebo. His death wasn't a guaranteed result, but for a man in his condition, switching out his pills created a good likelihood that he'd die."

"So, sometime during the day of his death, someone switched his pills," Meg said thoughtfully. "He was at a picnic after a busy day with other congressmen, aides, et cetera. And the pills are all gone, since Maddie was so diligent about that. But there's nothing we can prove — and we don't know who might've done it."

"It lends credence to the possibility that somebody made Lara disappear. She probably suspected the truth. And she probably has a good idea of who's guilty. But Angela will call with more information soon. The Walker party isn't due until tonight and it's still early, so let's do what we can do. Are you okay with going to the park?"

Matt was at the wheel but they were parked in front of their bed-and-breakfast as he waited for her opinion.

"We used to go everywhere around here," she said, stroking Killer, who lay quietly on her lap. "Lara loved the Jennie Wade House. Remember poor Jennie? She was the only civilian killed in the battle. She was baking bread for Union troops when shots came through the windows. She supposedly haunts the area, but . . . I've never seen her. And Lara loved the train station where Lincoln arrived. Also the Lincoln museum . . . Lee's headquarters and the park itself," Meg said. "So, yes, I guess going around the park is a good plan."

They drove for a while, starting at the visitor center, following their private trail, hers and Lara's, stopping at monuments. Each place they went, Meg tried to *feel* something. But all she felt was that she was spinning her wheels. If Lara was in hiding, the first place she would've gone was to Peter's. He would've kept her secret. But she sensed that he hadn't even known about her disappearance . . .

"Think you can find your Private Murphy again?" Matt asked.

"I'm told we only see the 'residual' hauntings of the men marching to or from battle when the sun has fallen, when mist lies over the land," she murmured.

Lara had seen those men when she and

Meg had gone to the battlefield together. Lara *claimed* she only saw them because Meg had described them so well, but Meg knew better. Lara, too, could see the dead. And she had the ability to enter Meg's mind.

Matt's phone rang. Angela. He put her on speakerphone.

"You do realize," Angela said, "that when people refer to the Underground Railroad, they don't always mean underground. Many people hid escaped slaves in their attics, smokehouses, barns and so on."

"Yes, of course." Meg wondered why Angela was pointing this out.

"But there were many places in the Gettysburg area that were part of the Underground Railroad. I've done a dozen computer searches with Will's help, and I have a list of locations you can check out — and a few you're not supposed to. I'm sending it to your phones in an email attachment. The problem you two have is that you're government agents, and if you go where you're not supposed to and someone wants you arrested — well, you'd better be damned good at pretending you were just tourists."

Matt started to thank Angela but she interrupted him. "Oh, and I've cross-referenced what you asked, Matt," she added. "So far, I haven't found what you're looking for, but then property is often purchased under corporate names, so I'm researching the corporations that recently purchased property in remote or heavily farmed areas in Adams County."

When Angela rang off, Meg asked, "What exactly is she looking for?"

He smiled. "Anyone associated with Congressman Walker's party who might own property in this area. Someplace that might sit over old foundations, or had tunnels for the Underground Railroad, or covered wells. That kind of thing."

Her heartbeat quickened. "Someplace you might keep a prisoner?"

"Yes."

"Or hide a body."

"I don't believe Lara's dead. Private Murphy said he felt her presence. She knew about you, right? Your talent? Maybe she even shared it. She saw Private Murphy, too, right?"

Meg nodded.

"That's my point. If she was dead, she would've reached you. She's alive, and she managed to enter your mind or appear before you that one time — but it's hard for her because she *is* alive. I really believe that."

"Let's head over to the Virginia Monument on Seminary Ridge," Meg suggested. "It was one of Lara's favorites."

Matt drove to the monument and they stopped. Dogs weren't allowed in the cemetery or the visitor center, but they could be taken onto the battlefield if they were leashed. Killer had hopped out every time they'd left the car — well behaved on his little leash. At the Virginia Monument, he barked and seemed anxious.

"Killer," Meg said, "what is up with you?"

She scooped him into her arms. He was silent but still shaking. He licked her face.

"Ugh," she muttered.

"Give him to me," Matt said.

"I'm okay."

"No. You need to use your gift to contact the living. You need to stand here and concentrate on Lara. Think of her as if you were trying to call her. Clear your mind and think of nothing else, nobody else, but Lara."

The Virginia Monument stood forty-one feet high; it was a beautiful equestrian statue of Robert E. Lee over a group of seven Confederate soldiers. It was the largest of the Confederate monuments.

Meg handed the dog to Matt and sank down on the monument where she and Lara had sat before, talking about the Civil War. Years later, Lara had said that while Richmond might have been the capital of the Confederacy, it was now more "Washington" than ever, what with the ninety miles between the two cities being nothing in this day and age.

Except for traffic, of course.

Meg closed her eyes. She tried to envision her friend, with her sunshine hair and sparkling green eyes, always striving to see both sides of an issue. She often deplored the fact that although the Civil War was more than a hundred and fifty years behind them, some people still had to fight against inequality, while others hadn't learned to stamp out their own prejudices.

The sounds around her dimmed as she concentrated. She felt the sun and heard birds and pictured her friend's face. In her mind, she could see Lara, smiling in the sunlight.

And then the sun dimmed. And she saw her in darkness, barely visible, lying on . . . dirt. Surrounded by darkness. Walls of dirt . . . and darkness.

She's dead, Meg thought, *dead and silent. Forgotten . . .*

Then she seemed to hear a pulse, a heartbeat. Lara wasn't dead; she was weak and starved and dehydrated, barely alive and yet . . .

"Meg . . . Meg, where are you? Help me . . ."

Alive. Yes, Lara was still alive. Still trying to reach out to her.

Alive . . . but for how long?

Lara lay on the floor, fevered, half awake and half asleep.

She was dying, and she knew it.

She wanted to fight; the will to fight was strong in her. But her body was giving way. She was nearly out of water and she hadn't eaten in days. She was so weak . . .

And yet, lying there, she suddenly had an image of Meg.

Meg is near.

She wanted to concentrate. She wanted to tell her friend there wasn't much time left. She tried . . .

She could no longer scream. She could hardly move. She knew that Meg wouldn't stop until she found her.

But now . . .

Now it seemed that when Meg found her, she'd be dead.

But then she could tell her some things . . .

Because Meg could speak with the dead.

15

Meg's eyes opened. "I don't know . . . Am I just making up what I want to see? I — I think she keeps trying to reach me. I think she's somewhere in the dark. Like . . . thrown into a well, a dirt-floor basement, something like that!"

Holding Killer, Matt sat next to her for a moment and she realized she was shaking. "Meg, I believe you did see her, and I believe she's alive — she's not coming to you as a ghost. Her mind is connecting with yours, and she's communicating with you the way you two did as kids. There've been lots of experiments with people who have extrasensory perception, and there's lots of evidence that it exists — which is far more accepted than that we might see the dead. Take a deep breath. We'll figure it out. We'll find her."

She looked at him and was thankful that he gave her strength. What she'd once seen as arrogance really was his stance on life; he always walked forward in confidence, spoke with honesty, maintained a clear vision.

She smiled. "If we find her — *when* we find her — and this is over, I'm going to need a vacation. With you, of course. I may be the new kid on the block, but . . ."

"You'll deserve it." He smiled back, using his free arm to pull her close. "Now, we're running out of time. We have to check into the MacAndrew farmhouse, look it over and then head to every location on Angela's list. With any luck I'm right — and someone in Walker's party owns land and on that land we'll find Lara."

They left the park. They'd spent about three hours there, but it was still early, only about one o'clock. By that evening, they'd be on official duty as part of the Walker family security. Matt was anxious to get there.

The MacAndrew farmhouse had been in the Confederate line of fire; while MacAndrew had sympathized with the North, he was also a Quaker and a pacifist. When the Confederates had arrived in need of a field hospital, MacAndrews, his wife and six daughters had set about tending the wounded. They'd welcomed the help of Confederate doctors.

When the Union forces had rolled

through, Northern doctors had worked with the Confederate ones and the injured Union and Rebel forces had lain side by side. The Rebels would become prisoners, but many had forged friendships with their Northern doctors and fellow patients that would last all their lives.

The farmhouse was large, with eight bedrooms upstairs and four more on the second level of the old barn, which was now a gathering place. Apparently, Congressman Walker's people would be in the main house, along with two members of the Capitol police, their own retinue, Matt, Meg, Angela and Jackson Crow. Other security would stay in the barn; there were four guard stations set up around the house itself, one on either side of the road, one in front of the house and one behind it.

It seemed impossible that anyone could get at Congressman Walker — not while he was at the MacAndrew house, at any rate.

They were met there by Larry Mills of the Capitol police, who'd already taken over; Maddie Hubbard had specifically requested that Meg be in the upstairs bedroom that connected to hers.

Matt would be across the hall, and Kendra and Ian Walker would be next to Maddie.

Larry Mills seemed to be a serious and competent man. He had a buzz cut and looked weathered and fit, thanks to eight years as a navy SEAL, he told them.

"They're not due in until eight," he said. "As you saw, I have the stations set up, and rooms assigned. They're bringing their security with them. A few of your unit are in the party, so I'm assuming you're in communication?"

Matt assured him that they were — and that they'd be back at the house before the congressional party arrived.

"That ain't much of a dog," Mills said, pointing at Killer. "He isn't a security canine of some kind, is he?" he asked dubiously.

Meg didn't really answer, but said, "You'd be amazed. He's got a great bark."

"Does he know the right people to bark at?" Mills asked.

"Oh, I think he does," Matt replied. "Trust me, he's an asset."

Mills grinned. "A German shepherd, a rottweiler — that's an asset. Him? He's an accessory."

They laughed politely and Mills scratched Killer's head.

Then Matt and Meg left for what remained of their free time.

Aside from Gettysburg, Adams County offered a number of "stations" on the Underground Railroad. As they got in the car again, Meg reminded Matt that one of them might be where Lara was hidden . . . Matt saw how anxious she was. Meg was now convinced that Lara was alive, but that she wouldn't be if they didn't find her soon.

"It's not going to be anywhere obvious, Meg," he told her. "Not a place that's on a tour. This has to be something very different. Obscure."

He'd just gotten in the car when Angela called. He immediately put her on speaker.

"We're heading out soon," Angela said. "We'll be riding in Walker's car. I estimate our time of arrival to be somewhere between seven and eight, but I'll keep you posted along the way. I'm calling you now because I found something you were looking for. Congressman Walker is the majority owner of a corporation called PTP, or Preserve the Past. They're not nonprofit, but they work closely with historic boards. PTP has bought and restored a number of places in Maryland, Virginia, West Virginia — and Pennsylvania. PTP purchased ruins in

Gettysburg about six months ago. The old farmhouse was condemned, and I'm assuming the corporation plans to build a re-creation of the home. There's also the ruin of an old mill nearby. Thought you might want to check it out. Carefully — and discreetly — of course."

"That's it!" Meg cried.

"Can you give me the address?" She did and he rang off, then turned the car around in a handy driveway and veered in the right direction. "Do you know the place?" he asked Meg.

"Not really, but I'm sure I've been by. But if it's just some ruins in a field and it's privately owned, we might not even have noticed it."

"Probably not," Matt agreed. "There's still a lot of farmland around here. A lot of history and tourism, but a lot of farmland, too."

As they approached the address Angela had provided, he saw that there were lines of cars parked on the road leading up to another farm, practically next door to it. There were all kinds of tents pitched out in the fields, while paddocks in front of an old farmhouse were filled with horses.

"The camp!" Meg said.

"Yeah, the living-history camp Sylvia

mentioned. A Union camp," Matt said. "That's where the medical reenactments she was talking about must be taking place."

He drove slowly, looking across the acreage. Men sat by the tents cleaning rifles. A command tent had been set up, and he could see a group of men in Union officers' clothing at a table. Spectators milled around, watching them. There was a blacksmith shoeing a large draft horse and cooks worked around campfires.

"Matt, the ruins are beside the encampment, so we can park with these other cars. That way, no one would notice us if they happened to go by."

She was right. It was perfect, especially since he could see that while an easily scaled wooden fence surrounded the neighboring property, the fence was covered with signs that read Private Property! Keep Out! Violators Will Be Prosecuted to the Full Extent of the Law!

"Well, I guess we're going to become lawbreakers," he said.

"We're investigators!"

"With no legal search warrant," he reminded her.

"Imminent danger. I heard someone screaming," Meg improvised.

"That's a stretch," Matt said. He found a

place near the road, directly beside the fence. They were in the midst of other cars, dozens of them. They could hear the speeches being given and the murmur of conversation from the Union encampment. There was an expanse of long grass before they could reach the remains of the condemned house on the property. And there were overgrown trees not far in, which meant they wouldn't be obvious for long, if anyone did look over.

"Should we crawl?" Meg asked.

"Nope, walk in like you own the place. No one will pay any attention to you."

He opened the car door. To his surprise, Killer, who'd been well behaved, hopped onto his lap and then out the door, not giving Meg a chance to grab his leash.

"Hey!" She jumped out her side of the car and went scrambling over the wooden fence and after the dog. Matt followed as quickly as he could.

Well, good excuse for trespassing. "I had to get my dog, Officer . . . He ran off!"

Meg could run, that was for sure. He could catch up pretty quickly, but by the time he did, they'd passed by the long, overgrown grass and made it to the shelter of the trees. He nearly collided with her as they crashed through the doorway. The door itself was broken and hanging ajar.

She'd stopped — because Killer had stopped. He stood in the hall and whined. He was uncertain of where to go.

"I'll take the left side of the house," Meg said.

"Be careful. It's crumbling, could cave in," he told her.

"Gotcha."

The ruins were dark, gray, forlorn. Anything of value had long ago been removed. His route led to a dining room. No dishes or serving implements there; even the chandelier had been taken away. But wooden cabinets showed where china and crystal had once been kept, and a lopsided table and broken chairs paid homage to meals once eaten by a family. Spiderwebs reigned supreme.

He moved on to an empty pantry and then to what had been the kitchen, a room with worktables, a sink with a rusty pump and a giant hearth.

Coming around from the other side of the house, Meg met him there. A narrow stairway went up to the second floor — the servants' stairs, he assumed. Another door that was also hanging crookedly on its hinges opened out to more broken steps, steps that led down to the basement, he thought.

Killer followed Meg, then stood in the doorway to the second set of stairs and whined.

"We have to go down there," Meg said.

"The place is condemned. Could be dangerous. We have to be careful," he told her.

"Yes, so I should go. I'm way lighter than you are. If the stairs are on the verge of collapsing, I have a far better chance of not falling through."

"We both go or no one goes," he said firmly.

"But me first. I can warn you of faulty steps." Killer solved the problem for them. He barked, and started down the stairs.

"Flashlight?" Matt asked her.

"Yes, of course. I know about being prepared. I just graduated —"

"Yeah, yeah," he said with a smile, "from the academy. All right, I'm shining my light down there, too. Use one hand for the railing. It may hold if the steps don't."

"I know," she muttered. He could tell that she was a bit annoyed, but he couldn't help it — he was a protector by nature.

Killer was down there now — and barking. Matt stood in the doorway and tested the first step; it seemed sound. He shifted aside to allow Meg to take the lead.

She moved carefully, but a moment later he heard a loud creak.

"Fourth step!" she called up to him.

"Okay," he said. Tension flooded his body. He found himself thinking of childhood fears — of monsters that lived in the darkness of basements. Any monsters here would be human. He was pretty sure there was no one down there with a knife or gun, but he didn't *know.* And Meg couldn't hold on to a rail, plus her flashlight — and reach for her gun with the necessary speed if something did raise its ugly head down there. Something or someone . . .

"I'm down!" she shouted. "The rest of the steps seem solid enough."

He followed her, still moving cautiously. Together, they beamed their flashlights around the place. It was typical of abandoned basements. A slanted shelf held lanterns; candles were piled in another box, half-melted into one another. A rope was strung across the space, hung with old clothes as if they'd been put there to dry in winter. Barrels, staves and crates sat in one corner; here, too, spiderwebs seemed to hold court.

"Watch it. Nice nesting place for a brown recluse," he said. "Nothing like getting your man, and then dying of a spider bite."

"There's nothing down here," Meg said, her tone disheartened. "I thought . . . I thought we'd find her. But this isn't even like the floor I saw. I mean, I thought I saw. She was on the ground, alone, passed out from hunger or dehydration or . . ."

Her voice trailed off. Matt suddenly wondered if he'd been wrong about Lara and wrong in making Meg believe that Lara might be alive.

He hated to lose faith like this, but she was probably dead. The killer must have taken greater care with her corpse, weighting it so well that she wouldn't float back to the surface. One day, someone fishing or diving in the river would come across her decomposed remains, her bones part of the riverbed.

He realized, though, that he had faith in Meg, if not in himself.

"We're going to find her. Let's keep looking down here," he said.

They did. They searched for a good hour, tapping the walls, hoping for a secret exit, the kind of thing that might have been used in slave days.

"We have to give it up now," Matt said at last. "We're almost out of time."

Meg nodded, and they headed back to the

stairs. But before they reached them, Meg paused, easing back against him and turning around.

"Killer, come," she ordered the dog.

He didn't seem to hear her. He stayed where he was, whining again. Meg walked back over to where he stood and stooped down to pick him up.

"We've searched, boy. We've searched all over. We can't find anything," Meg told him.

"Take him and go on up first," Matt suggested. "I can catch both of you if you fall — better than you catch me."

Meg almost smiled. "I'm just not sure about hauling you back up if another step does go," she said.

"I tested them all. Only the fourth one was really bad." When they emerged into the kitchen, he turned to her and laughed. "You're covered in spiderwebs. You look like hell."

"As I noted before, you have a talent with words — you always know the right thing to say," she told him sardonically. "You should see yourself. And Killer!"

The dog looked like a ghost dog; he, too, was shrouded in gray webbing.

"We've got to get this off before we return to the MacAndrew house!" he said. "You help me, and I'll help you."

"Don't you dare try to turn spiderwebs into something erotic!"

"I'll contain myself — as long as you exercise control, as well," he teased.

It took some time before they were both presentable.

"We didn't go upstairs yet," Meg said.

"No. She's not going to be upstairs." If she was there, he thought, they would've heard something. Unless she was dead.

And then, he knew, they would have smelled the odor of decomposition.

He didn't say that to Meg. And what she said next did make sense.

"I agree we won't find Lara, but we can tell if someone's been here recently."

"It's likely that if the PTP corporation bought the place, they've had people here, including local real estate agents," he said. "But you're right. We've come this far. Let's go up."

The upstairs of the house was as sadly haunting as the rest. The few pieces of furniture were broken and falling apart. Drapes were ragged and drooping from the windows. In one bedroom, Meg paused.

"What?" he asked her.

She was standing by a window and motioned him to come over. "Look, but don't touch. There are prints in the dust on the windowsill. Someone's been here. And there in the distance . . ."

Across the fields and roads, up on another hill, was the MacAndrew farmhouse.

"Well, whoever was here was certainly checking the view," Matt said. "That might've been a security precaution by Larry Mills or one of the other cops. Maybe they'd thought about stationing someone here to keep watch. It's hard to say, Meg."

"Lara's somewhere nearby," she said passionately. "I just know it!"

"We'll figure it out — and we'll get to her in time," he promised. He prayed he could keep that promise. But somehow, he felt that something was going to break soon.

Congressman Walker's speech was the next day. That was a catalyst, he thought. He wasn't sure how he knew or why, but that would be the catalyst.

"We'd better go."

When they were outside the house, Matt looked across the overgrown field and to the Union encampment. "Let's pay our new friend a quick visit," he said.

"Our new friend? You mean Sylvia Avery?"

"Yes. She should be at that encampment, in the vicinity of the medical tent."

He didn't wait for her to answer, but started across the field. Meg was behind him; Killer was not. He went back and picked up the little dog. Crawling through the fence, Matt was greeted by a man in a Union uniform. "Sir! Living history that way!" he said, and pointed.

"Thanks, thanks so much," Matt said, and the soldier tipped his hat. They walked past scores of people, some in casual summer dress, many in uniform — or in their daily clothes with Union or Confederate hats or other paraphernalia. But no matter what people were wearing, they were friendly and courteous as they walked around. Most seemed to be talking about what they'd seen or learned.

He supposed that people probably didn't come to these events if they weren't interested, if they didn't care about history — and if they didn't honor the fields of battle that had taken more lives than other wars.

He caught Meg's hand. She was wearing a pantsuit that was dignified and proper but didn't scream FBI agent. He hoped they looked like a couple of tourists fervent about Civil War history.

They passed an officer explaining the use of the Enfield rifle to a crowd, and then an infirmary. At last they came to a surgical tent. A man in a Union doctor's uniform was describing field surgery, saying that even the federal forces had been low on ether, the anesthesia of the day. Most of the time, the men were dosed with whiskey. Limbs were removed, flesh cut, a bone saw used. Tourniquets were employed to stop the bleeding. Good doctors, he told his audience, disinfected the wounds with some of the alcohol the injured were drinking; these doctors had discovered that they lost more men to infection after surgery than they did to the surgery itself.

He poked Meg; he could see that Sylvia Avery was assisting in the mock surgery.

The doctor finished his speech, announcing that he was Dr. Collin Ferber of Philadelphia, a fifth-generation surgeon, following in the wake of his ancestor, who had worked on the Gettysburg battlefield. The crowd responded with applause, then began to disperse. Matt took Meg's hand again and moved through the milling people to find Sylvia Avery.

"Well, hello, you did come by!" she said, obviously glad to see them both.

"It was an excellent lecture and show," Meg told her.

Sylvia beamed. "Thank you. We pride ourselves on historical accuracy."

"Do many of the reenactors actually stay

here at the camp?" Matt asked.

"Oh, yes, most do. We used to stay, except I have to admit, the more years that go by, the more I long for my creature comforts. Showers, soft beds and softer pillows and finding an excellent cup of coffee ready for me when I get up," Sylvia said. "Frankly, Jordan and I are too old these days to enjoy *too* much authenticity."

Meg smiled. "Not to worry. I know many younger people who like to camp at nice hotels."

"I was wondering, Sylvia, how do you feel about being on the battlefield? Men trooped all over these fields during the war. You're here at night sometimes, right?" Matt grinned. "At least until you return to the B and B."

"Do I see the ghost troops refighting the battle? Is that what you mean? Or limping away, weary and bloodied?" she asked shrewdly.

"Exactly."

"I think at one time or other, any of us who are out in the fields at night believe that we see soldiers, Yankees or Rebels, marching. Some people think they see the actual battles as they're being fought, men screaming and dying, bullets and black powder — the whole nine yards. Me? Yes, I guess in the darkness and the moonlight I believe I've seen soldiers," Sylvia said.

"What about strange noises?" Matt asked.

"Well, yes. A friend of mine who was out here a few days ago heard something. First she thought it might be one of the advance people, so to speak, the 'sutlers' or shopkeepers who sell reenactment clothing or weapons or antique items. They come and set up pretty early. During the anniversary of the actual battle, things get pretty hectic here, and they like to be prepared. Anyway, my friend told me she had a horrible night. She was sure she heard someone screaming, crying out through the night. In the morning, however, she felt like a fool. She'd gotten up several times during the night and walked around, but couldn't find anyone in distress. Another friend told her that she was hearing echoes of the past, the cries of men who died on the field, waiting for their own troops to find them among the dead." She smiled at them curiously. "Why? Are you seeing soldiers walking in the mist?"

"Oh, yes, I believe I see them, too," Meg said. "Is your friend here now?"

"I'm sorry, she's not. But she'll be here tomorrow if you want to come by. Oh, I forgot! That speech Congressman Walker is giving is tomorrow, isn't it? Anyway, if you get a chance, she'll be here most of the next week. And," she added with a wink, "when it's late at night, you'll know where to find me. A comfy bed at Peter's place."

"Thank you, Sylvia. I'm sure we'll see you again," Meg said.

Sylvia scratched Killer's head. "Love this dog!" she cooed. "Truly one of God's creatures, so damned ugly he's beautiful! Sorry, I didn't mean to be offensive."

"It's okay," Meg assured her. "He gets that a lot."

Matt felt his phone vibrating and excused himself to answer it. Angela.

"We'll be in soon," she said. "Anything? Any luck?"

"No, but we feel we're on the right track. We'll head back to the MacAndrew farmhouse now. See you there."

Meg was still chatting with Sylvia. He glanced at his watch, signaling that they had to leave. They said their goodbyes and returned to the car, but when they reached it, Meg paused, looking back at the ruins of the house in the neighboring acreage.

"I know she's not there. But she's somewhere nearby."

"I believe you. And I believe that we will find her," he vowed.

Time, he thought.

Time was everything now.

"I really think this is far too much fuss for one congressman," Ian Walker said.

Meg agreed — except that, one way or another, the answer to Lara's disappearance lay with this man. They were seated in the massive family dining room at the farmhouse; some of the agents and security people were outside, others were stationed around the house, and everyone had come in at some point for dinner, which had been catered by a local restaurant.

"Oh, darling, after everything that's happened?" Kendra responded. "And you're not just *any* congressman, you know."

"Well, I should have planned better," Ian said. "It was all this bizarre trouble with Ellery Manheim. I couldn't believe that he was guilty of anything, and that turned out to be true. He was as much a victim of this maniac as I was. And yet he resigned. He said he wouldn't mar my good name with any hint of scandal. I told him I was willing to stand up to anyone, that he's an innocent man. False accusations cause so many problems, and I didn't want Ellery to be a victim of anything like that. But I couldn't convince him to stay."

"He made the only logical stand," Maddie said. She clasped Ian's hand. "I know what you mean, but he did do the right thing. Not to mention the fact that he's already gotten a huge offer to write a book. Ellery is going to be fine."

Ian Walker stood suddenly. "Well, it's late, but no help for it. I want to see the site where I'll be speaking. I won't be in the cemetery, but I'll still be close to where Lincoln gave his Gettysburg address!"

"Incredible, isn't it? Lincoln never knew what an impression he'd make with his words that day," Matt said. "He'd intended to be brief — Edward Everett had already given a lengthy oration, and Lincoln didn't think the crowd could abide another long speech. He was also ill when he delivered it. Physicians later thought he might have had the beginnings of a mild case of smallpox. Also interesting — there are at least five slightly different versions of the speech."

Meg noted that he spoke casually, just making conversation, which they'd been doing since dinner. Before that, the place had been bustling with activity, as everyone went to their assigned rooms, police and security and FBI were all introduced to one another and luggage was brought in. She'd had a few minutes to spend with Maddie, who was delighted that her room actually connected with Meg's. "I'll feel so safe with you next to me," she'd told her. Meg just wished she could feel as confident. She wasn't afraid of an unknown situation; she was afraid of treachery.

Someone in that house was to be feared. She knew it.

"Lincoln was truly such a great man," Kendra said with enthusiasm.

"Garth Hubbard was the closest living politician to him I've ever seen," Ian Walker said, squeezing Maddie's hand in return.

"Well, you'll have to carry on in his stead, Ian, that's all there is to it," Maddie said, tears in her eyes.

"I plan to at least deliver a good speech. So, ladies and gentlemen, I understand that a number of you will accompany me? As I said, I want to see the platform where I'll be speaking. It isn't where Lincoln dedicated the Soldiers' National Cemetery, but I'm here to talk about our country getting together. About how we should stop with the bipartisan bull that's tearing us apart. Gettysburg is a fitting place for it, but . . . I'm trying to follow in giant footsteps. I *have* to speak well."

Jackson, standing quietly in one corner of the room, came forward. "Sir, you do realize that it's late and dark."

"And I have all of you," Ian said. "Special Agent Crow, I'll be bringing members of your unit and the Capitol police and my own people. We'll be fine."

Jackson nodded, but he clearly wasn't pleased.

"And ladies . . ." Walker went on, turning to Maddie and his wife. "You feel free to go to bed and get some sleep. We won't be long. I just need a feel for where we'll be. I announced earlier that I was planning to see the venue today. If it hadn't been for the current situation, which I will address, I would've been here hours ago, and we'd all be on our way to bed by now. I won't ask for much of your time, I promise," he said.

There was a scramble as people rose and the security forces split up; Angela and Meg were staying, while Jackson and Matt would be accompanying the congressman. Matt had a moment to speak with Meg before they left.

"I don't like this," he said. "Walker should stay in the house, which is surrounded by security."

"What can really go wrong? Who knows that he's going out there except the people who are here now? Walker himself is probably not at risk," she added.

"Cell phones. That information could've been shared with anyone by now," Matt said. Although they were alone in her room, he spoke softly, since Maddie had asked that the door between Meg's room and hers be kept open. She and Kendra were playing gin rummy in Maddie's room.

"But like I said, I don't think the congressman is in danger." She hesitated. "I know forensic units and our people and various police forces are investigating how those tongues could have shown up at the Walkers' house and at Ellery's. I have to assume that Ellery Manheim was set up by someone else, someone close to Walker. Whoever did this has been smart — but not smart enough. Eventually he's going to get caught."

"I don't like it, not one bit," Matt said again. "A sharpshooter in the right place . . ."

"I wish I could leave the house tonight," Meg told him. "Slip out while they're sleeping and you're gone. Lara's nearby, Matt, and I'm afraid she's close to death."

"Don't think that Jackson doesn't have people out there looking for her. The local police have also been advised. People are searching for her right now, people who know the area. Meanwhile, we'll keep our eyes on everyone in Walker's retinue. You'll be here, and I'll be with Walker and whoever he brings. No one, at least no one in that group, will have a chance to get to Lara tonight — wherever she may be. And the minute this situation is clear, we'll do nothing else until we do find her."

He didn't add the words *dead or alive,* which lay silently between them.

He gave her a kiss on the head. "I guess no fooling around tonight," he said. "Considering that there isn't much privacy."

"I suspect that's a good thing," she said. "Older people need their rest. *All* of them."

"Ouch. I'm only thirty-six," he said.

"An age of vast experience, as you frequently remind me."

He grinned and left her. "Don't wait up. Walker says he'll be quick, but I doubt it. And get some sleep. There'll be plenty of security throughout the night, but keep the Glock by your side."

"First thing I learned," she assured him.

Killer barked and wagged his tail as the two of them looked down at him.

"Take Killer with you, Matt," Meg said. "A dog has instincts people don't. He might be the deciding factor if something does go wrong, if someone *is* out there."

"If it makes you feel better, I'll take the dog."

"It does."

The party assembled downstairs. Meg stayed upstairs, watching, gazing out her window as they all got into cars. Walker would ride with Nathan Oliver, and Joe Brighton would remain at the house. Two members of the Capitol police were on guard in the house. Two would accompany Walker and Nathan Oliver, with Jackson and Matt following in their own vehicle. Two local police officers would lead the procession.

It really was a lot for one man, who was still no more than a possible blip on the presidential radar . . .

Meg watched the campaign manager, Nathan Oliver, leave with Walker.

The man was scary. Who the hell had a campaign manager who looked like he could take down an MMA fighter with a single move?

She wanted to call Matt back; she wanted to tell him she felt uneasy, that she sensed something was going to happen. She told herself that she shouldn't be afraid for him; he'd been through the military and he'd worked as an agent in the field for over a decade.

Angela walked up the stairs and met her out on the landing when the others had departed. "You all right?" she asked Meg.

"Doing fine. Maddie's playing cards. I promised I'd keep the door open between the rooms."

"I meant about Lara," Angela said. "Matt may have told you that we have agents here now, searching for Lara. They're not you, of course. After the speech tomorrow, you'll be free to join that search. We don't give up, Meg. We've never yet given up on a case, especially when a life is at risk."

"Thank you, and you're right — I feel I should be out there, too. But . . . I know I have to have faith in others. Maddie asked for me specifically, and I'm fine. As long as one of us is around at all times with a view on every member of Walker's party, I can manage."

"On a different but related subject . . . I hear from Matt that you bent a few rules today."

"Bent rules? Don't be silly! We had to chase after our dog. Well, whatever we did, it was to no avail, I'm afraid."

Angela shook her head. "It just means that we now know where Lara *isn't*. And that's a step forward."

I'm afraid we'll find her tomorrow, after the

speech, so no one will hear about her body being discovered and connect her with Congressman Walker.

Meg didn't say the words out loud. Instead, she told Angela, "I was close to her today. I know it. But we went through every inch of that basement. We looked for tunnels. We looked everywhere."

"Try to get some rest tonight," Angela said. "I'll see you in the morning."

Meg hurried back to her own room, smiling at the officer from the Capitol police who was on guard in the hall.

" 'Night, Special Agent Murray."

"Good night." She smiled, waving at him. She realized she liked the sound of her title. She hadn't had time to think about it yet.

In her room, she walked over to the half-open door. The card game was still going on.

"Everything okay?" she asked the two women.

"She cheats," Kendra Walker said, pointing her finger.

"I do not! She's a con artist!" Maddie joked in return.

Kendra laughed. "Well, I'm off to bed. Have a good night, ladies." As she left the room, Maddie yawned.

"You all right?" Meg asked.

"I'm happy as a lark." Looking at Meg, she suddenly frowned. "You've got something gray stuck in your hair."

"Gray?" Meg touched her head. *Spiderweb.*

"Hmm. I must've, uh, leaned against a wall somewhere. Anyway, if you're okay and going to sleep, I'll take a shower. Sleep well. Don't forget, I'll be just over there, with a Glock by my side — and I scored higher than the boys at the shooting range."

"Good night. And thanks."

"No problem." She was glad she'd so recently come from the academy. She was used to sharing accommodations, and the open door didn't bother her at all.

Still, she walked into the bathroom fully dressed in the sweats she'd be wearing to bed. She grabbed a hanger for her shirt and jacket and, undressing, pulled her Glock and its small holster from her waistband. She set them on the back of the commode, then hung up her clothing. After that, she brushed her teeth and stepped into the shower, armed with soap, shampoo and conditioner.

The water pressure was strong, the water nice and hot. She let it pour over her as she contemplated the day. It seemed almost impossible that she hadn't found Lara;

she'd been so certain that the ruined house was going to hold some kind of dank, dark prison.

But it hadn't.

She washed her hair and put conditioner on it, closing her eyes as she rinsed.

And in that moment she was attacked.

Her eyes were closed; the water had drowned out any sound. She'd never known that someone was coming; she would never have believed anyone would come after her in this house.

She didn't have time to chastise herself for her stupidity. She never even heard the shower curtain open. Hands went around her head and a rag soaked with chloroform was over her face before she could inhale to scream, before she could begin to fight.

There was an instant of fury at herself, but no time to fear, not even time to know she was going to die.

There was just nothing.

16

Matt had voted for Ian Walker. He hadn't known the man personally; he'd watched him speak and thought he was an excellent speaker and that he had solid, thoroughly researched plans. Of course, he usually saw him with Congressman Hubbard, and most people had imagined that when the time was right, the two of them would make a formidable ticket, Hubbard for president with Walker as his VP.

Hubbard's death had changed all that — and put Walker in the forefront.

That night, all he could think was that the congressman was a major pain in the ass.

Walker insisted on seeing the speaking platform and dais; he wanted to see where every person would be sitting, his wife and Maddie — who was really more important on this occasion than Kendra, since she was a beloved public figure. Then he wanted to know where every security team member would be.

He'd promised they'd be brief, but it was a good two hours before he and his security returned to the MacAndrew.

They were met by the security forces watching the house who assured them that the evening had been without incident. In the house, he found a man from the Capitol police force in the parlor, along with Joe Brighton.

"All quiet here?" Matt asked, holding Killer on a tight leash.

"Quiet as can be," Brighton replied. "The ladies all went to sleep. I'm assuming they wanted their beauty rest so they could be up bright and early tomorrow."

"I'll take over on watch here," Nathan told Joe. "You can spell me around three or four, all right?"

"I think we have enough security around here that you guys don't need to stay up," Walker said. "I have to admit that I was shaken by those tongues showing up. Obviously, someone really hates me or wants to see me go down. But yeah, you could all get some sleep. Me, I'm heading up to be with my wife."

Jackson nodded at Matt; he was free to go to bed. He'd check on Meg first.

Upstairs, he found that Meg had locked

her bedroom door. Smart move, he thought. She had to be safe in there.

But Killer, trotting beside him, wasn't satisfied.

The dog scratched at Meg's door and whined, then started jumping on Matt's legs, insistent that he do something, that he get the door open.

"Everything okay?" the Capitol police cop asked from the end of the hall. "The dog's going to wake everyone."

"I just want to check on Agent Murray. If the dog is upset, there's even more reason for me to do so."

"Knock on the door. I know she's inside there. I watched her go in and haven't seen her leave."

He knocked as softly as he could, and then harder. There was no response.

Matt moved down the hall to the door to Maddie's room. He tried the door. It, too, was locked.

By then, others began to come out of their rooms. Jackson and Angela, Kendra and Ian Walker, and then Nathan Oliver.

"I need this door opened," Matt explained. He had to make sure both of them were fine. He didn't give a damn about anyone's opinion or the consequences. He kicked the door to Maddie's room open and threw on the light.

Maddie Hubbard was in bed. She was sleeping deeply; she didn't wake up, even with the sound of her door being kicked in or the bright light suddenly streaming into her room.

Was the woman dead?

Matt rushed to her side and felt for a pulse; she was alive. He shook her arm, lightly at first. "Mrs. Hubbard. Maddie." She still didn't wake. He shook harder. Her eyes slowly opened, and she stared at him with confusion.

"You're all right," he said briefly.

He left her to the others and walked through the adjoining door into Meg's room. Killer was already there, barking insanely.

Matt turned on the light. At first, he thought she was in the bed. Then he discovered that it was just pillows and wadded-up blankets.

He looked at her window. It was wide-open. The evening breeze was gusting in.

And Meg was gone.

Meg woke slowly, fighting what seemed like swarms of spiderwebs in her mind.

Then she became aware of the cold, hard ground beneath her and the dank smell of earth. She was cold — naked, shaking, shivering. Next, she became aware of the wet feel of her hair, clumped around her body and her face. She tried to move, but it was difficult; her limbs felt as numb as her mind. She had to make an effort to get her eyelids to open, and when they did, she wasn't sure if they were truly open or not. She was surrounded by darkness. She tried to rise and realized she had to do it slowly. She wanted to leap to a defensive posture immediately, but it wasn't that easy.

She wasn't dead; she hadn't had her throat slit. She was in a dark place, lying on a dirt floor that felt like earth. She was cold because she was naked, and she couldn't have been there too long because her hair was still really wet. She remembered that she'd been taken in the shower.

She had nothing — no gun, no weapon, nothing — including clothes. She was somewhere . . . near the MacAndrew farmhouse. She had to be.

She managed to come to her knees, and then to stand carefully. She held very still, listening, but she could hear nothing at all. The night was completely silent.

Where the hell was she?

She reached in front of her, trying to discover what she could feel. Just more dirt.

She inched forward. Her mind raced in several directions. It was impossible! Impossible that someone had kidnapped her from the MacAndrew house. Her door had been open to the next room. There'd been a policeman in the hall. There was security all around the house.

Impossible! Yet here she was.

But she wasn't dead yet!

She gritted her teeth, fighting cold and fear. She reminded herself that she'd been trained, that she was in excellent shape.

And that Matt would return to the house . . . and he would discover she wasn't there, and he'd start a search that would continue until he found her. She *would* be found.

Unless the killer returned first.

She stood still, halting her blind groping for a moment. She remembered when they'd been at the Virginia Monument, when she'd sat on the step and closed her eyes and thought of Lara. She'd touched Lara's mind somehow . . . and she had seen this place. Dank and dark, filled with the rich scent of earth.

Lara had been here.

She dropped back to her knees. She had to take care with every movement. She couldn't afford to hurt herself. She began to crawl, reaching out tentatively, trying to feel for what was directly ahead of her. Finding only more earth.

Then she touched stone, and she was suddenly sure she knew exactly where she was.

The mill. The ruined mill by the stream that passed near the condemned property, which had recently been purchased by Walker's company. And Lara was here somewhere.

She was right! She heard a soft moan, so weak it was barely audible. She had to force herself to pinpoint the sound — and to move slowly and carefully toward it. Inch by inch. There was a stone object to her left, one of the old grindstones, she thought. She hit metal next and figured it was part of the mechanism. She moved around it with painstaking care.

And then, finally, she hit flesh.

Lara.

She'd found her at last. "Lara!" she said loudly. "Lara, Lara!"

The body stirred.

And then she heard her name.

"Meg! Meg, I knew you'd find me."

Meg let out a cry of relief and blindly slid her arms around her friend. "Yes, yes, I'm here. We're going to be okay."

Yes, they were going to be okay.

As soon as she figured a way out of here.

Lara had almost no voice left at all. When she spoke, it was in a scratchy whisper. "I don't know where we are. I was on my way home in DC and I called you. I was afraid because of that girl who'd been killed — her throat slit — I saw a van and I started to dial emergency. But I decided I was being ridiculous. Then I saw a car, a black sedan, and I thought that Walker had sent someone to see that I got home okay. And I walked over to the car and . . ." She paused for a moment, and the silence frightened Meg, but then she heard her friend draw another breath to continue. "Someone had been sent, all right. I didn't even see his face before I realized he'd come for me. I ran. I ran but he threw himself on me and then . . . then I was out, and I woke up here."

"So you don't know who it was?" Meg asked with dismay. "Or does it matter? Is Walker's whole household involved?"

"No, no, I don't believe so. We were in his office late that night — the five of us — fighting about the platform and I said something about how convenient it was that Congressman Hubbard was dead. Ian appeared to be shocked, then everyone was shouting that it was horrible that I could've said such a thing. It occurred to me that we'd all been at a picnic with him to benefit a kids' program the day he died. Maddie was worried about her husband, reminding him about his heart condition. He patted his suit pocket and said he always had his pills with him, he'd be fine. Meg, I'd started to wonder if someone that day had gotten hold of his pills and switched them with something else."

Lara was shaking as she spoke, her words a hoarse whisper. She was burning up with fever, Meg thought. She had to get them out of here.

Lara seemed to read her mind. "I've been all around this place," she said. "Over and over again. We're deep in the ground somewhere. There's no way out. There's stone in the middle and earthen walls all around. It's impossible."

"We're in the mill," Meg told her, "the ruins of the old corn mill."

"What old corn mill?"

"It's in Gettysburg. We're in Gettysburg, Pennsylvania. And I know exactly where we are. I wasn't very far away, searching for you today. No farther than a football field."

"Gettysburg . . ." Lara said. "I was in DC and now I'm in Gettysburg . . . How are we going to get out? We can't scale the walls. Trust me, I tried. At the beginning, I had a lot more strength. I tried, Meg. I screamed, I yelled, I tested the walls. They're just dirt, so you can't crawl up them."

"There are two of us now, Lara. We can get to that stone in the middle and one of us can climb on the other and —"

"Oh, Meg, I have no strength left! I can barely move."

"I'll lift you."

"I don't even know if I can stand up." She struggled to sit, grabbing Meg for support. Meg held her, and Lara groaned. "I was going to ask if you had an aspirin. You don't even have any clothes. Neither do I. No purse, no aspirin."

"We're getting out of here," Meg said desperately. She got to her feet and pulled Lara to hers. "I can be the muscle for both of us." She swore, supporting Lara as she staggered along. "Let's make our way to the stone. It's a container — a big stone container for the corn to go in . . . If you can get to the ledge and use the stone as leverage, I can crawl up."

"Oh, Meg, I'll try anything, but . . . I'm broken here."

"You're not broken, Lara. You're a fighter! You've fought for the underdog all your life.

Well, we're the underdogs here. Fight! We have to fight!"

"I'm ready when you are," Lara said on a shaky breath.

Meg led the way to the container for the corn that was once ground there. "Be careful. The mechanism must be faulty now. We don't want to end up milled," Meg said.

"Just get to the ledge, get over it to the other side so it acts like a counterweight, and I'll give you my arm," Lara told her.

"Yes."

"You have the strength . . ."

"Yes," Meg said firmly. She was glad of the brutal hours of training she'd gone through at the academy. She was strong. They were going to survive.

She raised Lara up, trying to angle her to stand on her shoulders. Lara giggled softly.

"What?" Meg asked.

Lara's giggle was of an hysterical sob. "This would make one helluva porn movie, wouldn't you say? Maybe a snuff-porn movie," she added grimly.

"Get up there. If anyone is getting snuffed, it's those responsible for all the deaths — and this situation."

"*All* the deaths?" Lara repeated. "All what deaths?"

Meg realized her friend didn't know about

the three women who'd died since her disappearance. This didn't seem the time to tell her. She didn't reply.

"Get up there!" she said instead, balancing her weight, trying to get Lara onto her shoulders, then standing, so Lara could grab the lip of the stone container.

"It's just beyond my reach," Lara said.

"Stretch!" Meg ordered her.

"I — I can't . . ."

"Stretch, damn you! I am not dying down here!" Meg snapped. "And neither are you!"

A second later, she felt Lara's weight lift from her shoulders. And after another few seconds, when she fumbled around in the darkness, she found Lara's hand. She took a deep breath. She was in good shape, excellent shape, and she prayed she could hoist her own weight with enough power to drag herself up to the ledge.

She clasped Lara's hand and braced against the stone with her feet. It wasn't going to be enough.

"Hang on!" she called to Lara. She took another deep breath and assessed her situation. She tried again. No, it really wasn't going to work. But then she heard Lara grunting, swearing, sobbing. She pressed her feet against the stone and used the leverage to hoist her own weight. She freed one hand from Lara's grasp and reached . . .

And she had it; she had the ledge. With tremendous force she pulled herself up.

They were still in stygian darkness, perched precariously on the ledge. Balancing carefully, she began to feel around. She found the platform by the ledge and dragged herself over, hoping that the wooden flooring would hold.

It did. She reached back for Lara, telling her to follow the sound of her voice. A minute later, she felt her friend's hand. They were both on the platform.

Meg lay back for a moment, breathing hard. And then she realized that she was seeing a pinprick of light. The moon was peeking through a hole in the mill's roof.

The light seemed to burst into her like a thrill of hope. She squeezed Lara's hand. There was no response.

"Lara!"

"Meg . . . I . . . I can hardly breathe."

"We're close, so close to help. Get up! Come on!"

Meg stood. She held Lara, who could barely make it. Her friend had obviously used the last of her strength to pull her up.

She kept still, not moving at all, and let Lara regain her balance. Her eyes adjusted to that little bit of light. There was a break, she saw now, in the giant barnlike doors to the place. Despite the rough flooring — the pebbles, splinters and everything else on the ragged wooden floorboards — she headed for the door, half carrying, half dragging Lara.

When she got to the doors and pushed her way through, the moonlight seemed so bright she had to blink against it.

But she'd been correct. They were at the ruined mill. And beyond it, she could see the ruins of the old house and, beyond that, the Yankee reenactment camp, quiet now in the night.

"Come on! I can see help just over there!" she told Lara.

She realized then that her friend had passed out, that Lara's entire weight was hanging on her. She gritted her teeth and lifted her up, starting across the overgrown grasses and bracken and through the trees. She was going to live — and see that Lara lived, too.

"Oh!" Maddie said in confusion. "Meg is gone? Gone — how could she be gone? She said she'd stay with me! Oh, dear, she must be so worried about her friend that she decided if I was sleeping she'd go out and look for her!"

"She didn't go past me!" the Capitol man insisted.

"No, it's obvious." Kendra Walker grimaced. "She climbed out her window and somehow got down to the back porch, which is right underneath this room. So much for the security people. Great job! She went out a window and disappeared."

"Meg didn't go out a window — not on purpose," Matt said firmly.

"I didn't hear a thing, and I came up and knocked on Maddie's door to check on her and she was fine. I assumed Agent Murray was asleep in the next room," Joe Brighton said. "Face it, Bosworth. She figured that if she slipped out by night, no one would know."

"Her gun and shoulder bag are gone," Angela said quietly.

"I don't care what's gone. Meg wouldn't leave. I know her. She wouldn't just leave. Even if she felt she should be looking for Lara Mayhew."

"All right, let's get out there and search for her," Jackson said.

"Search for her?" Ian Walker still seemed dazed. "That's . . . that's rather futile, isn't it? She'll come back when she's ready."

"Congressman Walker, you have plenty of protection here. My people and I will be heading out to search for our colleague," Jackson announced.

"But . . ." Kendra began.

"If my agent is sure that his partner didn't leave willingly, I believe him, and that's that," Jackson said.

"We could have your badge for this!" Kendra protested. "What if she *was* taken? You're going to abandon us? Maybe that's just what the kidnappers want! They want us to be defenseless, and if you go . . ."

"You're far from defenseless," Jackson interrupted. "Now, let's go. Matt, you lead."

"Mr. Crow is right," Ian agreed. "Kendra, we're fine. Joe, Nathan, you get out there, too, and join the search."

Matt called the dog. "Come on, Killer, time to find our girl," he said quietly.

Killer raced along with him. Downstairs, Jackson spoke to the men at the checkpoint, who'd seen nothing. But they'd been watching the road to the house, not the house itself. He returned to Matt. "The local authorities are all on the hunt. Where to?"

"The ruins of the old house. Meg was certain Lara was nearby when we were there. She *saw* her, deep in the earth." Jackson would, of course, know what he meant. "There has to be something that we missed."

"Let's do it," Jackson said. "We'll take a few cars. We can split up as needed."

Matt was already headed for his car, Killer at his heels.

Meg staggered into the Yankee encampment; there seemed to be no one around. She fell to her knees holding Lara and then struggled back up again. She made her way to the medical tent. She knew that at least she'd find a cot and blankets for Lara.

She burst into the tent, which was as quiet as the rest of the camp. The encampment tents couldn't be far and she'd venture over there later. But first, Lara.

She laid her friend on one of the surgical cots and wrapped a blanket around her. A Union doctor's uniform coat hung on the back of one of the chairs. She put it on; it was mammoth on her and scratchy — real wool, she remembered — but it was warm and it covered her. She looked around for something to conceal Lara. She'd have to leave her here alone while she went to get help, and she was afraid to do that.

Matt would have checked on her when he came back to the B and B. She was very certain that no one had broken into the MacAndrew house; the killer had been inside all the time. Matt would be on the hunt for her, but the killer would be, too.

"Halt! Who goes there?" she heard.

She turned around. A man in a private's uniform, carrying a lantern and an Enfield, was staring at her from just outside the tent.

Help was here.

"Sir, my name is Meg Murray, Special Agent Meg Murray. I need you to alert the camp. Please! My friend may be dying."

"Is this some kind of prank?" the man demanded, dropping his Civil War stance. "This is private property specifically rented for the encampment. It's not a playground for college games."

"This is no game!" Meg shouted. "I'm an agent with the federal government and I need your help now! Go and alert the camp. Get the cops here. Now! Do you understand me?"

The young man had come into the tent and saw Lara lying on the cot. He looked at Meg again, his eyes wide. "Yes, yes, I'm going right now." He left them at a run. Meg walked over and peered anxiously at Lara. She was so flushed, and when Meg touched her cheek, she felt as though she were on fire. But an ambulance would be here soon.

She was startled to hear a *thunk* — and then a sound that was like a groan, and every nerve in her body seemed to shriek

432

out a warning.

They'd been found. And not by Matt and the Krewe.

She had to do something; it was only a matter of time before someone came upon them. In the dim light filtering in from outside, she surveyed the surgical tent.

And then her eyes lit on the scalpel. A weapon, of sorts.

Meg picked it up and edged over to the flap of the tent. She heard a whisper, but couldn't identify the speaker. "They're here. They're here. Dammit, find them!"

"You said to keep them alive, you idiot!" The voices were low, but this one was oddly familiar.

"Rotting bodies smell. They can't be found until after . . ." She couldn't make out the rest of the sentence.

She strained to hear. There were two of them. If they were armed, she might not be able to bring both of them down with her scalpel.

She had to lead them away from Lara.

Meg drew the blanket up higher, hiding her friend's face, praying that Lara would look like a mannequin in the surgeon's displays.

Then she made a point of rustling as she walked out of the tent. And to her relief, she heard the whispers again.

"That way!"

"Let's go."

"The house?" Jackson said. "We'll search it again."

Matt closed his eyes and tried to think, to concentrate, to will Meg to use whatever she had, whatever skill or intuition she possessed, to tell him where she was. When he opened his eyes, he was staring across at the ruins of the old mill. Killer stood beside him, whining anxiously.

Then the dog started to bark. "No, that way," Matt said.

Jackson stayed behind to begin another search of the farmhouse. Angela had already gone in.

Killer raced ahead and Matt followed. They reached the old mill and he threw open the old doors, letting the moonlight flood in. "Meg!" he shouted.

There was no answer, but Killer was barking and running in circles. Matt headed over to some of the old broken millstones and the machinery to the rear. He trained his flashlight on the area; there was a deep pit with stone vats for the corn to be milled around a threshing floor.

"Meg!" he shouted her name again. The

sound of his voice, loud as it was, seemed muted. He found himself remembering their conversation with Sylvia Avery earlier that day — and how people had sworn they'd heard the ghosts of the battlefield crying out.

They hadn't heard ghosts; they'd heard the living. Lara Mayhew, begging for help.

But no one was here now.

"Killer, find Meg. Get her scent. Find Meg, boy, come on, you can do it."

The dog sniffed the floor in a fury. Then he dashed out.

As Matt hurried after him, he saw something shimmering on the ground. He paused to pick it up.

And then he knew. They had all missed it, but who would ever suspect . . .

The killers had been there before them. He could only pray that Meg had made her way out.

The dog was racing across the field toward the Union encampment, exactly where Meg would have gone for help. As he ran past the farmhouse, he shouted for Jackson and Angela.

He didn't wait for them but kept on running, his heart thundering in his ears.

He realized in that moment that he couldn't bear to lose her.

No. He wouldn't lose her. It was that simple.

Meg wasn't sure where to run. As she moved forward, she had to ignore the cuts on her feet — and the pain that streaked through her as she stepped on a nail by the blacksmith's tent.

She dashed by one of the sutlers' displays; it had been covered with canvas for the night but someone had left a pair of cavalry boots beside it. She swooped them up as she ran, trying to decide what direction to take. She heard something fall behind her; a rack set up for drying clothes at the laundry, she thought. They were close.

The soldiers' tents, where the hard-core reenactors were sleeping, were to the right, tucked away from the rest of the encampment. The road was the other way. If she tried running across the field to the soldiers' tents, she'd be seen. If she made for the road, she'd be an easy target, as well.

Definitely an easy target — for anyone with a gun.

And her pursuers would be armed. One of them, at least — she could tell by the voice — was security for Congressman Walker.

But the other . . .

She felt she should have recognized the whisper. There was something that teased at her mind. Something she couldn't quite place . . .

Matt reached the encampment with Killer.

The dog came to a dead stop, and Matt slowed just in time to keep from tripping over a body. He hunkered down to see that it was a young man dressed in a private's uniform. The sentry? There was a bloody gash on the man's forehead; Matt raised his voice and shouted for Jackson — who came pounding along behind him.

Jackson was already on his phone. "We need ambulances . . . every cop in the vicinity. Union encampment by the old mill and the ruins of the farmhouse," he said quickly, and crouched beside the body, too. "He's alive?"

"Yes, has a pulse," Matt said.

Angela was almost there and Killer was running toward the surgeon's tent where they'd watched the doctor and listened to the medical lecture. "I've got this — go," Jackson said.

Matt stood and started running again, following the dog, Angela directly behind him.

He burst into the tent, Glock drawn. There was no one inside the tent.

He saw a form on the cot. He stepped forward, his heart in his throat, and pulled the blanket away.

A woman lay there, blond hair filthy and matted, naked. She was covered in earth and dust.

Lara. Lara Mayhew. She hadn't gotten herself here. Meg must have done it.

Angela came into the tent and rushed over, immediately checking for a pulse. "She's alive. High fever. I'm going to get water, cool her down while we wait for the ambulance. Find Meg."

Matt nodded, whirled around and stepped out of the tent.

At least he hadn't tripped over her body yet!

But, he thought, *I'd know if she was dead! I'd know it.*

Meg was alive and she was out there, not far away, running by herself. And she might not have discovered yet what he'd figured out. Might not realize who was after her.

Killer barked.

Matt turned to the dog. "Killer, which way?"

She could have run to the soldiers' tents; she'd expect to find help there. And whether or not the men had their old guns loaded with black powder, those guns had bayonets attached to them.

But that part of the encampment was across a barren expanse of field. A sharpshooter could easily pick her off.

The same with the road. It, too, would leave her exposed, a target.

He took a moment to do what he always told Meg to do — concentrate. Envision her before him. See her, try to reach out for her.

He thought he heard her speaking . . . inside his mind. It was as though her mind were connecting with his. He could almost hear her reasoning, weighing her choices carefully.

I'm coming, Meg, I'm coming!

Killer was sitting by the tent, staring toward the woods.

Matt looked over, too. And as he did, figures began to appear before him. Soldiers. Some in Rebel uniforms.

And some dressed in Union garb. They were there by the woods, Private Murphy front and center. They were there, just as if they were assembled for war, except now they were no longer waging war against one another. They stayed on this hallowed field; perhaps they'd learned peace in death, as those who had survived learned peace, after the war, slowly and through the decades that had followed.

They beckoned to him. And he began to run again.

Once in the camouflage of the trees, Meg paused to catch her breath, still clutching the oversize boots. She wondered how it had all been pulled off, and started putting together the few facts she was certain of with what she'd begun to figure out. She knew that help was on the way; she could see that an alarm was being raised and that men were beginning to stir at the camp.

She allowed herself a fleeting smile. She could swear that she heard Matt's voice in her mind, reassuring her.

I'm coming, Meg. I'm coming!

He was out there; he was close. And he wouldn't be alone. The Krewe was a team. They were a team and they believed in one another.

Yes, help was out there.

But she didn't dare cry out; the killers were among those who might be seen as rescuers by anyone who happened to come upon them. She had no doubt that, even with other people, they might well have an opportunity to kill her before she could speak. Before she could reveal what they were . . .

She leaned against a tree and got her feet into the boots. When she'd done that, she moved deeper into the woods. She moved as quietly as she could, trying to keep from cracking branches or giving any other indication of her whereabouts.

She'd gone in about fifty feet when she came through the trees and to a clearing.

"Meg?"

She heard her name whispered by a terrified voice. A female voice.

She didn't reply; she waited.

Then she heard a soft, frightened sob. "Help me . . . someone help me, please." Looking around the trees, she saw that Kendra Walker, muddied and disheveled, was slumped by a tree, tears streaming down her face.

"Help me, oh, Lord, someone . . . help me!" she wailed again.

Meg was shocked. Had whoever spirited her out of the MacAndrew house taken Kendra, too? Had the killer finally snapped and decided to take out his boss's wife, along with all those who'd seemed to threaten him?

Or was Walker himself behind it all — and had he chosen tonight to rid himself of another burden?

The cries were heart-wrenching.

Meg crouched low and inched toward her. "Mrs. Walker — Kendra, you have to be quiet. Help is coming," she whispered, "but we need to be quiet until we see that it's — it's the Krewe that has come. Get up, please. We have to get farther into the woods."

"I — I can't!" Kendra told her. "My ankle! I had to get away when I realized it was . . . Joe. Oh, God, it was Joe all along, Joe Brighton!"

"Get up and lean on me. We need to move into the woods, where we can hide until we know it's safe."

Meg started toward Kendra but she stopped abruptly. She could see someone there in the night, slowly appearing.

It was the ghost she had seen before. The ghost of Genie Gonzales.

And Genie spoke.

"Don't trust her!" Genie said.

Kendra evidently didn't see Genie; she turned to look around, to find out where Meg was.

And then everything about her changed. The mask of tears was gone. She had a hard, vicious expression on her face and she seemed furious — not hurt at all.

"Damn you, Joe, get the little bitch!"

Meg whipped around to see Joe Brighton

442

behind her, wielding a long sharp knife. He smiled at her.

"Joe Brighton," Meg said. "Not a surprise."

The man acted confused. "Not Joe, it's Slash. Slash McNeil, at your service."

"Joe, quit acting like an ass. This isn't the time to fool around. Kill her! Kill the bitch and let's be done with this!"

"Slash," the man said, still smiling at Meg. It was a bizarre smile, cheerful and self-satisfied. "Slash — and I've been waiting."

He had a Bowie knife; she had a scalpel. He was a fit, strong man. But he couldn't get behind her to drug her again and carry her out a window and eventually down into a deep dark hole. They were face-to-face.

"I've watched. I've waited," he said. "Slash . . . Slash doesn't like playing with pills and leaving women alive in the dirt. Slash likes to feel the knife on flesh. Now . . . I have my chance."

"Damn you, Joe!" Kendra shouted.

"Shut up, woman!" Brighton growled, never taking his eyes off Meg.

"That's what happens when you deal with men who are sociopaths or psychotics," Kendra said. She shrugged, glancing at Meg. "Oh, well. I don't care if Joe has fun thinking he's the world's most famous —

uncaught! — serial killer. Slash. I got wind of his little idiosyncrasies, including murder, when I caught him one night about to attack a coed. I might have died myself if I hadn't convinced him I needed someone like him. My husband is a good man, you see, and a total fool — like most good men. He didn't see that he'd never get anywhere while Hubbard was alive. Now, Hubbard, that was tricky. But we pulled it off, didn't we . . . Slash?"

"We pulled it off," Slash agreed. "And the tongues were a smart idea, right? People can't talk without tongues, so that was my signature." He grinned. "I've read every serial killer study out there, so I know about signatures. Putting them at Manheim's place and yours — that was clever of you. It confused everyone." He sighed. "You should've at least let me take Lara's tongue," he told Kendra.

That chilled Meg deeply.

I'm probably about to die myself. I should be scared.

But without intending to, Kendra was giving her time — time to come up with a plan, a way to escape. It was a good thing that Kendra seemed to think Meg needed to know just how clever she'd been.

And that she, not her husband, was the

real power! "Yes, Slash, the tongues were a great plan of yours," Kendra said. "I always told Slash — even before I knew he was Slash! — that people, certain people, couldn't be allowed to talk. I guess that gave him the idea of taking their tongues when he started."

And Meg realized that Kendra Walker was as much of a sociopath as Brighton, and beyond any doubt, a monster.

She didn't want to be the vice president's wife; she wanted to be the first lady.

She'd gotten this man to do the work for her. Knowing he, too, was a monster, she'd exploited his sickness for her own gain. The man before her had now dropped his mask, just as Kendra had dropped hers — but what lay behind his eyes was true insanity. Behind Kendra's . . . lay a cold and psychopathic degree of control.

Which of them was the more dangerous? Meg wondered.

She had to move. She propelled herself into the clearing, toward him, scalpel raised and ready, and she caught him hard, right in the belly. It didn't kill him, but he was wounded and he was down. She could run again, scream for her life . . . and look for help while he gathered himself. She could try jumping on him, slashing him with the scalpel, but she'd learned in the academy to judge the strength of an opponent and take evasive measures when necessary.

In this case, it was necessary. She turned to make a calculated retreat.

She was stunned when she suddenly went flying herself.

Kendra Walker was standing over her, having tripped her, pure and simple.

"I would've told you more," Kendra said, scowling down at Meg. "What do I care now? Okay, so I like an audience. But you have become a major pain in the ass." She turned to the killer she commanded and said, "Joe, Slash, whatever the fuck, get over here now and finish this!"

Meg heard Brighton lumbering to his feet, groaning and cursing and coming for her.

The ghost soldiers of Gettysburg moved swiftly through the trees — literally through them at times — and Matt struggled to keep up. He couldn't even see Killer; the dog was all but buried in the tall grass, bracken and brush that covered the forest floor. His heart was beating furiously. He still didn't know exactly who else was involved, but he did know that Kendra Walker was in on it — whether her husband was aware of it or not. Matt couldn't tell yet just how much Walker grasped about what had been going on. Matt knew for a fact that it was Joe Brighton who'd done the killing. Ellery Manheim had been cleared of the murders — although he might prove to have been involved, too. The actual killing, however, had been done by one hand, and one hand alone. And Nathan Oliver, the giant who *looked* like a killer, had been with him and Congressman Walker when Meg was taken. As always, appearances could be deceptive . . .

Had Ian Walker planned the events tonight — to allow his wife and his henchmen time to slip Meg out of the house — and to ensure that when she found Lara, she could be with her friend for eternity?

He didn't know yet — he just knew who was involved because he'd found Kendra Walker's pendant on the ground at the mill. The silver pendant of the Washington Monument she'd toyed with when they'd met . . . At the moment, he didn't know and didn't care if she'd been working on her own or with Walker. Or if, perhaps, she'd acted on some remark he might have made about what would make his climb to the White House easier. She'd recognized the one man among her husband's retinue who would suit her purposes, a man who'd been willing to slash women to death in order to distract everyone, including media and police, from the murder that meant so much — that of Congressman Hubbard.

And Lara had suspected. She'd sensed that something wasn't right. And she'd been smart enough to realize that she'd needed to disappear, but she hadn't realized how quickly.

Running through the woods, he heard voices just ahead.

He burst through the trees to see that Joe Brighton was standing over Meg. Protocol said he should draw his Glock and tell the man to halt and drop his weapon.

But that would give Joe Brighton time to carry out his deed if he didn't drop his knife. And Matt couldn't risk shooting at such close range. Especially since Brighton wouldn't care if he died in killing Meg.

And then Meg would be dead.

Matt didn't call out a warning. He hurled himself straight at Brighton, bringing them both down a few feet past Meg. He'd taken the man by surprise; the Bowie knife flew into the dirt. He heard Meg scramble to her feet. The man beneath him was struggling to reach his own gun. Matt slammed him with a right hook against his jaw.

He turned just as Meg kicked the Bowie knife far from the man's grasp. Kendra let out a howl that sounded like that of a dying wildcat; she leaped at Meg.

But Meg didn't need help. She caught the woman by her shoulders and threw her hard against a tree. Kendra staggered to her feet. Meg headed back for her, a ball of energy and fury.

Meg had a damned good right hook herself.

Kendra Walker went down, sagging against the tree.

Matt heard Jackson's voice. He stood over the fallen Joe Brighton, panting and gasping as the ghosts of the soldiers moved through the forest like . . . wraiths.

He looked at Meg and she looked back at him, then scampered across the clearing, ridiculously clad in a too-big officer's jacket and giant boots. She flung herself into his arms and said, "I knew you'd come. I knew you'd come."

At their feet Killer barked excitedly.

Matt held Meg in his arms as if she were the most precious being on earth — which she was, to him. And then, as Jackson erupted through the trees and ran over to them, Matt ducked to pick up the little dog.

Jackson glanced at them and then at the two on the ground and nodded his relief. He stepped forward, ready to handcuff

Brighton and Kendra Walker.

Matt turned slightly. He smiled and lifted a hand. Soldiers in blue, and soldiers in butternut and gray, were disappearing, becoming part of the trees.

Private Murphy, inclining his head gravely, was the last to go. Matt mouthed the words *Thank you,* and the apparitions in the forest disappeared into the mists of night.

EPILOGUE

Meg was glad to be at Matt's town house — and to have Lara there, too. It was Lara's first night out of the hospital. Due to exposure and dehydration, she had pneumonia, and although she was still sick, she was doing much better. Nancy Cooper was driving up to be with her beloved niece, and they'd have dinner here, with Matt and Meg. Then Nancy would be with Lara when she returned to her home by the Capitol and packed up.

After that, Lara was going to Florida. She wanted to lie low and she no longer wanted to be in the public eye. She'd been offered a job at a new dolphin research facility near Miami, a small place where her PR skills would be vital. She'd always had an interest in marine zoology, as well as politics, and it was important that the public understand that the staff weren't torturing dolphins; they were taking in the old and the wounded and doing research on dolphin intelligence while delighting children and adults alike with the social antics of the sea mammals.

"A scandal like this hasn't hit Washington since . . . ever!" Lara said, curled up in an armchair and sipping tea. "I'm still doubtful. I can't believe that Ian Walker had no clue whatsoever that his wife was so fixated on the White House — or that she was willing to commit murder to get there. Well, to arrange for murders to be committed. Or maybe she didn't see it as murder. But I heard them talking once. Kendra and Ian, that is. And she was telling him that he should be the one making the bid for the White House, not Congressman Hubbard. But he said that as long as Hubbard was running, he was second man on the ticket and that was that. And . . . the next thing I knew, Hubbard was dead. Heart attack. I vaguely suspected Ian — or one of his aides. But when I was with that trio — Ellery, Joe and Nathan — they all seemed to be okay. So, while I suspected *something,* what do you in a situation like that?

"The night we were working so late, he was finishing up his Gettysburg speech, and that's when I saw how much he intended to change his policies and . . . his changes did not support Congressman Hubbard's platform. I didn't know if those guys had anything to do with Hubbard's heart attack. Still, I felt I had to get away, try to figure it out, keep my distance from them."

She hesitated. "I had no idea at the time that Joe Brighton — *Slash McNeil* — had already decided that I might have to disappear. And that he was out there, murdering and mutilating other women, so there'd be a real trauma on the national scene and that people would believe that I'd either left — or been a victim of the killer. Never mind that he'd apparently found a . . . an obscene calling as a serial killer. What I still don't understand is why he didn't just kill me at the start."

Meg watched as Matt came around behind Lara's chair. "Lara, you don't remember much from that last night in Gettysburg. You couldn't. You were burning up with fever and then you were in the hospital. Kendra Walker never admitted to anything. She immediately demanded a lawyer, called us liars and said she'd been trying to save Meg because she suspected Joe of being a killer. She's sticking to her story, but I doubt she'll get away with it. The prosecutors are organizing their evidence and their case with a vengeance. Walker claims he's absolutely innocent — but whether he is or isn't, he's retired from politics now."

"I think he might have had a sick feeling that things weren't right," Meg said, "but from what I gathered that night, she always 'wore the pants' in their family. He wouldn't have questioned her. He would've done as he was told." She shook her head ruefully. "I'm still staggered by the fact that they managed to get me out of the house that night," she said, catching Matt's hand and smiling.

"I went through all of this with Jackson and Angela, trying to straighten out the details," Matt said. "Kendra played up to Maddie Hubbard all the time, and she made sure that Maddie left her door open so she could run in to 'check' on her and that she spent time with her, as well. None of the security forces noticed her going in and out, and there was quite a bit of commotion. So, apparently, when she'd supposedly gone to bed and you'd gone to your room, she went to Maddie's and had Joe follow her — with the chloroform," Matt said. "Maddie was out like a light. All they had to do was make sure that Joe could get you when you were either asleep — or in the shower. Kendra made all the plans, always had. She knew when to be with Hubbard, how and when to switch his pills, and yes, she did have to

454

hope he died when he didn't get his digitalis. What I *don't* think she initially realized was that she got a true madman to do her deeds. I think Joe would've been happy to cut her throat in the woods that night. He's gone completely mad now, says there is no Joe Brighton, that his name is Slash McNeil."

"I think Kendra's her own kind of psychopath," Lara said.

Matt nodded. "No argument there. Anyway, she made her mistake with you, Lara. She didn't want your body showing up right away. She wanted your remains tossed when the time was right and . . ."

He paused for a minute, then said quietly, ". . .and sufficiently decayed to make identification difficult at first. But she was afraid of Meg, too, since Meg — Lara's best friend — was an FBI agent. Somehow she figured that she could get rid of her that night in Gettysburg — and that we'd all believe Meg had thrown her career to the winds to go and look for her friend."

"But who arranged for Walker's company to buy the property by the mill? That was obviously all part of the plan," Meg said.

"Joe did — after Kendra said they should have it. Kendra arranged to rent the Mac-Andrew farmstead for the day of the speech. She chose the room assignments. Meg, do you remember that your window was right by a trellis that ran along the wall from the back porch? Well, he just climbed down it with you over his shoulder. While he was doing that, Kendra was outside, ever so sweetly checking with the security men there and making sure they were watching the road for traffic — or for anyone trying to sneak in. No one was looking for anyone to sneak *out.* Brighton got you outside, walked down the field to a little ATV he'd purchased and dumped you at the mill. I suspect," he continued, "that Kendra told Slash he could kill you both after Gettysburg. The speech would be over. There was no danger of the public not adoring Ian Walker, and all would be fine."

"Do you know why Kendra ordered one of the dead girls' tongues to show up at her house — and then in Ellery Manheim's desk?" Meg asked. "And at his house?"

"I think so," Matt replied. He offered them a grim smile. "Manheim really was innocent. Kendra wanted him out of the house. He might get too close to the truth. Fortunately, she didn't think of everything. *Un*fortunately, neither did we. If we'd gone through all the footage of who was where when, we would've known that Slash wasn't at the Walker house on the night of the murders. We were looking for Manheim. But even if we'd gone through them all, Walker's three closest aides have their own residences, too, so they could've claimed they spent the night at their homes, where there weren't security cameras. Lucky for Ellery Manheim, he was in the Walker house on the nights that mattered."

Lara looked over at Meg and smiled. "My dear friend, you are the best. I love you so much. I kept believing that you'd find me. And you did."

"To be honest, at first I thought you were dead. Matt was the one who felt certain you were still alive. And he read your journal and decided that we needed to follow it. Even if Walker hadn't been speaking in Gettysburg, it was going to be our next stop."

"I guess you didn't plan on finding me the way that you did," Lara said drily.

"No. And . . . I guess I didn't actually find you. But we would have. I just don't know if we would have found you in time, otherwise. And so . . ."

"So . . ." Lara said. Something in her voice told Meg that she didn't want to dwell on this anymore. Lara suddenly smiled. "So there I was in a black pit — while you were getting it on with the government hottie!"

she teased. Then she frowned. "I don't understand. What did Joe get out of all this, doing everything Kendra said?"

"First, she got him by telling him that she knew what he really was — and what he was doing. And then, by allowing him to vent his craziness and even giving it a direction." Meg shook her head. "You should have seen her that night. My God, she was proud of herself."

"Scary as hell!" Lara said with a shudder. "I can't believe I'm alive."

Meg grinned, not even flushing. "Hey, the government hottie helped me find you."

"Hey, I'm sitting right here," Matt said. He grinned back at Meg. "I like being a hottie."

Meg groaned. "Don't let all this go to your head . . ." she pleaded.

Her voice trailed off as Killer began to bark. There was a knock at the door, and Matt rose to answer it. Nancy Cooper had arrived.

Matt opened the door, welcoming Nancy in; there were hugs all around, but none so tight as the one she gave her niece.

Then there was a lot of laughter and joy as they sat down to the roast dinner Matt had insisted he could prepare, which was excellent.

But it was an early night; Lara still tired quickly and she and Nancy needed to get to her place.

When it was time to leave, Lara hugged Meg fiercely and then Matt.

Meg stood with him in the doorway to watch them leave. Killer escorted them down the walk.

Matt started to return to the house, and Meg called the dog.

But the little guy stayed at the end of the walk. And Meg saw Genie Gonzales appear, then slowly stoop down to pet him.

Genie noticed Meg watching her. She lifted a hand, and Meg realized she was saying goodbye.

"Thank you," Genie said, gesturing at Killer.

"No, thank *you,*" Meg said.

Matt came to the doorway, just as Genie disappeared. She didn't merely fade away; it seemed that there was a beautiful flash of light all around her.

It might have been a blinking streetlight.

Meg didn't think so.

She knew Matt didn't, either.

After a moment, he said, "Come on, Killer. In for the night."

The dog looked out into the night a moment longer, then obediently trotted back into the house.

Matt closed and locked the door.

He leaned against it, trapping Meg in his arms, locking her into position there. He smiled. "Hottie, huh?"

"Oh, Lord," she murmured.

"Want me to prove it?" he teased.

"If you can," she teased back.

He released her and she headed up the stairs, aware that he was following her, that he knew her mind . . .

And was quite capable of proving that he was everything she wanted. Her lover, her partner.

And her life.

ABOUT THE AUTHOR

New York Times and *USA Today* best-selling author **Heather Graham** majored in theater arts at the University of South Florida. After a stint of several years in dinner theater, back-up vocals, and bartending, she stayed home after the birth of her third child and began to write, working on short horror stories and romances. After some trial and error, she sold her first book, *When Next We Love*, in 1982 and since then, she has written over one hundred novels and novellas including category, romantic suspense, historical romance, vampire fiction, time travel, occult, and Christmas holiday fare. She wrote the launch books for Dell's Ecstasy Supreme line, Silhouette's Shadows, and for Harlequin's mainstream fiction imprint, Mira Books.

Heather was a founding member of the Florida Romance Writers chapter of RWA and, since 1999, has hosted the *Romantic*

Times Vampire Ball, with all revenues going directly to children's charity. She is pleased to have been published in approximately twenty languages, and to have been honored with awards from Waldenbooks, B. Dalton, Georgia Romance Writers, *Affaire de Coeur, Romantic Times,* and more. She has had books selected for the Doubleday Book Club and the Literary Guild, and has been quoted, interviewed, or featured in such publications as *The Nation, Redbook, People,* and *USA Today,* and appeared on many newscasts including local television and *Entertainment Tonight.*

Heather loves travel and anything have to do with the water, and is a certified scuba diver. Married since high school graduation and the mother of five, her greatest love in life remains her family, but she also believes her career has been an incredible gift, and she is grateful every day to be doing something that she loves so very much for a living.